PATRICIA WENTWORTH
TOUCH AND GO

PATRICIA WENTWORTH was born Dora Amy Elles in India in 1877 (not 1878 as has sometimes been stated). She was first educated privately in India, and later at Blackheath School for Girls. Her first husband was George Dillon, with whom she had her only child, a daughter. She also had two stepsons from her first marriage, one of whom died in the Somme during World War I.

Her first novel was published in 1910, but it wasn't until the 1920's that she embarked on her long career as a writer of mysteries. Her most famous creation was Miss Maud Silver, who appeared in 32 novels, though there were a further 33 full-length mysteries not featuring Miss Silver—the entire run of these is now reissued by Dean Street Press.

Patricia Wentworth died in 1961. She is recognized today as one of the pre-eminent exponents of the classic British golden age mystery novel.

By Patricia Wentworth

The Benbow Smith Mysteries
Fool Errant
Danger Calling
Walk with Care
Down Under

The Frank Garrett Mysteries
Dead or Alive
Rolling Stone

The Ernest Lamb Mysteries
The Blind Side
Who Pays the Piper?
Pursuit of a Parcel

Standalones
The Astonishing Adventure of Jane Smith
The Red Lacquer Case
The Annam Jewel
The Black Cabinet
The Dower House Mystery
The Amazing Chance
Hue and Cry
Anne Belinda
Will-o'-the-Wisp
Beggar's Choice
The Coldstone
Kingdom Lost
Nothing Venture
Red Shadow
Outrageous Fortune
Touch and Go
Fear by Night
Red Stefan
Blindfold
Hole and Corner
Mr. Zero
Run!
Weekend with Death
Silence in Court

PATRICIA WENTWORTH

TOUCH AND GO

With an introduction by
Curtis Evans

DEAN STREET PRESS

Introduction

BRITISH AUTHOR Patricia Wentworth published her first novel, a gripping tale of desperate love during the French Revolution entitled *A Marriage under the Terror*, a little over a century ago, in 1910. The book won first prize in the Melrose Novel Competition and was a popular success in both the United States and the United Kingdom. Over the next five years Wentworth published five additional novels, the majority of them historical fiction, the best-known of which today is *The Devil's Wind* (1912), another sweeping period romance, this one set during the Sepoy Mutiny (1857-58) in India, a region with which the author, as we shall see, had extensive familiarity. Like *A Marriage under the Terror*, *The Devil's Wind* received much praise from reviewers for its sheer storytelling élan. One notice, for example, pronounced the novel "an achievement of some magnitude" on account of "the extraordinary vividness...the reality of the atmosphere...the scenes that shift and move with the swiftness of a moving picture...." (*The Bookman*, August 1912) With her knack for spinning a yarn, it perhaps should come as no surprise that Patricia Wentworth during the early years of the Golden Age of mystery fiction (roughly from 1920 into the 1940s) launched upon her own mystery-writing career, a course charted most successfully for nearly four decades by the prolific author, right up to the year of her death in 1961.

Considering that Patricia Wentworth belongs to the select company of Golden Age mystery writers with books which have remained in print in every decade for nearly a century now (the centenary of Agatha Christie's first mystery, *The Mysterious Affair at Styles*, is in 2020; the centenary of Wentworth's first mystery, *The Astonishing Adventure of Jane Smith*, follows merely three years later, in 2023), relatively little is known about the author herself. It appears, for example, that even the widely given year of Wentworth's birth, 1878, is incorrect. Yet it is sufficiently clear that Wentworth lived a varied and intriguing life that provided her ample inspiration for a writing career devoted to imaginative fiction.

It is usually stated that Patricia Wentworth was born Dora Amy Elles on 10 November 1878 in Mussoorie, India, during the heyday of the British Raj; however, her Indian birth and baptismal record states that she in fact was born on 15 October 1877 and was baptized on 26 November of that same year in Gwalior. Whatever doubts surround her actual birth year, however, unquestionably the future author came from a prominent Anglo-Indian military family. Her father, Edmond Roche Elles, a son of Malcolm Jamieson Elles, a Porto, Portugal wine merchant originally from Ardrossan, Scotland, entered the British Royal Artillery in 1867, a decade before Wentworth's birth, and first saw service in India during the Lushai Expedition of 1871-72. The next year Elles in India wed Clara Gertrude Rothney, daughter of Brigadier-General Octavius Edward Rothney, commander of the Gwalior District, and Maria (Dempster) Rothney, daughter of a surgeon in the Bengal Medical Service. Four children were born of the union of Edmond and Clara Elles, Wentworth being the only daughter.

Before his retirement from the army in 1908, Edmond Elles rose to the rank of lieutenant-general and was awarded the KCB (Knight Commander of the Order of Bath), as was the case with his elder brother, Wentworth's uncle, Lieutenant-General Sir William Kidston Elles, of the Bengal Command. Edmond Elles also served as Military Member to the Council of the Governor-General of India from 1901 to 1905. Two of Wentworth's brothers, Malcolm Rothney Elles and Edmond Claude Elles, served in the Indian Army as well, though both of them died young (Malcolm in 1906 drowned in the Ganges Canal while attempting to rescue his orderly, who had fallen into the water), while her youngest brother, Hugh Jamieson Elles, achieved great distinction in the British Army. During the First World War he catapulted, at the relatively youthful age of 37, to the rank of brigadier-general and the command of the British Tank Corps, at the Battle of Cambrai personally leading the advance of more than 350 tanks against the German line. Years later Hugh Elles also played a major role in British civil defense during the Second World War. In the event of a German invasion of Great Britain, something which seemed all too possible in 1940, he was tasked with leading the defense of southwestern England. Like Sir Edmond and Sir William, Hugh Elles attained the rank of lieutenant-general and was awarded the KCB.

Although she was born in India, Patricia Wentworth spent much of her childhood in England. In 1881 she with her mother and two younger brothers was at Tunbridge Wells, Kent, on what appears to have been a rather extended visit in her ancestral country; while a decade later the same family group resided at Blackheath, London at Lennox House, domicile of Wentworth's widowed maternal grandmother, Maria Rothney. (Her eldest brother, Malcolm, was in Bristol attending Clifton College.) During her years at Lennox House, Wentworth attended Blackheath High School for Girls, then only recently founded as "one of the first schools in the country to give girls a proper education" (*The London Encyclopaedia*, 3rd ed., p. 74). Lennox House was an ample Victorian villa with a great glassed-in conservatory running all along the back and a substantial garden-- most happily, one presumes, for Wentworth, who resided there not only with her grandmother, mother and two brothers, but also five aunts (Maria Rothney's unmarried daughters, aged 26 to 42), one adult first cousin once removed and nine first cousins, adolescents like Wentworth herself, from no less than three different families (one Barrow, three Masons and five Dempsters); their parents, like Wentworth's father, presumably were living many miles away in various far-flung British dominions. Three servants--a cook, parlourmaid and housemaid--were tasked with serving this full score of individuals.

Sometime after graduating from Blackheath High School in the mid-1890s, Wentworth returned to India, where in a local British newspaper she is said to have published her first fiction. In 1901 the 23-year-old Wentworth married widower George Fredrick Horace Dillon, a 41-year-old lieutenant-colonel in the Indian Army with three sons from his prior marriage. Two years later Wentworth gave birth to her only child, a daughter named Clare Roche Dillon. (In some sources it is erroneously stated that Clare was the offspring of Wentworth's second marriage.) However in 1906, after just five years of marriage, George Dillon died suddenly on a sea voyage, leaving Wentworth with sole responsibility for her three teenaged stepsons and baby daughter. A very short span of years, 1904 to 1907, saw the deaths of Wentworth's husband, mother, grandmother and brothers Malcolm and Edmond, removing much of her support network. In 1908, however, her father, who was now sixty years old, retired from the army and returned to England, settling at Guildford, Surrey with an older unmarried sister named Dora (for whom his daughter presumably had been named). Wentworth joined this household as well, along with her daughter and her youngest stepson. Here in Surrey Wentworth, presumably with the goal of making herself financially independent for the first time in her life (she was now in her early thirties), wrote the novel that changed the course of her life, *A Marriage under the Terror*, for the first time we know of utilizing her famous *nom de plume*.

The burst of creative energy that resulted in Wentworth's publication of six novels in six years suddenly halted after the appearance of *Queen Anne Is Dead* in 1915. It seems not unlikely that the Great War impinged in various ways on her writing. One tragic episode was the death on the western front of one of her stepsons, George Charles Tracey Dillon. Mining in Colorado when war was declared, young Dillon worked his passage from Galveston, Texas to Bristol, England as a shipboard muleteer (mule-tender) and joined the Gloucestershire Regiment. In 1916 he died at the Somme at the age of 29 (about the age of Wentworth's two brothers when they had passed away in India).

A couple of years after the conflict's cessation in 1918, a happy event occurred in Wentworth's life when at Frimley, Surrey she wed George Oliver Turnbull, up to this time a lifelong bachelor who like the author's first husband was a lieutenant-colonel in the Indian Army. Like his bride now forty-two years old, George Turnbull as a younger man had distinguished himself for his athletic prowess, playing forward for eight years for the Scottish rugby team and while a student at the Royal Military Academy winning the medal awarded the best athlete of his term. It seems not unlikely that Turnbull played a role in his wife's turn toward writing mystery fiction, for he is said to have strongly supported Wentworth's career, even assisting her in preparing manuscripts for publication. In 1936 the couple in Camberley, Surrey built Heatherglade House, a large two-story structure on substantial grounds, where they resided until Wentworth's death a quarter of a century later. (George Turnbull survived his wife by nearly a decade, passing away in 1970 at the age of 92.) This highly successful middle-aged companionate marriage contrasts sharply with the more youthful yet rocky union of Agatha and Archie Christie, which was three years away from sundering when Wentworth published *The Astonishing Adventure of Jane Smith* (1923), the first of her sixty-five mystery novels.

Although Patricia Wentworth became best-known for her cozy tales of the criminal investigations of consulting detective Miss Maud Silver, one of the mystery genre's most prominent spinster sleuths, in truth the Miss Silver tales account for just under half of Wentworth's 65 mystery novels. Miss Silver did not make her debut until 1928 and she did not come to predominate in Wentworth's fictional criminous output until the 1940s. Between 1923 and 1945 Wentworth published 33 mystery novels without Miss Silver, a handsome and substantial legacy in and of itself to vintage crime fiction fans. Many of these books are standalone tales of mystery, but nine of them have series characters. Debuting in the novel *Fool Errant* in 1929, a year after Miss Silver first appeared in print, was the enigmatic, nautically-named *eminence grise* Benbow Collingwood Horatio Smith, owner of a most expressively opinionated parrot named Ananias (and quite a colorful character in his own right). Benbow Smith went on to appear in three additional Wentworth mysteries: *Danger Calling* (1931), *Walk with Care* (1933) and *Down Under* (1937). Working in tandem with Smith in the investigation of sinister affairs threatening the security of Great Britain in *Danger Calling* and *Walk with Care* is Frank Garrett, Head of Intelligence for the Foreign Office, who also appears solo in *Dead or Alive* (1936) and *Rolling Stone* (1940) and collaborates with additional series characters, Scotland Yard's Inspector Ernest Lamb and Sergeant Frank Abbott, in *Pursuit of a Parcel* (1942). Inspector Lamb and Sergeant Abbott headlined a further pair of mysteries, *The Blind Side* (1939) and *Who Pays the Piper?* (1940), before they became absorbed, beginning with *Miss Silver Deals with Death* (1943), into the burgeoning Miss Silver canon. Lamb would make his farewell appearance in 1955 in *The Listening Eye*, while Abbott would take his final bow in mystery fiction with Wentworth's last published novel, *The Girl in the Cellar* (1961), which went into print the year of the author's death at the age of 83.

The remaining two dozen Wentworth mysteries, from the fantastical *The Astonishing Adventure of Jane Smith* in 1923 to the intense legal drama *Silence in Court* in 1945, are, like the author's series novels, highly imaginative and entertaining tales of mystery and adventure, told by a writer gifted with a consummate flair for storytelling. As one confirmed Patricia Wentworth mystery fiction addict, American Golden Age mystery writer Todd Downing, admiringly declared in the 1930s, "There's something about Miss Wentworth's yarns that is contagious." This attractive new series of Patricia Wentworth reissues by Dean Street Press provides modern fans of vintage mystery a splendid opportunity to catch the Wentworth fever.

Curtis Evans

Chapter One

"A motherless girl—" said Miss Hildred.

"There is always so much to be considered." She pushed her pince-nez crooked and added, "No one can take a mother's place."

Sarah Trent agreed.

The hands of the clock on the mantelpiece pointed to the hour. Seven. They had been at it for a solid thirty-five minutes, and she hadn't the faintest idea whether she was going to get the job or not. She didn't quite see herself being a mother to a girl of seventeen, yet the greater part of the thirty-five minutes had been taken up with a dissertation upon Lucilla Hildred's motherless state.

When Miss Marina Hildred had said a thing once, she invariably said it all over again with embroideries, additions and appendices. Her original statement that she had been unexpectedly called to the guardianship of a young great-niece whose mother and stepfather had been killed in a motor accident was by now so overlaid with anecdote, family history, and explanations which made everything a great deal more difficult, that Sarah had practically stopped trying to follow her. She looked away from the clock and met Miss Marina's eyes. They were large, prominent eyes of a light greyish green with short, colourless lashes. They gazed expectantly at Sarah through the pince-nez which were always crooked.

Sarah was obviously expected to say something. Would she get the job if she said that she would be a mother to Lucilla? Jobs were most damnably difficult to get. Ought she to have made herself look dowdy? A matron's hat? With an inward shudder she said,

"Your niece—"

Miss Marina interrupted.

"Ah—there I must correct you. Lucilla is not really my niece—my great niece I should say."

"Your great niece—"

Miss Marina put up a plump, wrinkled hand with a good many rings on it.

"Ah no—forgive me. I am afraid that I have misled you. Lucilla calls me Aunt. Her poor father—he was killed in the war. So sad—such a fine young fellow. There is not a photograph of him here or I would show it to you. A terrible sacrifice. Let us hope there will never be another war.... Where was I?... Oh yes—poor dear Jack. He and Henry always called me Aunt—his elder brother, my nephew Henry Hildred from whom Lucilla inherited the property—or at least, as I was explaining, not really my nephew. Their grandfather's first cousin is what I really am—Henry and Jack's grandfather—but of course a good deal younger, because there was five years between my father, Admiral Hildred, and his elder brother, and he was getting on for forty when he married. So I suppose I am first cousin twice removed to Henry and Jack, and first cousin three times removed to Lucilla, but I've always been Aunt Marina to all of them. And of course when Lucy and her husband—I never really knew him well, but he was a most charming man—when they were both killed in that dreadful accident—and you may say what you like, but I can never believe that we were intended to travel at sixty miles an hour. Poor Lucy—this craze for speed! There they were, both killed, and my cousin Mr. Geoffrey Hildred and I left guardians."

Miss Marina paused for breath. She again appeared to expect Sarah to say something.

Sarah said, "Yes—"

What *did* you say to slabs of genealogy? She hoped her "Yes" didn't sound half-witted. They wouldn't want a half-witted companion or governess, or whatever it was they did want for Lucilla Hildred.

Sarah's voice was one of her strong points. It was full and rather deep. When she said "Yes—" Miss Marina was favourably impressed. Miss Trent listened well. Miss Trent did not talk too much. She did not gush like that Miss Smilax whom Barbara Lawrence recommended, or lay down the law like the Miss Gregory whose testimonials were so unexceptionable and to whom she had taken such a dislike. Miss Trent was a gentlewoman. Miss Trent had a good manner. She began to feel that Miss Trent would do. She must do her duty by Lucilla, but if she had to interview many more people like that Miss Gregory, she felt sure that she would be obliged to send for Dr. Drayton. She felt sure that Mercer would think it necessary. Only an hour ago Mercer had said in quite a worried way, "You're not looking at all your usual, ma'am. I only 'ope as how we shan't have to send for Dr. Drayton."

A tremor of nervousness passed over her. Mercer hadn't been her maid for fifteen years without knowing just how she ought to look. It wasn't good for her to have so much responsibility and to be answered back as that Miss Gregory had answered her. Miss Trent made no attempt to answer back. A gentlewoman can express sympathy without gushing. She did not consider that Miss Smilax was a gentlewoman. She would not have liked Lucilla to acquire that gushing tone. By no means. She pushed her pince-nez until they slanted from her left eyebrow to her right cheekbone and said,

"You were with Lady Constance Manifold for two years?"

Sarah said "Yes" again, but this time she smiled and added, "You read her letter—didn't you?"

There were three letters lying in Miss Marina's black cashmere lap. She always wore black, but since she was in mourning for Lucy Raimond, once for a few months the wife of that Jack Hildred who had been killed in the war and was not really her nephew but a first cousin twice removed, Mercer had taken off the black silk which had originally trimmed the cashmere and substituted two wide strips of military braid. In Miss Marina's code, which was also Mercer's, braid was mourning and silk was not. Lisse frilling was mourning, and Miss Marina's short neck rose from a white lisse frill. Her face above it was as pale and plump as a well floured scone. The colour of her hair was known only to Mercer, who presented her to the world in a faded auburn wig untinged with grey. In the lobes of her small, close-set ears were a pair of black enamel studs, each set with a small twinkling diamond. The brooch which matched them fastened the lisse below her second chin. Lucy, though never a favourite, was being duly mourned.

The three letters were rather precariously placed, Miss Marina being too stout to have much lap. There was a grey sheet on which Mrs. David Emerson spoke of Miss Trent's kind and sympathetic attention to an invalid child. There was Mrs. Moffat's rather curt and restrained recommendation on dark blue paper with a black initial in one corner. And there was Lady Constance's thick white sheet. Miss Marina took it up and turned it over. In a large sprawling hand Lady Constance spoke very highly of Miss Trent.

"You were with her two years?"

Sarah said "Yes" again.

"She doesn't say in what capacity," said Miss Marina, turning the sheet.

Sarah smiled. She had a very pretty smile.

"Well," she said, "I don't know what I was exactly. I didn't go there as a governess—I'm not certificated, you know—and I didn't go there as a nurse, because I never trained as a nurse. Eleanor had been ill, and she wasn't supposed to do lessons, but I read with her, and when she was better I played tennis and golf with her, and taught her to swim and to drive a car. I stayed till she was nineteen."

"That was Lady Constance's daughter?" said Miss Marina.

"Yes—Eleanor Manifold. All my jobs have been rather like that."

"Oh—" said Miss Marina. She pursed up her mouth until little wrinkles ran from it in all directions. It sounded very suitable. It really did sound very suitable, only—

"I shouldn't want Lucilla taught to drive a car," she said in an agitated voice.

"That would be just as you like, of course."

"Geoffrey doesn't agree with me—my cousin, Mr. Geoffrey Hildred who is Lucilla's other guardian—but after such a terrible accident I could not possibly consent to Lucilla learning to drive. I told my cousin so only yesterday. I hope you agree with me, Miss Trent. I hope I could rely on you to tell Mr. Hildred that it wouldn't do at all. I hope I could rely on you to do that?" The plump, white hands shook a little, and Lady Constance's notepaper crackled.

Sarah said, "I expect it would be better to wait."

Her deep voice had a soothing sound, and Miss Marina gave a sigh of relief. Miss Trent was an amenable young woman. Miss Trent wouldn't make difficulties. Geoffrey was a very clever man, but he didn't understand her feelings, and he couldn't be expected to understand a young girl like Lucilla. She hoped that he would approve of Miss Trent. It was he who had insisted that Lucilla's companion should be young— "Cheer her up—take her about—make her play games—shake her out of herself. You don't want some old cat of a governess, Marina. You want a nice, jolly girl, old enough to have sense in her head, but not too old to make Lucilla play."

She looked at Sarah Trent and wondered how old she was. Twenty-four—twenty-five—twenty-six? It was very difficult to tell young women's ages nowadays. *Jolly* didn't seem quite to fit Miss Trent. She wondered if Geoffrey would think her pretty. She herself had never got used to this short hair. She thought Miss Trent's hair was short. She was wearing an odd-shaped cap which showed dark waves on one side and came right down over her ear on the other. Eyes, and brows, and lashes were all of the same dark brown. Miss Trent was as sunburned as it was the fashion to be. Miss Marina looked complacently down at her own pale hands. Miss Trent's hands were very brown indeed. She had a fine bloom and good white teeth, but she was certainly too sunburned. The colour of her skin was one shade of brown, the oddly shaped cap and the neat tweed suit were another, and the hair and eyes a third.

"A decided brunette," was Miss Marina's verdict. "The Hildreds have always been so fair. It's not unpleasing in its way. I wonder whether Geoffrey—"

She coughed a slight embarrassed cough and said,

"Geoffrey—my cousin Mr. Geoffrey Hildred—is most anxious about Lucilla. She was at school—I think I told you she was at school—but he insisted on her being taken away. After such a shock he said she would need great care."

Sarah's tongue ran away with her.

"I should have thought school would have been the best place for her," she said bluntly. Good Lord! A wretched girl has a shock, and you drag her away from her normal school life where she wouldn't have time to think about it and put her down in a lonely country house with an old lady who does nothing but rub it in! Well, men were fools enough for anything!

The old lady apparently had a gleam or two of common sense.

"I thought it would have been better if she had gone back—after the funeral, you know—and Dr. Drayton agreed with me at first, but afterwards he thought Geoffrey was right."

Miss Marina went on talking about Geoffrey Hildred. He was a solicitor with a London practice, and it was very good of him to spare so much time to Lucilla's affairs, but he was so conscientious, and so anxious that Lucilla should have young companionship.

"Of course if Ricky could be here all the time it would be nice. He's twenty-four—just a nice difference in their ages. But he's in his father's office, and of course that keeps him very busy. Geoffrey is *really* my first cousin, you know, and not removed at all, though so much younger—but then of course his mother was my grandfather's second wife, a Miss Mallow of Deeping, a very old family but no money, and she died quite young poor thing, so there were no more children, and perhaps it was just as well. Geoffrey's boy, Ricky, is said to be like her, but I'm not very good at seeing likenesses myself. He's fair, and the Hildreds have always been fair—fair or auburn." She put up her hand and patted the faded wig a little self-consciously. "Lucilla is very fair," she said; and then, "I was hoping Geoffrey would have been here by now. I can't think what can have kept them. I know he will be anxious to meet you. They ought to have been here half an hour ago. What train were you catching, Miss Trent?"

"I'm driving," said Sarah. "A friend lent me a car."

"All alone—in the dark—all the way back to town?"

Sarah gave Miss Marina's dismay a very surface attention. Was she going to get the job, or wasn't she? As far as the old lady was concerned she was, but it seemed pretty plain that it was Cousin Geoffrey who ran the show. Her spirits, which had risen considerably, sank a little. Would Cousin Geoffrey think her young enough—or too young? Would a touch of lipstick have improved her chances? It might have finished her with the old lady. It was a bitter bad business making a good impression. She smiled at Miss Marina, who was recounting anecdotes of Ricky's infancy.

And then the door opened and Geoffrey Hildred came into the room.

Chapter Two

SARAH CAME AWAY walking on air. She was engaged, and she was going to get twenty pounds a year more than she had had with the Manifolds, and that meant that if Bertrand really got a new car, she could make him hand her over *The Bomb*. How little could she decently ask him to take? Fifteen? No, that was too much. Smith only offered him fifteen last year. *"Ten*—and he can take me out to a show on the proceeds." The ten would have to come out of her precious nest-egg, but the extra twenty would make it possible to run *The Bomb* and still put away what she had always put away. No improvidence for Sarah Trent. She had had a look at being down and out and she wasn't taking any risks. Respectability, and a nest-egg—these were her twin aims. To be able to pursue them and yet indulge herself with *The Bomb* was a miracle of good luck. Her colour glowed and her eyes sparkled so becomingly that Watson shut the door upon her with regret, and reported in the servants' hall that the governess was a looker and no mistake.

Sarah started *The Bomb* with a joyous hand. A feeling of ownership glowed in her. Bertrand could say what he liked, but *The Bomb* always went better for her than for anyone else. Anyhow she'd never actually exploded or laid down and died, like she had with Bertrand's last girl but one.

"Joy!" said Sarah to herself; and then, "Damn!" because *The Bomb*, after starting like an angel or a Rolls and thus enabling Watson to close the door, suddenly coughed, spat, and faded into a discouraging silence just where the drive turned into the straight.

Sarah pressed the starter again. It sounded wonky, but you never could tell with *The Bomb*—she hated getting cold. "And I oughtn't to have sworn at her. She hates that worse than poison."

"Angel!" said Sarah in her deepest, softest voice. "Angel *Bomb*, don't let me down."

She pressed the starter again, and *The Bomb* got going with bewildering suddenness. There was a horrid noise and a horrid lurch, after which she proceeded in a series of bounds.

"Joy!" said Sarah and accelerated.

The long drive ran down hill. *The Bomb* gathered speed. There was a bank on either side and overarching trees. It was pitch dark, but Sarah's heart was as bright as the headlights. Another twenty pounds a year and a car of her own! Pride of ownership inflated her.

"I hope the brat's not half-witted. I'd like to have seen her before we clicked. Anyhow beggars can't be choosers, and I'm in luck, luck, luck!"

The lodge gates came in sight, with the road beyond them and the dark hedge on its farther side. And then with appalling suddenness someone screamed and fell. It was all just in one flash of time—the sound of a cracking branch, and the fall, and the scream. Something cut the beam of the off-side headlight and went down through it into the dark. The something was registered in Sarah's mind as a head with a nimbus of fair hair. She pulled the wheel over violently and jammed on her brakes. *The Bomb* ran into the left-hand bank and stopped. It all took no time at all to happen. Crash, scream, stop, and the head with the fair floating hair—they were all there together without any time going by.

Time began again when Sarah got the door open and jumped out. Her legs didn't shake. If they had belonged to her, they would probably have been shaking like anything, so perhaps it was just as well that they didn't belong to her. Her hands didn't belong to her either, but one of them had got hold of her pocket-torch and was turning the narrow pencil of light to and fro. The light moved quite steadily. The hand was quite steady. From a very, very long way off Sarah was looking for the head. It was like the worst sort of awful nightmare. When a nightmare was as bad as that, you generally woke up. Meanwhile she had got to find the head.

The ray picked out the gravel of the drive stone by stone. It picked out a dry fallen leaf, the ghost of a leaf, with a shadow like spilled ink. Every pebble had its shadow too. And then the light was on the soft fair hair. The hand that wasn't Sarah's didn't shake at all. It moved the torch, and the torch moved the ray. There was all that fair hair, and a white face, and a body that belonged to the head. The body was clothed in something woolly and black which came right up to the chin and down to the wrists.

Sarah put out her left hand and felt. The head appeared to be quite firmly attached to the body, and the body jerked as she touched it. The ray, crossing the face again, showed the eyes open and blinking. In a fusing flash of rage Sarah's limbs became her own again and Sarah herself ceased to be about a thousand miles away. She was kneeling on the gravel path shaking a black woolly shoulder and demanding in a voice of fury,

"Blithering idiot! What did you do that for?" And then, still at boiling point, "Are you hurt?"

The shoulder heaved and the owner sat up.

"Wh-what happened?"

"Don't you know?" said Sarah.

The shoulder heaved again, this time with a giggle that turned into a sob.

"Of c-course I don't."

Sarah used some regrettable language.

"You blinking little idiot! Didn't you see my lights—didn't you *hear* me? People who've been stone deaf for *years* can hear *The Bomb*. I suppose you know you're pretty lucky to be alive. You haven't broken anything, have you?"

"N-no," said the voice with a catch in it, "I d-don't think so."

Sarah took her hand away and got up.

"You'd know if you had. Get up and see if you can walk! I'm Sarah Trent, and I suppose you're Lucilla Hildred. Now, where did you fall from, and what were you doing there anyhow?"

Lucilla scrambled up, said "Ouch!" and giggled again. "Nothing's broken. I was up on the bank. I wanted to see you pass."

"And how did you think you were going to see me in the dark?"

"I'd got a torch—I was going to shoot it at you as you passed."

"Nice child!" said Sarah. "You might have made me run into the bank. If that's what you wanted, you've done it all right. *The Bomb* is probably a corpse, and if I hadn't been pretty nippy with my brakes, you'd have been one too. What's the bright idea?"

"I didn't—" said Lucilla. "I mean there wasn't any idea—I mean I only wanted to shoot you with the torch and see if you'd jump. You see, it takes no end of a nerve to be any good at looking after me, so I thought I'd better find out whether it was any use letting you come. I mean if I really lay down and screamed, I suppose Aunt Marina and Uncle Geoffrey wouldn't make me have you."

"I don't know. Are you going to try?" said Sarah.

It would have given her the greatest possible pleasure to box Lucilla's ears. They appeared to be rather above the level of her own and temptingly near. She swept the ray across her face instead. Pale face, pale hair, round pale blue eyes that blinked against the light. A long thin slip of a girl in heavy black. She let the torch fall again.

"You haven't told me what happened," she said. The anger had gone out of her and she felt rather cold.

There was an odd little silence, rather a breathless little silence.

"I fell," said Lucilla in a small uneven voice.

"How did you fall?"

"I don't know—I just fell. I didn't mean to."

That was what Sarah had been wondering. A good deal depended on it. If Lucilla had meant to fall, no extra salary was going to drag Sarah Trent into her affairs. And then quite suddenly she was sure that Lucilla hadn't meant to fall. Her every instinct told her so. Lucilla's giggle told her so, and Lucilla's really brazen cheek. She might be a little beast, but she wasn't a would-be suicide.

Sarah gave a laugh of pure relief.

"Well, are you going to lie down and scream?" she said.

Lucilla giggled in the dark.

"I don't think so. You can come on appro if you like. I suppose they've engaged you. Uncle Geoffrey wanted a young one, and Aunt Marina's hated everyone she's seen so far. Can do."

"How do you know I'll come?" said Sarah.

"Well, you wouldn't let a little thing like this put you off—I mean, would you? I knew you'd do as soon as you called me a blinking idiot. A real proper governess would have said *'My dear child!'*" She broke off and gave a whistle of dismay. "Oh golly! I shall be late for dinner! I say, they've not let you go without any food, have they?"

"I'm supposed to be dining with a friend," said Sarah. "Sometime, you know, in the remote future, if I ever do get back to town."

"Will she wait for you?" said Lucilla.

"Oh yes, he'll wait," said Sarah.

Chapter Three

BERTRAND COULD WAIT, and Bertrand certainly would have to wait. If she got back by nine, *The Bomb* would be doing her proud. The picture of Bertrand Darnac waiting for his dinner till nine o'clock made Sarah feel warm and pleased all over. "*So* good for you, Ran darling," she murmured as *The Bomb* turned the corner into the main road.

She felt at peace with all the world. Aunt Marina was a pussy old thing. When Sarah stroked her, she would purr. Uncle Geoffrey was going to eat out of her hand. She knew the symptoms. Lucilla was undoubtedly a little devil, but she would probably be quite an amusing little devil. Over and above all this, and the twenty pounds, and the prospect of acquiring *The Bomb*, there was the heady exhilaration which is natural when you think you have killed someone and then find that you haven't. It was amusing to be alive, and it was going to be very amusing to see Bertrand's face when she arrived hours late. If *The Bomb* hadn't behaved like a perfect saint after being run up the bank, Ran might have waited till closing time. "Noble, angel *Bomb!*" said Sarah in a much more affectionate voice than she had ever used to Mr. Bertrand Darnac. And with that *The Bomb* spluttered, slowed down, and stopped dead. The most horrible suspicion assailed Sarah. Bertrand had sworn that the tank was full. It now appeared probable that he had been thinking about last week. It was a waste of time looking for a spare can. You drove *The Bomb* on luck, not on good management.

Five minutes later Sarah was convinced that her luck was out. *The Bomb* was dead to the world, and no motorist ever stopped for you now, because if they did, you would probably turn out to be a bandit. The days were gone by when any young woman could stop any passing car however lordly. No, the only chance was a house, and it didn't seem to be a very good chance. It wasn't a housey road. It was dark, and straight, and overshadowed by trees.

Sarah took out her torch and flashed it about. On this side of the road the trees bordered an open common—two or three of them, and then a gap, and half a dozen more and some gorse bushes. "Blasted heath!" said Sarah viciously, and turned the torch across the road. Here the trees were much bigger. They bulged up against the sky and hung low down over the grass verge. She went across to have a nearer look, and found that under the drooping branches, all black and shadowy, there ran a high stone wall. "Somebody's park. That means a house, and that sort of house means a garage, and a garage means petrol." Pleasant visions of an obliging young chauffeur rose before her. Chauffeurs were always very obliging to Sarah.

Well, well, the next thing was to find a gate. It might quite easily be a quarter of a mile away. It was a good two miles from the Manifolds' main gate to the one that came out on the Godswick corner.

Sarah set off up the road, and almost at once she came upon a gate. The trees receded and two ghostly pillars loomed up. There didn't seem to be a lodge, and the gate stood open. She began to walk up what was evidently not a main drive. It had not been swept for some time. She trod on dry leaves and snapping twigs. The trees closed in above her, shutting out the sky. It was awfully early in the year for the leaves to be so dry. Could there possibly be so many in October, or had this blighted park lain unswept since goodness knows when—a year—two—three—ten—or twenty? The idea that she might be walking briskly up to a house that hadn't been lived in for years was an extremely daunting one. "On the other hand, it may be full of the most delightful people who are going to be my friends for life. If you've got umpteen drives, and you haven't got umpteen gardeners, the leaves just have to lie. Forward, Sarah my child!"

The drive came out on a flat place where the bulk of a big house just showed against the sky. There was a little light in the sky, but there was none at all in the house.

Sarah switched out her torch, because it made her feel conspicuous. The place was very lonely and the house was very dead. A star looked over the edge of a chimney-stack, and no smoke blurred it. Sarah shivered. She hated a house that wasn't anybody's home any more.... And a complete wash-out as far as petrol was concerned.... On the other hand, there might be someone living in the stables, or there might be a caretaker lurking in a kitchen wing.

She began to walk round the house in the direction in which she supposed the back premises would lie, and she hadn't gone twenty yards before a light flashed high up above her head. She had been looking up at the house. The light flashed and was gone. She was left with the startled impression of a long narrow window and a spark that broke the blankness of its panes. She stood still and continued to look up.

Then all at once the light showed again. It was lower down, and it was nearer the front of the house. It stayed a little longer, and it was not so bright. Someone was moving about in the dark house with an electric torch. The narrow window probably lighted a staircase. The beam had touched the glass and dazzled there. Now the person who carried the torch was crossing one of the ground floor rooms. The windows were shuttered, so the light showed only in a faint line here and there. If it hadn't been so dark, she would not have seen it at all. There was a knothole in one of the shutters.

"No good standing here, Sarah," said Miss Trent with decision.

She put on her torch again and examined the side of the house. Just under the narrow window which had showed in the first flash, her own small feeble ray discovered a door. It was the sort of door that leads to a garden room, a quiet, unassuming door with three steps leading up to it. But the interesting thing about this quite ordinary door was that it was ajar. It slanted in under the ray and showed a full hand's breadth of shadow between its edge and the door-post.

Sarah went up the steps and lifted her hand to knock. She lifted her hand, but she stopped it just short of the panel. She had been thinking about a caretaker. But does a caretaker wander round in the dark with a torch? All at once Sarah felt quite sure that he didn't. He would have a candle, or one of those lamps with a tin reflector, or a stable lantern. The thing that had flashed and dazzled on the pane just over where she was standing now was none of these things. It was an expensive up-to-date electric torch—"And I wouldn't mind having half as good a one myself."

She discarded the caretaker. What then? Owner? Burglar?

Sarah let her hand fall to her side. It was a lonely place to meet a burglar. She would have liked to run for it. The broken-down *Bomb* seemed a haven of safety—"And I suppose you'll just sit there till a milk-float comes along in the morning. I should if I were you, and give Lucilla the whip hand once and for all." After all, it *might* be a caretaker, or an owner, and if he hadn't got petrol himself, he would at least know where you could get some. She turned off her torch, pushed open the door, and walked in.

It was dark as a winter midnight. She walked a few steps and stopped to listen. There was nothing to listen to. She felt before her and touched a door with glass panels. Well, she would just have to have a light. She wanted to see without being seen, but she couldn't afford to make a noise, and she was bound to make a noise if she went barging ahead in the dark.

The light showed that the glass panel was on her left, while a little farther along on the right there was a swing door covered with old green baize and studded with tarnished brass nails.... That was her way.

The torch went out again before she pushed the door. When it had closed behind her, she thought longingly of the dark drive with the rustling leaves under foot. The silence here was an old, settled silence. She wondered how long it was since anyone had broken it. And then she remembered the torch. Whoever was carrying it must have passed this way, and not so long ago. Sarah's heart warmed towards the torch-bearer as she felt her way forward, one hand on the wall and the other outstretched before her face. The wall felt damp. Her fingers clung to it.

She turned a corner, felt a draught blowing down, and saw facing her the pale shape of an open doorway. It broke the darkness as a window breaks it. There was not enough light to show her where she was or what place she was in, but since the faintly seen doorway was a long way off, she guessed that she had come into the hall of the big house.

Well, there was a room with an open door, and there was a light. She hadn't come as far as this to turn back. But as she moved silently across a smooth polished floor, thought conjured up a flaring headline: EMPTY HOUSE MYSTERY. MURDERED WOMAN IDENTIFIED AS SARAH TRENT.... She wondered if it would be WOMAN or GIRL. Just when did you stop being a girl? BEAUTIFUL GIRL FOUND MURDERED. The plainest and most bun-faced female was beautiful as soon as she became news. On the other hand, her hair was probably turning snow-white at this very moment, in which case she would figure as WHITE-HAIRED MYSTERY WOMAN. That was a nasty thought.

At this point she reached the doorway and stood looking through it into the room beyond. It was a big room full of shadows. A bright, keen ray seemed to cut it in two. The torch from which it came was out of sight, screened from her by the open door. Everything either above or below the ray was vague and formless. There was something that might have been a chandelier high up in the gloom. There were blurs that might have been chairs and a table, but the darkness hid them like deep water. The ray itself helped to hide them, it made so sharp a contrast. Its white brilliance cut the empty air and came to rest in a wide diffused circle upon brown panelling with a linenfold pattern. The ray was motionless, but in the room, hidden by the door, someone moved. A slow footfall went to and fro—a slow, loitering footfall.

The headlines ceased to comfort Sarah. Petrol no longer lured her. The footfall filled her with a most vehement desire to scream and run away. "Atavism," said a modern Sarah to a Sarah whose very, very remote ancestors had screamed and run. The modern Sarah stood her ground.

And then suddenly the ray moved. Someone had taken up the torch and was coming into sight. She saw the black outline of a man's head and shoulders. The light slid over the tall backs of a number of chairs that were ranged against the wall. It crossed the corner of a long bare table and then swept up and came to rest on the wall which faced the door.

The room was a dining-room, the large old dining-room of a large old house. The man leaned against the far end of the long table, with his back to Sarah and the torch in his right hand. The light moved across the panelling and touched the gilt frame of a portrait.

The next moment Sarah very nearly did scream, because she saw in the ray what she had seen in the off-side headlight of *The Bomb* not half an hour ago. She saw a round white face and a nimbus of flaxen hair. She thought she saw Lucilla Hildred, and it frightened her out of all reason. With extreme suddenness she ceased to be modern. She gasped audibly and ran across the hall with outstretched groping hands, feeling for the way by which she had come and by some miracle of good luck finding it. The baize door swung to let her through and swung again behind her. She tripped on the step and very nearly fell. Panic snatched at her, but with flying feet she drew away from it. Over the rustling leaves, down the dark drive, and out between the ghostly pillars she ran, to draw up panting beside the derelict *Bomb* and curse herself for a fool.

Chapter Four

SARAH STOOD IN the damp road and wondered how much longer she would have to stand there. She had got her breath again, but her pulses still thudded. Why on earth had she suddenly taken leave of her self-control and run like a rabbit? She repeated the word with a vicious emphasis—"a blithering *rabbit*." She had never done such a thing in her life before—"and if you're going to make a habit of it, Sarah my girl, you'd better get into a home for the half-baked and stay there!" Her legs were actually shaking still, and she hadn't the remotest idea why. "Oh, for goodness sake wake up and behave like something human for a change!"

She sat down on the running-board and looked about her. It was very dark indeed. The sky was a little less dark than the trees, but that was all that could be said for it. The road was damp under her feet, but the leaves in that blighted avenue had been rustling dry. There must have been a shower whilst she was having her heart-to-heart talk with Aunt Marina and Uncle Geoffrey. It couldn't have been much—enough to damp the road, but not enough to penetrate those overhanging trees. Well, the question now was, did she and *The Bomb* just quietly moulder here till daylight, or would someone come along and rescue them?

The night was as still as it was dark. If a car did come along she would be able to hear it about half a mile away, and if it went by without stopping, it wasn't going to be Sarah's fault. She disliked this place as she had ever disliked a place in all her life. The proximity of those ghostly pillars and that rustling drive was definitely unpleasant. She wanted to get a long way away from them as quickly as possible. The dead stillness of the night offered her no encouragement to suppose that she had any immediate prospect of being able to get away from them. An echo of her nursery days came back to her: "I want—" "Then want must be your master, Miss Sarah." The only balm was the thought of Bertrand Darnac waiting for his dinner.

It may have been ten minutes later, or it may have been no more than five, that she heard the first faint beginnings of a sound. It began like the stirring of a pulse, and it was so small a sound that it was almost lost in the clammy silence. She had to listen for it, straining, and even then for a moment or two she wasn't sure. It is queer how a sound grows. There was the moment when she wasn't sure, and the moment when she was and the space between. Then she was on her feet looking for the car that was coming down the road. The sound grew. Away in the distance there was a faint glow. The direction puzzled her until the headlights shone across the road and then swung round, dazzling her with their two bright beams.

The car hadn't come down the road at all, it had turned into it from a side road. For one horrid moment she had wondered which way it was going to turn, the next she was out in the middle of the road with her arms spread wide.

Mr. John Brown was in a hurry. He was travelling fast. He said something short and sharp and jammed on his brakes, and as he did so, Sarah jumped for the side of the road. It had been a nearer thing than she had meant it to be. The virtuous fury of the pedestrian boiled in her. He must have skidded that corner at forty, the blighted road-hog!

Mr. Brown opened the near-side door and descended into the road. He was in a hurry, and he was as angry as a man may be. He didn't think he'd hit the girl, but he wasn't absolutely sure. It had been a near thing, and he'd got the wind up. He looked about him, and immediately a furious voice said,

"You nearly killed me!"

Mr. Brown immediately became a great deal angrier than he had been before. The girl sounded most vigorously alive, and he could therefore give his whole mind to being angry instead of having about three-quarters of it taken up with the most repellent and, as it turned out, unnecessary visions of a coroner's court. He had a quiet drawl when he was angry. He used it now as he said,

"You were rather asking for it, weren't you?"

Sarah felt an unwilling stab of admiration. She remembered her own fury with Lucilla; she remembered calling her a blighted little fool. She admired the calm of Mr. John Brown. She said frankly,

"Yes, I was—but I'd got to stop you."

"And may I ask why?"

Sarah was not pleased. He ought to have responded to her frankness, instead of which there he was, all politely furious like a person in a play. She felt a most unregenerate desire to put out her tongue or throw a stone. Women have these savage impulses. Sarah controlled hers with regret.

She said "Petrol!" pitching the word at him as if it had been the stone which she had renounced.

Mr. Brown said "Oh—" and then more briskly, "Where's your car?"

Sarah having indicated the whereabouts of *The Bomb*, he passed round the back of his own car and proceeded to detach the spare can from the running-board on the off side. There was no more talk until *The Bomb* was refuelled. Then Sarah said, "Thank you," and Mr. Brown said, "I shouldn't do it again if I were you—you might get killed." After which he went back to his own car and waited for Sarah to drive away. As soon as *The Bomb* was out of sight he backed into the space in front of the ghostly pillars, turned his car, and also followed the road to town.

Chapter Five

YOU CAN GET a meal at The Lizard during most hours of the day or night, and you can call that meal anything you like. The waiters themselves stop alluding to breakfast at twelve-thirty or so, to lunch at half past three, and to dinner somewhere round about ten o'clock, but they have no objection to your calling your food by any name you fancy. As a natural consequence, nobody minds what you wear. There is a garage just round the corner.

Sarah tidied up at the garage, used the lipstick which she had denied herself in order to impress Aunt Marina, cocked her hat at a slightly more rakish angle, and proceeded to her rendezvous with Mr. Darnac.

The Lizard was neither full nor empty. As a matter of fact Sarah had never seen the Lizard really empty. Whenever you came, or whenever you went, there were always odd people having odd meals or odder drinks. Bertrand was neither eating nor drinking. He sat humped in his chair with all the appearance of a person who has just died of boredom. "Boredom and extreme bad temper," thought Sarah delightedly.

She approached the table with a catlike tread, sank noiselessly into the second chair, and said in a clear, brisk voice,

"When's the funeral, Ran?"

Mr. Darnac sat up with a jerk. His eyes opened. He ceased to resemble a corpse and became very obviously alive, exasperated, and French.

"But *vois tu*, Sarah, this is—what do you call it?—the top-lid. Have you, perhaps, any idea what time it is?"

"'M—it's twenty-three minutes and a half past nine, and I'm simply starving. I hope you've got lots of money, because I'm going to be a very expensive guest. Just tell Henri to get me some of the thickest soup they've got, and then to keep right on bringing me things till I say no. Everything on the menu. Ran darling, how frightfully cross you are!"

Bertrand Darnac frowned until his very thin, mobile eyebrows looked as if they had been ruled across his forehead with a piece of charcoal. He was a tall, dark young man of three or four and twenty, and ordinarily of a pleasant and vivacious ugliness. He gave the order to Henri in the grand manner of serious offence and turned back to find Sarah smiling at him seductively. It amused her that Bertrand should be in a temper, but she had no notion of allowing him to stay in one. She was bubbling over with her adventure, and you really can't bubble over to a person who is being all stiff and proud. She thought complacently about the lipstick and smiled her best.

"Where have you been?" said Mr. Darnac with offence.

"Where *haven't* I been? Darling Ran, if I talk before I have something to eat, I shall swoon."

The eyebrows relaxed a little.

"You do not look at all as if you were going to swoon."

"Under the rouge her face was of a ghastly pallor" murmured Sarah. "I've got a new lipstick. How do you like it?"

"It is good. Yes, just right. You must continue to use it."

"Perhaps Aunt Marina won't let me," said Sarah. She greeted the arrival of the soup with a radiant smile. "Henri, you have saved my life. Now, Ran, I'm not going to say another word till this is all gone."

Mr. Darnac permitted himself a slight snigger.

"If you can keep from talking, my dear, that will be a—how do you say?—knock-out."

Sarah made a face and then went on eating. If Ran thought he was going to draw her, he wasn't. She finished the last drop, laid down her spoon, and looked up to find that he was doing exactly the same thing. They both laughed.

"*Enfin*, Sarah," said Bertrand Darnac, "you are too bad! I have been here since half past seven, and first I think 'She will be late, because girls are always late, but she will not be more than half an hour late, because she likes her dinner.' Oh yes, you do, my dear. That is one reason why I ask you to dine. Those girls who say no to everything— what a bore that is!" He made a quick grimace. "And when I am hungry and could eat everything on the menu! But the girl, she says no to this, and no to that, and no to the other, and then how can I eat my dinner? I must go to bed hungry."

"Well, you needn't to-night. I'm not saying no to anything, and if this is an omelette, I'm going to have my fair half of it. What sort of omelette is it, Henri?"

It was a shrimp omelette, and Henri gave her a good deal more than her fair share of the shrimps.

"And now," she said when he had gone again—"now, my child, you can congratulate me."

"On what?"

Sarah ate a shrimp with crisp enjoyment.

"I've got the job—*and* a rise. And I'm going to buy *The Bomb*, so you'd better get busy about a new car, because I shall want her at once. In fact I think I'd better just keep her. They want me to go down next week, and she'll be useful to run about in meanwhile."

Bertrand Darnac grinned.

"And what do I run about in—meanwhile? *Mon Dieu*, Sarah, you have the cheek!"

"'M—" said Sarah. "Ran darling, you're letting your omelette get cold."

"Never mind about my omelette—I am talking about my *Bomb*. MY *Bomb*, Sarah!"

Sarah shook her head.

"No, darling—*mine*. I'm buying her here and now."

"Oh, you are buying her? And what do you pay me, my dear?"

"A fiver?" said Sarah casually. "I say, Ran, if you're really not going to eat that omelette, I could do with a spot more."

"There is nothing doing—I am going to eat it myself. There is also nothing doing about the fiver."

"Now look here, Ran, you won't get more than that for her anywhere, but I'll go to six pounds if you're really hard up."

Mr. Darnac's mouth was full of omelette. His eyes twinkled impishly and he shook his head.

Sarah leaned back with a frown.

"Seven?"

Mr. Darnac shook his head again.

"Eight?"

"C'est ridicule!"

"Talk English! That's what you're here for, isn't it? Eight pounds, and that's my last word."

Bertrand smiled amiably at her across his empty plate.

"You are very amusing."

"All right," said Sarah. She leaned towards him, her eyes wide and candid under dark arched brows. "All right then, ten—and that really *is* my limit. Nobody will give you more than that. You know that perfectly well. Ten—and we do a show to celebrate it."

"Oh, a show…. And who pays?"

"I do—out of the ten pounds," said Sarah happily.

Henri approached with a casserole.

It was at this moment that Mr. John Brown entered the room. Having followed *The Bomb* to the garage, he had been obliged to wait outside until Sarah emerged. If he had not done this, he would not have been able to keep track of her further movements. When she did emerge, he let her get a little way ahead and then followed at a crawl. From the corner he was able, with a good deal of relief, to see her go into the Lizard. He then had to turn his car, go back to the garage, and park.

He entered the Lizard, crossed the floor whilst Sarah was helping herself to *poulet aux champignons*, and sat down at the next table. On the dark road he had been merely a shadow. In the lighted room he appeared as a man of rather more than average height with a quiet, easy way of moving and the look of having spent a good deal of his time out of doors. The brown was very deeply tanned into a skin which might once have been fair. His eyes looked light in contrast, though they were really of quite a deep grey. His hair was brown, with a touch of grey at the temples. His age might have been anything between thirty-five and forty-five. His clothes, though unobtrusive, had an air that was not quite English.

He caught Henri's eye as Bertrand Darnac helped himself, and presently he gave an order, picking up the printed menu and indicating what he wished with a finger that looked very brown against the white card. He sat a little behind Sarah, and to her right. Without appearing to watch her he could observe her profile—the arch of her brow, the bright changing colour that glowed on her cheek, and even the effect of the new lipstick which emphasized the curve of her mouth. He could also see Mr. Bertrand Darnac, and he could hear nearly everything they said. Sarah was talking with animation about her interview with Aunt Marina and Uncle Geoffrey. The names reached Mr. John Brown perfectly distinctly as he gave his order to Henri.

Presently, when Henri was gone, he was able to listen undisturbed … "A nice pussy-woolly old thing," Sarah was saying. "I'm frightfully good at old ladies. It's one of my assets. They love me passionately because I let them talk all the time and just say yes or no with early Victorian respectfulness about once in five minutes or so."

"Is Uncle Geoffrey also going to love you passionately?" said Bertrand impudently.

Sarah nodded.

"Darling Ran, when I said you could congratulate me, I didn't just mean the job—I meant Uncle Geoffrey. I came, I saw, I conquered—you know, just like that. He went down like a ninepin, and if I want to be Mrs. Geoffrey Hildred, I can. So there we are!"

Bertrand frowned a little.

"That is what you say quick work."

"I might do worse," said Sarah calmly. "Much, much worse."

"An old man!"

"That's just what he isn't, my child. He's not old at all—a nice mellow fifty or so, and awfully good-looking—fairish grey hair, bright blue eyes, nice ruddy complexion, very hale and hearty, rather like the squire in a musical comedy, only he's not a squire, he's a solicitor with a London practice. There's money in it, my child. It's frightfully comic, because he looks as if he'd lived in the country for generations."

Bertrand frowned a little more.

"You will have to—how do you say?—watch the step, my dear. These old boys, they are dangerous. He may make love to you, but when it comes to marriage—" He shrugged his shoulders.

Sarah gazed at him earnestly.

"Advice to the young girl who is about to enter the wicked world for the first time! '*Ma fille*, it is your father who speaks. He has *been* there and he knows.'" Her tongue shot out and back again. Mr. Brown saw it in profile, a nice, bright red, pointed tongue. "Ran darling, here's a new idiom for you—'Go home and boil your head!' Your Sarah wasn't born yesterday."

Bertrand shrugged again.

"Well, I have warned you." He broke suddenly into a grin. "He will have his work cut out, that one. Do you know, when I first met you I thought to myself, 'My Aunt Constance, she has been jolly well had!'"

"Thanks, Ran darling."

"I saw you there—what shall I say?—*gouvernante* to my Cousin Eleanor, and I thought, 'Oh la la, she is a lively one that Miss Sarah!

There will be some fun for you, Bertrand my boy!' And if anyone had told me that I should know you—how long is it—six months?—that I should take you to the dinner, to the dance, to the theatre, to the night-club, that we should walk ourselves in the woods, that we should drive by day and by night in our little *Bomb*, and at the end of it I should not have so much as one kiss to remember—*ma foi!* I should have told him, 'Sir, you are a dam liar!'"

Sarah looked at him reprovingly.

"Well, that just *shows* you. It's a very good lesson for you, my child. Respectability's my strong suit. If I hadn't a most beautiful blameless character, how do you suppose I'd ever get a job?"

Bertrand groaned.

"Respectable!" he said. "Mon Dieu, Sarah—what a word! Are you a *concierge*, or the mother of a family, that you should be *respectable*?"

Sarah put out her tongue again.

"Respectable I am, and respectable I stay."

He threw up his hands.

"With those eyes, and those lips, and that colour!"

Sarah turned her head and gazed appreciatively at her own reflection in the mirror behind Mr. Brown. She did not see him at all. She only saw her own bright eyes and heightened bloom. She turned back to Bertrand with a pleased smile.

"Nice—aren't they?" she said, and then arrested Henri as he passed. "Biscuits, cheese, and butter—lots of butter. And white coffee for me, and black for Mr. Darnac."

They helped themselves, and then Bertrand said,

"And what becomes of me when you have gone to make the eyes at your old country squire?"

"I don't make eyes," said Miss Trent with dignity. "I don't have to. And I suppose you'll go back to the Manifolds, carry on with your job of learning how to speak English, and finish up by marrying Eleanor according to plan."

He shook his head.

"No, I shall never do that," he said seriously.

"And what will the families say if you don't?"

He made a lively grimace.

"They will not like it, but they will, as you say, lump it, my dear. Without any joking at all, that is what they will have to do. It is very *embêtant* for everyone that the property must come to me and the money to Eleanor. If we liked each other, it would be all very nice and easy—so my little mother thinks. She is still in her heart a good deal English, though, as you know, she has really never lived here. She writes to her brother and suggests that I should come over on a long visit and learn the English and make friends with *ma belle cousine*."

"I was there when the letter came," said Sarah, laughing. "Major Manifold was most awfully cross. He hates visitors, and he hates the idea of anyone marrying Eleanor. He'd like her to be just a little girl always. But Lady Constance was pleased."

Bertrand nodded.

"Well, that is how it is—I do not like Eleanor, and Eleanor does not like me. When I hold her hand it is as if I held a piece of cold fish. How can one embrace a large, pale, cold fish? I ask you, my dear!"

Sarah said, "Nonsense!"

"No, it is the truth. And besides I do not think it is eugenic for cousins to marry. I have written to *maman* about that. I am very strong for the eugenics."

"You wouldn't have thought about them if you'd liked Eleanor. And she's not in the least like a fish."

"For me she is. And *vois tu*, Sarah, I do not ask the impossibilities. It is necessary that I should marry a girl who has money—that is understood. I do not demand that I should be love with her passionately, as for example I could so very easily be in love with you."

"The kind compliment is noted!"

Bertrand frowned at her levity.

"I do not demand that—I have said so to *maman*. I ask only that she should not remind me of cold fish." Quite suddenly his gravity broke up into a grin. "Why should I not marry your Lucilla Hildred?" he said.

Chapter Six

SARAH TRENT ARRIVED at the Red House in the middle of a fine October afternoon. She drove herself in *The Bomb*, with her luggage crammed to the roof behind her. Having studied a map commandeered from the reluctant Mr. Darnac, she had discovered a new and much shorter way to the house. When she came down to interview Miss Marina, she must have driven in circles round the village of Holme instead of coming through it. She had no idea that the entrance to the Red House was only a stone's throw from the last cottage in the village street.

The house itself stood high, and the drive sloped sharply. She looked with dislike at the banks on either side of it. They were thickly overgrown with trees and shrubs. Dark drives appeared to be the fashion in the neighbourhood of Holme.

The house was a square building in the Georgian style, the red brick which had originally given it its name being almost entirely covered by Virginia creeper, which flamed in every shade from scarlet to deep maroon. Coming on it suddenly at the turn of the drive, it was almost as if the house was on fire.

The Bomb was allotted a stable, and Sarah a room next to Lucilla's. It was a pleasant room, if a little too pink for Sarah's taste. As she gazed at it, she felt as if she had known Mrs. Raimond all her life. She knew just what type of woman has a rose-coloured carpet on the floor, a wall-paper with pink and mauve sweet peas profusely interlaced, and pink and white striped curtains at the windows. There was a pink wash-basin with hot and cold water laid on, a rose-coloured shade over the electric light, pink candles on the dressing-table, a pink pin-cushion, and a bright pink eiderdown.

"Golly!" said Sarah.

It appeared that Miss Marina was resting, and Miss Lucilla was down on the tennis-court. Sarah proceeded to the tennis-court by way of a lawn, a rose-garden, and a flight of steps.

Lucilla was playing tennis with a young man, and Uncle Geoffrey was watching them. In the sunlight she thought him even better looking than she had done before, and most undeniably pleased to see her. He said,

"Well, well—this is great!"

And then, before he could say anything else, Lucilla came up with her partner and he was introducing them.

"This is Lucilla, and this is my son, Richard. But perhaps you've already met."

Sarah opened smiling lips, but she looked at Lucilla before she spoke. The child was wearing a white shirt and a short black skirt, with black stockings and white tennis shoes. Her face, which had been so pale in the light of Sarah's electric torch, had the prettiest wild-rose flush. Her hair, as soft and fine and fair as a baby's, stood out all round her head like a halo. Her round innocent eyes met Sarah's and said a very plain and insistent no.

Sarah's smile widened. She beamed amiably at the little group and said,

"I think Lucilla was out."

"So you didn't meet?" Uncle Geoffrey's tone was very pleasant.

"I was out with Ricky," said Lucilla abruptly, and then suddenly the colour ran right up to the roots of her hair. She dropped her racket and stooped to pick it up again.

"Odd child," thought Sarah. She took a look at the third Hildred, and decided that he wasn't nearly so good-looking as his father. If Lucilla was having an affair with him, she was a little fool and it was high time she had someone to look after her. She thought Master Ricky looked a good deal of a milksop, a pale watered down edition of his papa—tall, slight, fair, and very well pleased with himself, with the pale blue eyes which make you think of skim milk.

Presently, while Lucilla and Ricky finished their game, Geoffrey Hildred talked very sympathetically about his ward.

"I hope you'll rouse her—take her about, get her out of some of this heavy black. Miss Hildred is old-fashioned and she doesn't realize how bad it is for Lucilla to live under a perpetual reminder of her loss. It's all very sad, very regrettable, but everyone has his own life to live. I don't mind telling you I have been very deeply concerned about Lucilla. There have been times when I have been afraid, but—well, it isn't necessary to go into that now. You will, I am sure, do her a world of good. But there's just one thing—"

Sarah gazed at him in the manner of the earnest neophyte awaiting instruction. As she did so, she felt quite sure that she was receiving full marks for tact and womanly sympathy. Uncle Geoffrey's fine blue eyes dwelt on her with approbation.

"Just one thing," he pursued. "You have your own car, I believe. Well, I am afraid that at first—yes, at any rate at first—Miss Hildred would rather you did not take Lucilla out in it. There is an old Daimler, and a very trustworthy chauffeur who will be at your disposal whenever my cousin is not requiring him, but for the present she is much alarmed at the idea of your driving Lucilla."

Sarah's face fell. It sounded unutterably stuffy and hum-drum.

"There are many pleasant expeditions which you could make," said Mr. Hildred consolingly. "It is really no distance to the sea. It is a pity you were not here earlier, but really the weather is so wonderful that bathing is still quite possible. That would be excellent for Lucilla, quite excellent. I hope you swim."

Sarah swam. She had swum with Eleanor Manifold. They talked about the Manifolds.

When Lucilla had finished her game, she took Sarah round the garden. As soon as they were out of sight, she looked sideways out of those round blue eyes of hers and said,

"They're all potty about cars. If they'd known you had nearly run me over, you'd have been in the soup."

"*I?*" said Sarah indignantly.

Lucilla's gaze became full, wide, and innocent.

"Of course," she said. "Tearing down the drive like that and knocking me over!" She began to giggle. "You know, Aunt Marina thinks cars ought to be forbidden to go more than five miles an hour by Act of Parliament. If you're ever really desperately keen on stroking her the right way, you try saying you think so too. It's never been known to fail."

"Thank you," said Sarah.

"You needn't. Look here, you didn't go and promise only to take me out in the Daimler with Morris driving it as if it was a hearse, did you? A push-bike's better fun than that. I've got a new one, but the other's still quite rideable. Here—this is supposed to be the spot view, if you're keen on views."

They had come suddenly from a path between crowding bushes to the open top of a knoll. It was surprising to see how far they were above the village. The thatched roofs looked like a line of haystacks grouped about the church. You could see the road with its hedgerows and elm trees, and you could see woodland, and yellow reaped fields, and pasture where the grass was green again after the rain, a stretch of pleasant, peaceful country losing itself towards the horizon in the autumn haze.

"That's Holme Fallow," said Lucilla, and pointed. Her voice changed on the name as if she forced it a little.

Sarah looked first at her and then along the line of the pointing finger. An odd child Lucilla. She saw the road running on away from the village, and, perhaps a mile away, the chimney-stacks of a house lifting from amongst trees. It looked to be a big house with a park about it. The road forked and enclosed the park as a stream divides to encircle a rock.

Sarah looked at the chimney-stacks, and had thoughts. She said, "What is Holme Fallow?"

"It's mine," said Lucilla.

"Yours?"

Lucilla's hand dropped to her side. She went on looking at Holme Fallow.

"Yes, it's mine, but I've never lived there. I shall some day. I hate this house—don't you?"

"No—why should I? Why do you hate it?"

Lucilla gave a laugh which was not in the least like the schoolgirl giggle of a little while before. It had a dry, unmirthful sound.

"Oh, it's a first-class house—central heating, hot and cold water in all the bedrooms, and every modern convenience, like the house-agents' blurb always says. It doesn't belong to me, thank goodness. It was my step-father's, and the Guardians have taken it on from the nephew who came in for everything. He's in India, so he doesn't want it himself."

"Would you like to live at Holme Fallow?" said Sarah idly.

Lucilla flushed and was silent. Then she said,

"Nobody's lived there since the war. I was born there, and then—my great-grandfather died—and Mummy married my step-father—and Uncle Henry never came home."

"You mean he was killed?"

"No, he wasn't killed, but he never came home. He had shell-shock and he couldn't keep still. He had to go on travelling all the time, and he never came home. He died about six months ago." She had spoken in a low, expressionless voice. Suddenly it changed and came alive again.

"Would you like to go over and see the house? They won't let me go alone, because Aunt Marina's an old fusty-fuss, but no one could object to my going with my chaperon."

"Am I a chaperon?" said Sarah laughing.

"You ought to know. You're either a chaperon or a governess, and we might just as well get it quite dear at the very start that I'm not going to be governessed." She shook back her hair and tilted an impudent head.

Sarah laughed again.

"I'm not really set on being a governess," she said.

"No—you don't look like one, thank goodness. I was going to make your life a hell on earth, but I'm calling it off for the present. We'll go and look at Holme Fallow to-morrow and sleuth the burglar."

Sarah had more thoughts—very quick, disturbing ones. She hoped her voice was all right when she said,

"What burglar?"

Lucilla clutched her arm and swung it to and fro.

"Why, it was the day you were here. You know, when you came down to see the Guardians and nearly killed me. Whilst you were doing all that, someone was burgling Holme Fallow. You see, there's a caretaker called Snagge, and he went out at six and he didn't come back till eleven, because he'd been in to Ledlington to the pictures. And he didn't notice anything that night, but next day he came up here all of a doodah and said the place had been burgled. There were damp footmarks up the steps to the side door, and in the passages, and all over the parquet, and a desk had been broken open and what not. Aunt Marina was in a most frightful fuss. A car had been driven right up to the house, which was pretty fair nerve, but I suppose they knew Snagge would be out. Everyone in the village knows that he and Mrs. Snagge go in to Ledlington on Thursday evenings. They've been doing it for years, so I expect the burglar knew. And the village policeman, who is a nice fat old grampus called Minnow, says he thinks it was a gang, because another car had been standing by the west drive and there were marks where petrol had been spilt."

Sarah breathed an inward *"Golly!"* Then she opened her mouth to speak and shut it again. The suspicions which had come to her when she first beheld the chimney-stacks of Holme Fallow were being most painfully confirmed. She had most undoubtedly seen the burglar at his burgling. But would it really be a good plan to say so? Would it really give her what you might call a good start with the Guardians? She had a horrid feeling that it would not. They would probably think, and say, that she ought to have sought out Mr. Minnow and told him what she had seen instead of blinding off to town to meet Ran. Silence looked very golden to Sarah Trent. She closed her lips firmly and let Lucilla go on talking.

Chapter Seven

THEY WENT NEXT DAY to Holme Fallow. It took much longer on a bicycle than it had done in *The Bomb*. Sarah remembered where she had turned, but instead of following the left-hand fork of the road Lucilla kept straight on until they came to a lodge and a pair of iron gates.

Mrs. Snagge came out of the lodge to let them in. She was a little woman with a long sharp nose and a tight mouth.

Lucilla leaned on her bicycle and said good morning.

"This is the way the burglar came in," she said to Sarah.

Sarah looked at the big gates which Mrs. Snagge was opening.

"Aha! That's where the fun comes in!" said Lucilla. "I say, Mrs. Snagge, did you tell Minnow how the burglar got in?"

Mrs. Snagge pursed up her lips.

"There's no saying—" she began, but Lucilla cut her short.

"Oh yes, there is. You know, and Snagge knows, and I know, that you left the gates open."

"I'm sure, Miss Lucilla—" The woman's voice shook, but Sarah thought it was with anger. Her eyes were resentful too.

"So am I," said Lucilla sternly—"quite, quite sure. You always do leave them open when you go into Ledlington, because it saves trouble when you get back late." She laughed a little. "You needn't be afraid—I shan't give you away."

Mrs. Snagge sniffed and gulped.

"And what difference could it have made when all's said and done, with the other drive that's never had no gates to it, not in my time nor in Snagge's anyway, and nothing to stop anyone going up it day nor night?"

"Well, the burglar came *this* way—didn't he?" said Lucilla, and then she jumped on her bicycle again and rode up the drive.

Sarah followed her. The drive was newly gravelled and neatly swept. The marks of the burglar's tyres must have been quite easy to see.

They came out upon a wide flat space before the house and left their bicycles leaning against the wall.

There is always something mournful about an empty house. Holme Fallow was beautiful, but it looked dead. The ground-floor windows were shuttered, and those above shut close, and blank. Lucilla looked up, frowning, and then led the way round to the side door which Sarah remembered only too well. That was where the other drive came up, and this was where she had stood in the dark and seen the lighted window spring suddenly into view. Those were the steps which she had mounted.

Silence continued to be golden.

They went along the passage and into the big hall, which was nearly as dark as it had been at night. No—once your eyes got accustomed to the change, it was only dusk that filled it and not darkness. The stairs went up at the far end, and they went up into the light, as if there were a window which lighted them just round the turn. They went up to a small landing, divided, and went on again. The window which lighted them was round the left-hand turn.

Sarah nodded. Yes, of course, that was it—that was the window at which she had seen the light, and the burglar had been coming down the stairs.

Lucilla came close up to her and put a hand on her arm.

"Do you have feelings about houses? What does Holme Fallow feel like?"

Sarah considered. She had come into it happily enough, and then she had been frightened. But that was because of the burglar; it had nothing to do with the house. She tried to put all that out of her thoughts and start fresh. After a moment she said tentatively,

"It's—old—"

"Some of it's sixteenth-century. The front is Queen Anne."

Sarah tried again.

"It's—friendly—" Some houses weren't friendly, especially empty houses. They made you feel as if you were pushing in upon their private affairs. Holme Fallow was friendly.

"Yes," said Lucilla. Her hand dropped from Sarah's arm. "Some day I shall live here." And with that she went on across the hall and opened the door which had been open when Sarah came that way before.

The room beyond was quite dark now, but Lucilla crossed it without having to grope her way. The next moment a long streak of light broke the dark and widened there. The middle shutter went back with a creaking sound and the daylight came in. There was bright, warm sun outside. Lucilla opened all the other shutters, and dusted her hands on her skirt.

"Snagge's a lazy hound," she said. "He ought to have all the windows open on a day like this." Then she turned back to the room and waved a grimy hand. "Family portraits—" They hung round three sides of the room in heavy tarnished frames.

A tall fair youth in the riding-clothes of the eighteen-fifties, and opposite to him something very fair and fragile in ringlets and a crinoline.

"Great-grandfather and great-grandmother at the time of their marriage." Lucilla's voice was quiet and serious. "She didn't live very long. *He* only died the year I was born.... That's my grandfather. He was their only child, and he was killed out hunting before he was thirty. That was done when he was twenty-one."

Sarah looked and saw another fair young man with a scarlet coat, and breeches which looked as if they must have been too tight to ride in.

"That's my father and his brothers, when they were all children."

This picture was the last on the wall facing the windows. It showed John Hildred's three children. Lucilla named them in order of age.

"That's Uncle Henry. He was about five. And that's my father next to him. He was three and a half. And the baby is Uncle Maurice."

Henry Hildred had his hand on his little brother's shoulder. He stared haughtily out of the picture—a very fair, handsome child with an air of having bought the earth. Jack, in a linen smock, had an apple at which he seemed to look longingly, whilst the baby Maurice, in an embroidered muslin dress, sat placidly on the grass at their feet. They were all fair and rosy, with the same grey-blue eyes. Jack and Maurice were round and chubby of face.

Sarah was looking at the baby.

"I didn't know you had an Uncle Maurice. Your aunt didn't mention him. She talked about Henry and Jack."

"Jack's my father," said Lucilla. "She doesn't talk about Maurice much, because it makes her cry, and she wouldn't want to cry when she was interviewing you. She was most awfully fond of him."

"Is he dead?"

"They don't think so, but of course he must be."

"Who's *they*, and why don't they know?"

"Well, he was missing in 1918, but Aunt Marina always swore he wasn't dead."

"But why?"

"Oh, because she just couldn't bear it, I suppose. She thinks he's alive, and what's more Uncle Geoffrey thinks so too."

"But why? I mean why doesn't he come home if he's alive?"

Lucilla frowned.

"They think he's wandering about in the States, or Canada, or somewhere like that. You know, Uncle Henry kept wandering and wouldn't come back, so that makes it seem more likely. And then a client of Uncle Geoffrey's told him he'd met someone who was most awfully like the Hildreds, and he and Aunt Marina made up their minds it was Maurice. But I'm sure he's dead."

Dead.... The word echoed in Sarah's mind as she looked at the picture. What a damnable thing war was. There was Henry, who had been a wanderer on the earth and couldn't face his home, and he was dead. And the jolly round-cheeked little boy with the apple was Jack, and Lucilla's father, and he was dead too, somewhere in France, a long time ago. And there was Maurice, the fat happy baby, and he was either dead like Jack or a wanderer as Henry had been, with shattered nerves perhaps or memory gone.... Whom the gods would destroy they first make mad.... Would the world ever be mad enough to plunge into that vortex of blood and misery again....

"And that's their mother—my grandmother," said Lucilla, and pulled her round to look at the chimney-piece. The portrait of Mrs. John Hildred looked down the length of the room. Sarah might have seen it a dozen times, but she had kept her eyes away. She had to raise them now and wonder, as she had wondered over and over again, why she should have taken fright and run when the ray of the burglar's torch had touched such a sweet and smiling face.

"I'm supposed to be awfully like her," said Lucilla. "She was a Hildred too—a cousin from miles away back in the family tree. It's poisonously dull to marry a cousin—don't you think so? But they didn't have time to get bored, he was killed so young. Do you think I'm like her?"

The likeness was evident, though not so startling as it had seemed when the beam illumined the face alone. Seen in daylight, the long flowing dress in the fashion of the nineties, the style of the hair, and the air of gracious maturity all made for difference. Eleanor Hildred had borne her three children when this portrait was painted. She smiled down from it as a young mother smiles, watching her boys at play.

"Yes, you're like her," said Sarah, and wondered again why she should have panicked and run away.

Chapter Eight

MR. GEOFFREY HILDRED and his son seemed to be making a stay of some length at the Red House. They went up to town, but they came down again. Sarah concluded that she was on appro, and that Miss Marina hadn't felt equal to vetting her alone. It is fairly grim to have the eyes of a whole family earnestly focussed upon all that you say, or do, or are, from the way you eat your breakfast banana, through your reactions to (*a*) a practical joke, (*b*) winding interminable balls of wool, (*c*) being accidentally banged over the head by Ricky at tennis, down to your capacity for staying the course of Aunt Marina's reminiscences without going to sleep as ten o'clock approached. Sarah hoped that she was comporting herself as well as was to be expected, and that the family interest would shortly become less intense. Miss Marina was becoming attached, and Uncle Geoffrey very assiduous and admiring. But she thought Ricky didn't like her, and she didn't much care whether he did or not. He inclined to moon about after Lucilla, and was probably jealous. Sarah had been extremely glad to hear that it was poisonously dull to marry a cousin.

It was on the third evening that Mr. Hildred mentioned Mr. John Brown. Miss Marina was knitting a grey and white striped muffler, and

Lucilla was being taught how to play bridge by the other three. They had finished a rubber and Ricky was shuffling for a new deal, when his father remarked.

"There's a client of mine just come down into this part of the world."

Miss Marina dropped a stitch. This always happened if she took her attention off the row she was knitting. She said "Oh dear, dear!" in a perfunctory manner; and then, "What did you say, Geoffrey?"

Ricky let the cards fall with rather a bang, and Lucilla kicked him under the table.

"I said a client of mine had just come down to Holme, Marina."

"Why?" said Miss Marina, her knitting in mid air.

Sarah was also wondering why. There did not seem to be any particular reason why anyone should come to Holme. It had a church, a cemetery, a general shop, some thirty cottages, and an inn called the Cow and Bush.

Mr. Hildred supplied the reason.

"He's an artist and he wants to paint the autumn tints, and he's also a great hand with his camera—does studies of wild life and all that sort of thing."

"Oh!" said Miss Marina in a worried voice. "Lucilla my dear, I think there are three stitches down. If you wouldn't mind—"

"It's such foul wool!" said Lucilla.

"My dear—what a *word*! Thank you so much. What is this gentleman's name, Geoffrey?"

Ricky dropped the cards again. His long pale face looked as sulky as a long pale face can look.

"His name is Mr. John Brown," said Geoffrey Hildred—"Mr. John C. Brown. He has, I believe, written a number of books about birds and animals. He's an American over on a visit, and the more money he spends here the better. He seems to be very well off. It's astonishing what some of these writers make. He was consulting me as to his liability to income tax if he stayed on this side. I was perfectly amazed."

"There's nowhere for him to stay at Holme," said Miss Marina. "Thank you, my dear, I shall be able to get on nicely now. Oh dear, there's another stitch gone! You left them rather far up the needle. Perhaps Miss Trent—"

The comforter passed to Sarah.

Mr. Hildred replied to the first part of his cousin's speech.

"He's at the Cow and Bush. He says he wants to sample an English village inn, but I should think he would soon have enough of it. I think we might ask him to dine. He's a very pleasant fellow. And Lucilla, my dear, I've given him permission on your behalf to go where he likes on your property. He is hoping to get some good photographs of migratory birds. It's a queer taste, but he seems very keen about it."

Sarah handed back the comforter with the stitches rammed well down.

"I say, are we going to play another rubber or aren't we?" said Ricky Hildred crossly.

Lucilla giggled a good deal over her lesson. She ran her fingers through her hair and said "Marvellous!" when she had three aces. She scowled and informed the table that her hand was "putrid" when its highest card was a knave. And she revoked whenever it was humanly possible to revoke. She seemed to enjoy the game very much, and was more than loth to go to bed.

Sarah went up when she did. She was feeling pleased with life. Uncle Geoffrey had held her hand in a lingering clasp, and Aunt Marina had called her my dear when she said good-night. Ricky could look as much of a cross spoilt child as he liked; it didn't matter in the least to Sarah Trent.

She was just going to get into bed, when the door was opened with a sort of quick push and Lucilla came in without knocking. She shut the door as quickly as she had opened it and stood with her back to it, her left hand still on the handle. She seemed to be trying for her impudent grin, but it trembled and broke. She caught her lower lip between her teeth and stared defiantly at Sarah.

"What on earth's the matter?" said Sarah.

The child was in her nightgown—blue, to match her room. Her fair hair stood up, and her feet were bare. She went on staring for a moment, and then she relaxed, let go of the handle, and took a running jump on to Sarah's bed, where she snuggled down with the pink eiderdown pulled round her.

Sarah said, *"Well!"* and Lucilla nodded. She was smiling now, but she didn't speak. It struck Sarah that the reason she didn't speak was because she couldn't. There had been no colour at all in her face, but either a little pink was coming back to it now, or else the eiderdown which she was clutching round her gave her some reflected colour. It was bright enough in all conscience.

"Well!" said Sarah again.

This time Lucilla spoke. She echoed Sarah's *"Well!"* in a voice with a catch in it.

"What's the matter?" said Sarah. The child was giving her cold feet.

"Nothing."

"Lucilla, has anything frightened you?"

The pale arch of Lucilla's eyebrows lifted a little.

"Of course not!" The eyes under the lifted brows were wide and innocent. She pushed back the eiderdown and stretched.

Sarah had an odd sense of relief from strain. The impudent smile was back again as Lucilla cocked her head on one side and said,

"Isn't this all too pink for words?"

"Why did you come?" said Sarah, sitting down on the edge of the bed.

"An urge," said Lucille trippingly—"just an urge. A sort of "If I don't see my darling Sarah this minute, I shall pass right out' kind of feeling. Don't you ever get an urge like that?"

"No, I don't," said Sarah. "And you ought to be asleep."

"'Macbeth hath murdered sleep, the innocent sleep,'" Lucilla's voice was suddenly a rather creepy whisper.

Sarah put a hand on her shoulder and shook it.

"Dry up! I don't want to have nightmares, if you do."

"Ow!" said Lucilla. "That hurt! All right, we won't talk about Shakespeare any more. It just shows you're not a governess, because any proper govvy would be most frightfully pleased at my knowing that quotation. We'll talk about your lovely pink room instead. Do you love it passionately?"

"Do you?" said Sarah dryly, but behind the dryness she was wondering, and a little afraid.

Lucilla giggled.

"Strike me pink I do! I believe if I had this room instead of mine that it might have a real effect on my moral character. You know—rose-coloured spectacles and all that sort of thing. I could have lovely rosy dreams about the good deeds I was going to do next day, and then when

Annie called me in the morning I should just bound out of bed and do them before the pinkness evaporated."

Sarah looked at her pretty straight.

"You mean you want to change rooms?"

Her arm was caught and squeezed. Lucilla's hands were cold and urgent.

"*Darling* Sarah—would you like to? You're here to cheer me up, you know, and how can I possibly cheer in a blue, blue room? If I have to undress in it, and sleep in it, and get up in it—well, it means I'm in the blues half my time, doesn't it?"

"What was behind all this nonsense? Sarah felt that she would very much like to know. A single fact emerged with unmistakable plainness—Lucilla didn't want to sleep in her own room, and she did want to sleep in Sarah's. Well, Sarah had no objection. She preferred blue to pink, and that was about all there was to it. She said so, and the colour came back into Lucilla's face with a rush. The cold hands gripped her hard for a moment and then let go.

"*Darling* Sarah! And you won't tell anyone? They're such fusses, and Aunt Marina would want to know why and all that sort of thing."

"Well, the girl who calls us will know," said Sarah.

Lucilla nodded.

"I'll square Annie. She won't give it away if I tell her not to. We can change over again to dress if you like, so you needn't move any of your things. Ouf! I'm so sleepy! I don't suppose I shall wake till the tea comes. Good-night, *darling* Sarah."

The two rooms were next to each other, but there was no connecting door. Sarah came out of her own room into a long passage with a glimmering light at the far end. Half a dozen steps took her to Lucilla's door, which stood ajar. She pushed it open and found that the light in the ceiling had been left on. It shone through a pale blue bowl, which gave rather the effect of moonlight. What a stupid woman Mrs. Raimond must have been!

Sarah shut the door and looked about her. She could imagine wanting to scream with rage if she had to live for ever surrounded by nothing but pale blue, but there didn't seem to be anything to be frightened of. Yet Lucilla had certainly been frightened.

Sarah looked under the bed after the time-honoured manner of the nervous spinster. Lucilla's deserted slippers stood there side by side, pale and fluffy and blue. She opened a couple of cupboards and rummaged in them. They contained nothing more alarming than Lucilla's frocks.

The room was about the same size as the one she had left, but since it occupied the corner of the house, it had an additional window. Both rooms had two windows looking upon the garden, but Lucilla's room had a window to the side as well. All the windows here had blue and white striped curtains, and all the curtains were drawn. Sarah pulled them back and discovered that behind the blue and white stripes all the windows were shut and latched. Surely to goodness the child didn't sleep with her windows shut! This would have to be gone into. They were old-fashioned sash windows, very large and heavy, but as they were fitted with pulleys there was no difficulty about moving them. Sarah ground her teeth with rage to find that even the pulley ropes were blue. She could imagine Mrs. Raimond saying, "How sweet!"

She opened the two windows that looked on the garden, switched out the lights, and got into Lucilla's bed. She was sleepy, but behind the sleepiness there was a curious puzzled feeling just touched with fear. If she hadn't been so sleepy, she would have laughed at herself, because there was of course nothing to be afraid of. It was the unreasoning fear which tinges the air of a dream with a murky something which will neither show itself nor yet be gone. Mist—fog—sleep—fear—

Sarah was never sure whether she had really been asleep or not. If she had not crossed the line, she had been very deep in that foggy borderland where thought and feeling are blurred and nothing is very real. The first sound came to her by way of this blurred thought. It may have called her back from actual sleep; she did not know. The first thing she knew was the sound, and it seemed as if it were a very long way off. She began to come back out of the foggy country, waking slowly and reluctantly. Then all at once she was really awake and listening.

There was nothing to listen to in that first waking minute. She thought that she had been wakened by a sound. She rose on her elbow to listen, and the room was as still as if everything in it were asleep except herself. The open windows let in a very faint murmur of leaves moved by some light passing air, but that was not the sound which had called her back from sleep. Yet she did not know what sound it was that had called her back.

It was at this point that Sarah told herself firmly that she had been asleep. The sound wasn't a real sound at all. She had dreamed it and so waked startled from her dream. She sank back on to the pillow again. The light air went to and fro outside, the leaves rustled, and she began to go down into the misty places of sleep.

Then the sound came again.

She waked sharply. One moment she was very nearly off, and the next she was broad awake. This time the sound did not stay behind in any dream. It was in the room. No, not in the room—at the window—at the shut window which looked to the side of the house. Sarah's first coherent thought was one of thankfulness that the window was shut. She had so nearly opened it, but the air blew cold from the east, and, with the other two windows already wide, she had let it be.

She threw back the bed-clothes and sat up. The sound came from the shut window, and it was like the sound of claws scratching on the glass....

She could have laughed with relief—a cat that wanted to come in. And then a quick chill thought—relief had come too soon—a cat doesn't scratch at a door or a window. A dog scratches when it wants to come in; a cat pats with a paddy paw.

The scratching came again with a sort of scrabbling rush. A dog never made a noise like that, and no dog could be on a window ledge so high above the ground.

Sarah got out of bed. She wondered whether it was a bat. It was a really horrid thought, because there were two wide open windows, and if it was a bat that wanted to come in, the way was clear. It would be fatal to put on the light, because bats were always attracted by a light. Without really thinking what she would do, she found herself at one of the two open windows, dragging at the pulleys. The catch went home with a little click. When she had got the second window shut, she stopped again to listen. There was no sound, and she could see nothing. The night was very dark and cloudy. From the other side of the room she had been able to see the break which the tall windows made in the solid blackness of the wall. Now that she was standing close up to them, she could discern one kind of darkness of the sky, and another of the trees. And the shadow under the trees was a deeper, blacker darkness still.

She left the two windows which she had shut and went to the one from which the sound had come. She did not go very near it. From a yard away she stared at the dark glass and could see nothing. And then, as she stood there, something flung itself against the pane in that same scrabbling rush and there was the sound of claws against the glass. She gave an involuntary cry, and in a flash the thing was gone.

She went and sat on the edge of the bed. She wanted to get away from the window, and she wanted to think. She felt as if she would be able to think better if she got away from the window, and if her legs stopped shaking. It was pleasant to think that all the windows were shut and hasped. Presently she would go over to them and draw the curtains. Just now she wanted to sit still and think.

The Thing which had dashed itself against the window within a yard of her was certainly neither cat nor bat. The ledge was narrow. A cat must have overbalanced and fallen, and the Thing was too big to be a bat. The scrabbling claws had struck the pane about half way up and so swept down it and across. An owl—it might have been an owl. But Sarah had stood within a yard of the glass and seen nothing that was lighter than the dense blackness and shadow of the trees which fringed the drive on this side of the house. She was used enough to owls, but they commonly hunt by moonlight. She had never heard of an owl trying to get into a house. The Thing had dashed itself with force against the pane, and she had seen nothing except a stirring of the darkness. If it had been an owl, she thought she would have seen its eyes, or at the very least some blurring of the glass where the wings and the breast feathers must have been pressed up against it.

How did she know what she would have seen? She thought she would have seen something. She thought the ruffled breast feathers of an owl and the under side of the wings would show light against the glass, and she thought there would have been some green or tawny gleam from the fierce, startled eyes. But she didn't know—she didn't know anything at all. Then she laughed to herself a little angrily. She did know one thing. She knew why Lucilla had wanted to change her room.

She sprang to her feet and switched on the ceiling light. It was like coming out of a nightmare—the dark—and the unknown scrabbling

Thing—and her own scaremongering thoughts—and then the silly blue room with its artificial moonlight streaming down from the ceiling.

Sarah went boldly to the windows and drew the striped curtains across them. She left the side window to the last. If the creature was attracted by the light and came dashing against the glass again, she might get a sight of it. She stood, as she had stood before, about a yard away and waited.... Five minutes—ten—she didn't know how long, but it was a slow, dragging time. She heard a clock strike in the house below. An old wall clock, striking solemnly in the sleeping house. She counted twelve strokes. Then she went forward and pulled the curtain across the window.

Chapter Nine

SARAH SLEPT UNTIL Annie came in with the tea. She woke with the feeling that she had had a great many dreams, but she could not remember what they were. She saw Annie looking at her with round eyes of surprise, and told her to open all the windows and let in some air. She hadn't slept with her windows shut like that since those very far off nursery days before the crash when old Nanna was an undisputed autocrat and didn't hold with letting the night air in.

The open windows admitted a fresh, soft air and a stream of sunlight.

Annie had hardly gone before Lucilla trailed in, clutching Sarah's pink eiderdown in one hand and a wobbling cup of tea in the other. Just as she reached the bed, she began to giggle and the cup slid. Lucilla shrieked, made an acrobatic recovery in the course of which she dropped the eiderdown, and finished up by thrusting the cup and saucer at Sarah, who was glad enough to get them away from her.

"*Darling!*" Lucilla sat down heavily on Sarah's toes and draped the eiderdown round her. "I'll have my tea now please." She took the cup and sipped from it, looking over the brim with round, solemn eyes. "And how did my darling Sarah sleep?"

"How did you expect me to sleep?" said Sarah.

Lucilla took a large, noisy mouthful of tea and gulped it down. Her eyes had changed though; Sarah could have sworn to that. She could not have sworn to what the change portended. Oddly enough, she thought it was relief.

"Well?" said Sarah after a moment. "What about it? How did you expect me to sleep in here?"

Lucilla's face shut up. The laughter went out of it. Everything else went too. It was just a face, with a nose, two eyes, and rather a secret mouth. She finished her tea and put down the cup. She looked sideways at Sarah.

"Did you lie awake and long for your lovely pink room? It's a beautiful room to sleep in. I slept like a top."

Sarah sat up and caught her by the wrists.

"Now, you little fiend—look at me! Were you playing tricks last night?"

"*I?*" The blue eyes were as round as saucers.

"Yes, you. Were you playing tricks?"

The relief flashed out again. This time Sarah was sure of it.

"What sort of tricks?"

Sarah let go of her, jumped out of bed, and ran to the east window. The sun streamed in through it, very pleasant and golden. The trees which bordered the drive were golden too in their autumn dress, with here and there the dark green of pine, holly, and yew. They had all been black together when the clock struck twelve. But she was not concerned with the trees. She was looking at the bare half inch of window-ledge beyond the sash. Nothing that went on legs could have clung there to dash itself against the glass. "It was an owl," said Sarah in the daylight.

She leaned out of the window and looked along the side of the house. There were other windows—a bathroom, a spare room, Ricky's room. His was the farthest away. She wondered if he had heard anything. Below, and a little to the left, was the porch which covered the side door. It had a flat top with a low stone balustrade. From the level of the porch a ledge about eight inches wide ran round the house, swelling out into a cornice above the ground-floor windows. A cat might have come along that ledge and then climbed up the creeper to Lucilla's window. There was an ampelopsis flaming in crimson and maroon, and an old wistaria with a gnarled stem that spread about the corner. Yes, a cat could very well have climbed to the window. By no conceivable means could it have clung to that half-inch ledge whilst it dashed itself against the pane.

She heard a breath taken, and turned sharp round to find Lucilla at her elbow. If she had been less quick, she might not have surprised the expression which she did surprise. She felt that afterwards. At the time she was only concerned as to the meaning which that expression might have. She thought it was fear, but there was more to it than that, and what the more might be she couldn't tell. She stopped thinking that it was Lucilla who had played tricks in the night, but not in time to stop the words that were already on her tongue.

"Was it you?"

The expression was gone in a flash. An ingenuous surprise took its place.

"Was *what* me?"

"Something banged on the glass," said Sarah, watching her.

A sudden colour ran up to the roots of Lucilla's hair. She took a breath which came near to being a gasp and blinked her eyes as if she had been hit. She repeated Sarah's words unsteadily.

"Something—banged—against the glass?"

"Yes," said Sarah.

Lucilla caught her by the arm with two very cold hands. They gripped hard. She said,

"What?"

Sarah said, "I don't know."

"You heard it?"

"Yes."

"You're sure?"

"Of course I'm sure."

"Did you see anything?"

"No."

Lucilla let go of her arm, turned in a wavering sort of fashion, and went back to the bed. When she got there, she went down in a crouching heap with her head on her arms and her shoulders heaving.

Sarah looked at her, frowning, for a moment. Then she took the pale blue tumbler from the shelf above the blue china wash-basin and filled it at the ridiculous pale blue tap. It went through her mind that it must have annoyed Mrs. Raimond not to be able to arrange for a flow of sky-blue water. She told Lucilla to sit up and have a drink, and when there was no response, informed her that the alternative was a tumblerful of cold water down her back.

Lucilla sat up with amazing suddenness. She said "Beast! You wouldn't!" And then she grabbed the glass and drank from it.

When she had finished, Sarah said seriously,

"What's all this *about*, Lucilla?"

"I don't know," said Lucilla in a small flat voice. Then she said, "You did hear it?"

"It was an owl," said Sarah in her firmest voice.

Lucilla seemed to put that away—Sarah thought it didn't interest her. She said again,

"But you *did* hear it?"

"Yes, of course."

"Cross your heart?"

"Yes, you little idiot!"

"You're not saying it just to please me?"

"Why should it please you?"

There was a silence. The door behind which Lucilla lived opened a very little way. Sarah was aware of the door, and she was aware that it was opening. She thought it didn't open very often. She wondered if it was the real Lucilla who looked out at her through the chink, wary but driven into speech.

"If you heard it—" The child paused, steadied herself, and went on. "If you did hear it—then it wasn't—just—me."

Sarah kicked herself for not having got there before. She said at once in a steady, every-day voice,

"Of course it wasn't you. Don't be an ass. I don't know what it was, but it made the hell of a row. I thought it was going to break the glass. I expect it was an owl."

The chink went suddenly and the door was shut. Lucilla made an impudent face.

"Governesses shouldn't say hell—not in front of the child anyway."

Chapter Ten

THEY MET MR. JOHN BROWN in the woods that morning. He seemed to have been sketching. At any rate he had with him a block and a paint box in a ramshackle old satchel which hung dangling from an untidy canvas strap. It was the paint box, a corner of which stuck out through a gaping tear, which enabled them to feel quite certain that the stranger loafing through Lucilla's woods was the client who had Uncle Geoffrey's permission to sketch there.

Sarah was rather amused by the way in which Lucilla went up to him.

"Are you Mr. Brown?"

Mr. John Brown said that he was.

"I'm Lucilla Hildred. My uncle told us you would like to sketch here. This is my friend Miss Trent."

Lucilla was being rather grand, because she was shy, and she wasn't at all used to being shy.

Mr. John Brown responded politely. He said it was very nice of her to let him wander about. He smiled slightly, and his eyes, which seemed lighter than they really were against the deep brown of his skin, looked at her for a moment as if they were looking right through her—an odd piercing look with a hint of amusement in it. And then he wasn't looking at Lucilla any more. It was Sarah who was being looked through and wasn't sure that she liked it. It may be said at once she hadn't the slightest idea that this was not their first meeting. When she had stopped his car by the east drive of Holme Fallow, she had been aware of no more than a shadow and a voice—Mr. John Brown had taken good care of that. At the Lizard she had not seen him at all. Not that it would have mattered to Mr. Brown if she had. He had good enough reasons for not wishing her to remember that she had seen him in the neighbourhood of Holme Fallow that night, but anyone may go to the Lizard, and she was welcome to remember that she had seen him there. As it turned out, she had not seen him.

She looked at him now for the first time, and might have liked him if he had not made her angry by looking through her and looking amused. He was well enough—the sort of man she rather liked—not young, not old—forty or something less. He looked hard and fit, and quite extraordinarily brown, and he wore his old tweed suit easily. But what in the name of all that was outrageous did he find amusing about Sarah Trent? He had a quiet, pleasant voice and an American accent. The motorist who had been stopped by Miss Trent had had no accent. Sarah did not think of this, because she had no reason to think of it. She was engaged in being angry with Mr. John Brown. She did not in any way connect him with the motorist.

He had now turned back to Lucilla.

"Mr. Hildred has very kindly asked me to dinner to-night."

"Are you coming?" Lucilla had stopped being grand. She now looked and spoke with the naive directness of a child.

"I should like to come very much," said Mr. Brown.

And that was all. They went one way, and he another.

He came to dinner in the evening, and made a very good impression. Miss Marina took a great fancy to him. What she chiefly desired was a good listener, and Mr. John Brown listened very well indeed. During dinner he lent a respectfully attentive ear to one of her longer stories, the one about the house which her parents had so nearly taken when she was in her early teens and which turned out afterwards to have a skeleton buried in the garden.

"Such an escape! And so much more suitable that it should have been the Bishop of Blackminster who took it."

Mr. Hildred said, "Nonsense, Marina!" and Lucilla asked "Why?" rather pertly, but Mr. John Brown went on listening a little vaguely but still very respectfully while Miss Marina told him all about the skeleton being the skeleton of the gardener's wife.

"Only of course he wasn't gardener there any longer, because the whole thing had happened about thirty years before, and he said the poor thing had run away to America with their lodger, and all the time he'd killed her and buried her in the garden. So wasn't that a merciful escape?"

"For her, or for him?" said Ricky with his rather sniggering laugh.

Lucilla kicked him under the table, and Miss Marina flowed serenely on.

"For my parents, dear boy. My mother was very nervous and delicate, and I'm sure such an unpleasant thing as a skeleton in the garden would have upset her very much. I've often heard her say that she would have insisted on my father leaving at once. She had a feeling that the lodger might be there too. But it shows, does it not, Mr. Brown, that murder will out?"

Quite seriously and respectfully Mr. John Brown disagreed.

"Not always, Miss Hildred," he said. "A great many murders are never found out at all. They are too carefully planned and too cleverly carried out."

To Sarah's surprise she felt a shiver run over her. She and Mr. Brown were on one side of the table, with Lucilla and Ricky opposite. Uncle Geoffrey had the head and Aunt Marina the foot. It was as if a little cold wind had moved in the room. Sarah's spine crept. She looked across to Lucilla and frowned. What was the matter with them all? The girl looked as white as a bit of paper. From her left, Mr. Hildred said,

"Rather a ghastly topic for the dinner-table, Marina. Lucilla will be having bad dreams." He began with pleasant ease to talk of a play he had seen in town. Was Mr. Brown fond of the theatre?... Well then, he should certainly not miss such first-class acting.

In the drawing-room Miss Marina approved of Mr. Brown. She produced her very highest award. "My dear, I think we may say—*a gentleman*. Do you not agree with me?"

Sarah agreed. Lucilla giggled.

Miss Marina went on talking happily about the decadence of manners, and how rare it was to meet anyone whom you could call a gentleman—"I mean, of course, my dear, outside one's own circle and social connections"—until the men came in.

It was later in the evening that Sarah found herself a little apart from the others with Geoffrey Hildred. He was, she found, an enthusiastic collector of china, and he had taken her to the far end of the room to show her what she privately thought an extremely ugly plate. Uncle Geoffrey, it appeared, admired it with passion. It was Lucilla's property, having been one of her mother's wedding presents, and he feared very much that it had never been properly appreciated. Lucilla, of course, was too young—"And poor Lucy's taste—well, well, I mustn't say anything about that now, poor thing." He discoursed instead upon ceramics in general, and Chinese art in particular. He handled the plate lovingly, and made Sarah feel the glaze. It was a long time before she had an opportunity of saying more than "Yes," and, "I see." All the Hildreds seemed to like being listened to, and in a general way Sarah did not mind listening. Uncle Geoffrey's discourse was interesting enough, but she had something to say, and she thought this might be a good opportunity of saying it. She waited as long as possible and then plunged.

"Mr. Hildred—may I ask you something?"

He looked first surprised and then rather pleased.

"My dear Miss Trent, of course, of course." There was a moment when Sarah wondered whether the "Miss Trent" would be forthcoming, but there it was, quite conventional and proper. Uncle Geoffrey's blue eyes beamed affectionately upon her as he assured her that he was at all times at her disposal. "Anything I can do, or anything you want to know."

"Thank you very much, Mr. Hildred, it's very nice of you. I want to ask you something about Lucilla. Is she very imaginative?"

Uncle Geoffrey looked distressed. His beaming gaze clouded a little.

"Now what exactly do you mean by that?"

"Just what I say." Why must people always beat about the bush? None of the Hildreds seemed to be able to give a plain answer to a plain question.

"Imaginative? You don't by any chance mean—untruthful, Miss Trent?"

Sarah didn't start, because she wouldn't let herself start. She had the impulse, but she controlled it. She looked down the long room. Miss Marina was knitting. Lucilla leaned shoulder to shoulder with Ricky at the card-table, where Mr. Brown was doing a trick. She seemed a happy, care-free child.

There was a little angry warmth in Miss Trent's voice as she said,

"I meant just what I said—is Lucilla imaginative?"

He seemed to find it difficult to answer her.

"I don't know—it is so difficult to define. It depends on what you mean by imaginative. Do you, for instance, mean the power to visualize something that really exists, or do you mean a faculty for being obsessed by what has no existence at all?" He looked at her very gravely, and again Sarah was startled.

"Mr. Hildred—what are you implying?"

His voice was as serious as his look.

"I am not implying anything at all—I am trying to clarify your question."

"You haven't answered it," said Sarah bluntly.

"I think you must answer it yourself," said Geoffrey Hildred, and with that he crossed the room and pined the group at the table.

Mr. John Brown could do the most amazing card-tricks. He had a quiet, easy patter and a quickness of hand that defied detection. The evening passed very pleasantly.

When he said good-night, Mr. Brown looked at Sarah with the same hint of amusement which had annoyed her so much in the wood and said,

"I think there is a friend of yours at the Cow and Bush."

"Of *mine*?"

Sarah was so astonished that she forgot to draw her hand away. John Brown held it in the same light, firm clasp with which he would have held any small creature such as a bird or a mouse. He was an adept at holding things so that they could neither hurt themselves nor get away. He held Sarah's hand, and felt her start when he said in his pleasant, quiet voice,

"Isn't Mr. Darnac a friend of yours?"

"Ran!" said Sarah, stupefied. Then she remembered about her hand and pulled it away.

"If that is what you call him"—said John Brown, "He said he was hoping to see you to-morrow."

"Well!" said Sarah when he was gone. *"Of all the impudence!"*

Ricky sniggered, Lucilla giggled, and everyone looked at Miss Trent in an interested way.

Her colour rose with pure rage. How dared Ran came down to Holme like this? It wouldn't lose her her job, but it might have done. She thanked heaven that Aunt Marina was looking benevolent—Uncle Geoffrey not quite so benevolent, but quite bland.

"A friend of yours, my dear?" enquired Miss Marina. "And I don't know if I quite caught the name."

"Darnac," said Sarah—"Bertrand Darnac. He's a nephew of Major Manifold's, and it's like his nerve to come down here without being asked. I hope you really do believe that I didn't ask him." She spoke to Aunt Marina, but she looked at Uncle Geoffrey. He was frowning.

"If this man is annoying you—"

Sarah's flush was subsiding, but her laugh still sounded angry.

"Oh, he's perfectly harmless. Just a bit of a brat, you know."

"Darnac?" said Miss Marina. "Now that sounds French. But if he is Major Manifold's nephew—"

"Major Manifold's sister married a Frenchman called Darnac—an old Huguenot family. This lad's over here partly to put a polish on his English, and partly—" She hesitated for a moment and then decided on frankness. After all it was only what everyone knew. "Well, partly because the Darnacs and the Manifolds both hoped that he and Eleanor would take a fancy to each other."

"My dear—*first cousins!*" said Miss Marina, scandalized.

"Well, it's the property," said Sarah. "Eleanor will have a lot of money, but the place goes to Bertrand unless the Manifolds have a son. Old Mr. Manifold left it that way. He was very fond of Ran.'

"And are they engaged," said Miss Marina—"this young man and his cousin?" Her voice sounded disapproving.

Sarah laughed and shook her head.

"Oh no—they don't like each other a bit. Eleanor thinks he laughs at her. She's rather serious. It's aggravating for the family, because Ran falls in love so easily. I should think Eleanor's the only girl he's ever met that he hasn't made love to. He's quite a nice lad, but he wants smacking." She turned to Geoffrey Hildred. "I'm awfully sorry he's come down here like this."

She got a benign smile.

"My dear Miss Trent, you mustn't distress yourself—there's really no need to—no need at all. We shall be very pleased to see your friend. Some young society is just what Lucilla needs."

Sarah's colour rose again. She wasn't going to be responsible for Ran and his behaviour.

"He makes love to every girl he meets," she said. "That's why it's so annoying about Eleanor. But she's the *only* exception. He's certain to make love to Lucilla."

"That will be very amusing for Lucilla," said Uncle Geoffrey.

Chapter Eleven

WHEN THEY WENT UPSTAIRS Sarah wondered which room she was going to sleep in. She entered the pink room, and Lucilla followed and shut the door.

"Well?" said Sarah.

Lucilla put her hands together after the manner of the infant Samuel.

"Angel darling Sarah—" she began.

"I suppose that means you want to sleep in here again. No one ever calls you an angel unless they want you to do something disagreeable."

Lucilla looked at her coaxingly. Her black taffeta frock made her skin look very white, and her hair very pale and golden.

"Angel darling Sarah, it won't be disagreeable—not to-night."

Sarah's eyebrows went up.

"How do you know?"

The joined hands sprang apart and sketched a sort of fluttering movement.

"Just like that—an intuish. Don't you ever have them? What Miss Markleton called an inward monitor. She was the mistress we all hated most. It's a pity you don't know her, because she could have given you splendid lessons in how a govvy ought to talk."

"Lucilla, do stop talking nonsense!"

"I was only explaining about the inward monitor."

"Oh—" said Sarah. "And the inward monitor says I shall have a good night if I go and sleep in your room?"

"Yes, that's what it says."

"Why?" said Sarah.

Lucilla cocked her head a little on one side.

"When I asked you about it out in the woods, you said you pulled back all the curtains and put the light on."

"Yes."

"*Well—*" said Lucilla, as if that explained everything.

"Well what?"

Lucilla sighed.

"Darling Sarah, you're not being very clever. If you drew the curtains and put the light on, anyone could see that it was you who was in my room and not me."

"You think there was someone outside?"

"Sure of it," said Lucilla.

"Why?"

The fair head was shaken.

"Who?"

It was shaken again.

Sarah remembered the ledge that ran round the house at the porch level. Ricky Hildred's room was at the next corner of the house. It was a trick that a boy might play. She said,

"Do you think it was Ricky?"

Lucilla did not shake her head this time. She spoke instead. She said, "No," and then, "Not Ricky. It happened when he was away."

"Then who?"

"Someone who wanted to frighten me." The words were hardly audible. Lucilla's eyes watched her. They said, "Do you believe? Do you?"

Sarah didn't know what she believed. She believed that Lucilla had been frightened. She didn't like the feel of things. There was something horrid, something that moved just out of sight. She didn't like it at all. Lucilla was hiding behind a door which sometimes opened a very little way and then closed again. She thought Lucilla had been frightened because she was not sure that the Thing which had come dashing against her window in the night was a real thing or some horror of her own imagination. Her fear had been allayed as soon as she knew that Sarah had heard just what she herself had heard, and now she seemed quite sure that whatever it was it would not come again. Someone wanted to frighten Lucilla, and it wouldn't come again if it was Sarah Trent who was there to be frightened and not Lucilla Hildred....

Sarah couldn't get any farther than that. She said briskly, "All right, sleep in here if you want to," and let it go at that.

In the blue room she left the side windows shut and locked, and opened the other two windows an inch or two at the top and bottom. She slept all night without moving or dreaming.

It was next day that she had a very disturbing conversation with Geoffrey Hildred. Lucilla and Ricky were playing tennis. Sarah had expected to play too, but on being very pointedly invited to go for a walk with Uncle Geoffrey, she thought that she had better comply. She changed therefore into tweeds and came down to find him waiting for her with rather a serious expression. He talked to her for a time about her life with the Manifolds, about books, and about the changing tints of the countryside.

They took a path which led by way of stile and field-gate through open meadow land, very green with the grass that had grown after the heavy September rainfall. It was an afternoon of bright sun and scudding cloud. The wind must have been very high up, for where they walked it was hardly noticeable.

Geoffrey Hildred pointed out to her how the Holme Fallow woods dipped down to the meadow land on the one side and spread out towards open heath upon the other. Pines mixed at first with deciduous trees, then marched alone, becoming more and more scattered until they finally disappeared. The chestnuts were golden, the oaks deep bronze, and the beeches brown. The pines stood dark among the other trees, and black where they cut the sky.

"It is beautiful, is it not?" he said. And then, "Lucilla has a beautiful home."

Sarah said, "Yes, lovely," and wondered what was coming next. She didn't think she had been brought out here to admire Lucilla's woods. She hoped earnestly that Uncle Geoffrey hadn't led her here to give her the sack. She didn't think so, but you never could tell. She lent an attentive ear.

Geoffrey Hildred was looking at her very seriously.

"Miss Trent—last night you asked me a question about Lucilla. I didn't answer it, partly because you took me by surprise and I did not want to say anything which I might afterwards regret, and partly because it didn't seem to me that either the time or the place lent themselves to any serious talk."

"Golly!" thought Sarah to herself.

Mr. Hildred proceeded.

"Now, however, after having had time to think it over, I have decided to have a talk with you. I don't really think it is quite fair to keep you in the dark. You are young, but you appear to me to be sensible and practical."

"Dear sir, these kind words—" murmured Sarah to herself. She continued to regard her employer attentively.

"You are, in fact, just the friend whom Lucilla needs and whom we hoped to secure for her. She does need a friend, Miss Trent—" He broke off to fix a distressed gaze upon Sarah.

Sarah said "Yes?" very quietly. The word was a question, and Geoffrey Hildred nodded.

"Yes," he said. "She's had a shock, you know, and she needs steady, cheerful companionship—and care."

"What kind of care, Mr. Hildred?"

He went on as if she had not spoken.

"Miss Hildred has doubtless told you that she considers it a great pity that Lucilla should have been taken away from school."

"Yes."

"Miss Trent, I am going to tell you in the strictest confidence why Lucilla was taken away from school. Miss Hildred doesn't know what I am going to tell you, and I don't wish her to know. It would only worry and upset her, and she feels the responsibility of being one of Lucilla's guardians quite enough as it is. But I think you ought to know that I removed Lucilla from school because the head mistress asked me to remove her."

"Why, Mr. Hildred?"

"Because, Miss Trent, on two separate occasions the girl's room was found to be on fire."

A flood of the most disturbed feeling surged up in Sarah's mind.

Geoffrey Hildred met her look with one of grave concern.

"I felt as you do," he said—"I felt that it was impossible. I told the head mistress that I really could not believe such a thing. She told me that she could not argue about it. She had thought the first occurrence an accident, and she would join me in hoping that the second fire was also accidental, but she thought that Lucilla would be better at home for a time, and she begged that I would remove her at once. I had of course no choice. I brought her home, and she has seemed to me quite natural, quite normal."

"Mr. Hildred, was she very fond of her mother?"

He looked a little surprised.

"It is rather strange that you should ask me that. You mean, was she so fond of her mother that the shock of her death might have had an unbalancing effect? Well, the point is, I think, well taken, and I think that my answer would be no. I don't mean to say she wasn't fond of her mother, but they were very little together. Mrs. Raimond's second marriage set up rather a difficult situation. Raimond was a very jealous man. He disliked anything that reminded him of the fact that his wife had been married before. Lucilla went to school early, and spent her holidays with Miss Hildred or with school friends. She came down here only for a few days at a time. You see what I mean—there was no very strong bond. Mrs. Raimond was one of those people who—" He stopped himself. "Well, well, she's dead, so I won't say what I was going to say."

"I see," said Sarah. "Mr. Raimond was jealous, and so Lucilla— What a shame!"

"Yes, it's been hard on the child," said Geoffrey Hildred. "And her holidays with Marina—well, you know she's the soul of kindness, but it can't have been exactly lively for a young girl. That is why I shall be pleased if you will bring some young life about the house. I'm letting Ricky off as much as possible, and if this young fellow who followed you down here—this young, what did you say his name was, Darnac?— well, if he's a nice young fellow, we shall be very pleased to have him come about the house. There's tennis, and there are some quite good expeditions all round, and you can run into Ledlington and go to the pictures. You see what I mean, my dear? I want you to take the lead a bit if you will—treat yourself a little more as if you were a daughter of the house—Lucilla's elder sister in fact—and make up pleasant little parties. Marina and I will be really grateful. There—that's what I wanted to say to you."

Sarah looked at him with frank pleasure.

"I think you're most awfully kind," she said, and meant it.

Chapter Twelve

BERTRAND DARNAC did not let the grass grow under his feet. When Sarah returned from her walk with Geoffrey Hildred, they found him making agreeable conversation to Miss Marina, who was quite obviously a good deal smitten. Like most old ladies she had a great indulgence for agreeable and personable young men. Bertrand's ugliness was of the attractive kind, and he could make himself very agreeable indeed.

Mr. John Brown was also there, paying a polite call.

Miss Marina was not as pleased as usual to see her cousin and her dear Miss Trent, because she was in the middle of explaining the whole network of the Hildred family relationships to "that nice Mr. Darnac and that pleasant Mr. Brown." She did not at all want to be interrupted, and of course two fresh people coming into the room cannot help causing an interruption—gentlemen (this was still Miss Marina's phrase) must rise to their feet, and there must be introductions; the atmosphere is changed and the thread of interest broken.

No, Miss Marina was not at all pleased. Her pince-nez dropped and became entangled in the long steel and jet chain which went twice round her neck and slid down into her lap. By the time she had pushed them back on to her nose, to which they always clung very precariously and with a decided tilt either to one side or the other, she found that the party had split into two groups, and that she was left with Mr. Brown as sole auditor.

"Yes, Miss Hildred—you were saying?"

His attention placated her somewhat. The trouble was that she was not quite sure what it was that she had been saying. She had certainly got past the cousinly relationship between Lucilla's great-grandfather, herself, and dear Geoffrey—"my cousin, Mr. Geoffrey Hildred"—and she had narrated at length the marriage and premature decease of Lucilla's grandfather, John Hildred the second.—"Such a shocking accident, Mr. Darnac." But she was a little uncertain as to how far she had proceeded with the characters and fates of poor John's sons, "my nephews, Henry and Jack." She liked talking about Henry and Jack, but she couldn't talk about Maurice, because even after all these years it still made her cry.

Mr. Brown said gently, "You were telling me about your nephews—"
Miss Marina rubbed her nose.

"Yes, yes, I was. But though I call them my nephews, you must understand that they were really the grand-children of my first cousin, who was a great deal older than I, you know, and they always called me Aunt, but I don't want you to be confused about them."

"No—I see—" said Mr. Brown.

"And my nephew Henry—only you will remember that he wasn't really my nephew—my nephew Henry only died a few months ago, after a most sadly wandering life. He never recovered from the war. And poor dear Jack, who was Lucilla's father, was killed in 1916—or was it '15? He was married in 191, I know. He was only twenty, Mr. Brown. Lucilla was born in 1916, and her birthday is in January, so it must have been in 1916 that he was killed, because she was only four or five months old at the time. And poor Lucy—her mother, you know—didn't marry again for nearly three years. And I remember the date of her marriage perfectly well, because my poor Toto died the day before—a most attached spaniel whom I had for fifteen years—and that was in April 1919. Toto died on the fourth, and poor Lucy married Guy Raimond on the fifth."

"And your other nephew?" said Mr. Brown, still very gently.

Miss Marina's pale eyes became suffused with moisture. There was a little pause, the sort of pause which indicates that the bounds of discretion have been overstepped. A tactful visitor should have changed the subject. Instead, Mr. Brown leaned a little nearer and said,

"You had a third nephew, hadn't you, Miss Hildred?"

Miss Marina fumbled for her handkerchief. She held it against the tip of her nose and said in an uncertain voice,

"Yes—Maurice."

"Won't you tell me about him?"

Miss Marina looked at him with reproach. Nobody ever talked to her about Maurice, because they knew that it made her cry, and if she cried, she would be upset and Mercer would scold her and send for Dr. Drayton. He oughtn't to ask her about Maurice like that. She looked at him reproachfully. And then an odd thing happened—she didn't want to cry any more. She found herself saying, "He was such a dear little boy," and it was an ease to her heart to say it.

Mr. Brown said, "Yes?"

"Such a very dear little boy. I saw a great deal of him then, but afterwards he went to school. I was living at Bournemouth, you know. I have lived there for many years—I am only here now on Lucilla's account. So once the boys went off to school I only saw them now and then. I did see Henry once after the war—it was on the Riviera—but the last time I saw Jack—Lucilla's father, you know—was on his sixteenth birthday. And I never saw Maurice after he was fifteen. He was missing in 1918, and we never heard any more, but I've never been able to believe that he was dead."

John Brown looked away quickly. Miss Marina drew a long sighing breath. She felt a strange relief. After a moment she began to talk about Lucilla.

Mr. Darnac had drifted to the window, where Miss Trent was, ostensibly, showing him the view. Mr. Hildred having been called to the telephone, Sarah was wasting no words upon scenery.

"*Really*, Ran—of all the outrageous nerve!"

"What would you?" said Mr. Darnac with a fine gesture, "You go—I follow. It is of a simplicity."

"Oh, is it? Well, just let me tell you, my lad, that you might quite easily have got me the sack!"

Mr. Darnac smiled an ingratiating smile.

"Adored angel, you look most beautiful when you are angry. The colour rises, the eyes sparkle, the eyebrows arch themselves, *et voila*, you are of a beauty so entrancing that you strike me dumb."

"I hadn't noticed it," said Sarah. Then she laughed. "Ran, you really are a priceless ass!"

Mr. Darnac grinned delightedly, showing very white teeth.

"That is all right then. You have, what you say, come off it—we are reconciled. Yes, yes, you must be, for I am bursting with things that I wish to say to you, and you would not like it that I should burst."

"I shouldn't mind."

"My angel, it would compromise you very seriously. No, no, we are definitely reconciled—the brass rags are parted no longer, as you say."

"I don't."

Mr. Darnac waved that away.

"Let us be serious. I have a thousand things to say to you before the old gentleman comes back. You are not yet, how do you say, affianced?"

"I don't say that either," said Sarah.

Mr. Darnac frowned portentously.

"Will you be serious! I tell you I have a thousand things that I wish to say."

"Well, why not say them, my dear Ran?"

He struck an attitude.

"Ah! Then I am no more *darling* to you—you have only this cold *dear* for me! The old gentleman he has—how do you call it?—cut me out!"

Sarah regarded him with mocking indulgence.

"Darling Ran, you never were *in*, so he couldn't cut you out. And he won't like it a bit if he hears you calling him an old gentleman. You're not telling me any of those thousand things, you know."

"I come to them, and the first one it is a question. How do you find yourself here?"

"Very comfy, thanks."

"They are amiable to you?"

I If you like to put it that way."

"What is wrong with how I put it?"

"Well, *I* should say they were very nice to me."

Mr. Darnac rolled the word about his tongue as though it were a sweet whose flavour he disliked.

"Nice—nice! Oh, *mon dieu*, what a word! A *nice* cup of tea—a *nice* day—a *nice* girl—a *nice* dance—a *nice* dinner! Oh la la! But now, Sarah, tell me—that Mr. Brown over there who makes his court to the old lady, who is he? Is he a friend of the family?"

"He's a client of Mr. Hildred's. He has come down here to sketch."

"Does one sketch in the middle of the night?" said Bertrand.

"What do you mean, Ran?"

They were sitting in the broad window-seat, half turned towards the sunny garden. Their heads were close together and their voices low. Sarah's breath came a little more quickly.

"Ran, what *do* you mean?"

"Well, he intrigues me, that one. But you have not answered what I asked you—is he the old friend of the family?"

"No, I told you he wasn't. Mr. Hildred is a solicitor, and he's just one of his clients."

Bertrand nodded.

"Very well then, he intrigues me very much. He also has a room at my Cow and Bush, you understand."

Sarah raised her eyebrows.

"*Your* Cow and Bush?"

"*Ma foi*, yes—since I am living there. If you had not a heart of stone, you would be touched by my devotion. It is not everyone that would stay at a Cow and Bush for you, my angel. Well, *j'y suis et j'y reste*. And in the next room to mine there is this Mr. Brown. Do you know this Cow and Bush? See—the stair goes up from the hall, and at the top of the stair on the left-hand side there is my room, and on the right-hand side there is his room. The landlord he shuts his door at half-past ten and we all go to bed. We have drunk beer and we sleep. But me, I do not like beer, and so I do not drink it and I do not go to sleep. I read a book, I sit at my window, I put out my light and look at the moon and think about all sorts of things—perhaps I think about you."

"Fiddlesticks!" said Sarah.

Bertrand looked hurt.

"I find your disposition very hard and unfeminine. I tell you that I think of you alone at midnight, and you say 'Fiddlesticks!'"

Sarah laughed again.

"Get along with your story, my child! You've nut in the local colour very nicely. Now let's get down to what happened. I suppose something really did happen?"

He nodded.

"I sat there, and I thought how much I hated beer and how much I adored you, and the moon went behind a cloud, and perhaps I got a little sleepy. And then all at once I heard something."

"What?"

"I did not know. I looked out of the window. There was a little light, but not very much. I saw someone get out of Mr. Brown's window and climb down the wall. There is a pear-tree fastened against it, so it is quite easy for anyone to climb up and down. Well, he went down into the garden, and he went away round the house walking like a cat without any sound at all. I do not know what that first sound was— perhaps he knocks something over. But there were no more sounds. I think to myself, perhaps it is a burglar and he has been stealing Mr. Brown's money, so I go to his room and I knock upon the door. There is no answer. Then I take a candle and I go in, and there is no one there. And then I wonder about this Mr. Brown, and I go to bed and I go to sleep, and I do not know at what time Mr. Brown comes back. That was the first night that I was here. I have been here three nights, and every night this Mr. Brown has climbed out of his window. I find it irregular, even a little—what do you say?—fishy."

It was at this moment that Geoffrey Hildred came back into the room.

"A call from my office," he explained. "I am on holiday, but unfortunately they know where I am. You can't really get a holiday unless you can get away from the telephone. Marina, my dear, I'm thinking of cutting the wires."

"My dear Geoffrey!" And then, "Mr. Brown was just asking me whether we hadn't any photographs of the boys—of Henry and Jack. He thinks he may have met Henry some years ago. But I was telling him that we haven't any photographs at all—not here. Poor Henry never would be photographed, and the others were so young when they—when Jack was killed. Poor little Lucilla's father, you know. He was only twenty. I have some snapshots taken when they were children, but I haven't got them here. But of course there would probably be copies up at Holme Fallow—wouldn't there, Geoffrey?"

"I don't know of any," said Geoffrey Hildred, "unless—" He turned to Mr. Brown. "Now that's a very funny thing, Brown, we had a burglary up at Holme Fallow the other day—the house broken into, a man's muddy foot-marks all over the place—and the only thing interfered with was an old desk which held papers and photographs. The lock had been forced. I don't really know why it was kept locked, because there was nothing of value in it, but I suppose the fellow hoped to find something worth having, and then perhaps he was disturbed or something alarmed him. Anyhow nothing of any value was taken. Everything in the desk had been turned over, but it is quite impossible to say whether anything is missing."

"I see," said Mr. Brown in his quiet way.

Chapter Thirteen

MR. BROWN and Mr. Darnac stayed to tea.

Sarah was not quite sure afterwards who first started the idea of a picnic. She had been a good deal taken up with her own thoughts, and when she emerged from them it seemed to be a settled thing that there was to be a picnic, and the sooner the better, because no one could expect such wonderful weather to go on for ever. It would have to be a lunch picnic, because the evenings had begun to close in. The only point which hadn't been decided was where they should go. The question was being debated by the Hildred family, with the three outsiders as audience. The choice seemed to lie between the Roman camp on Burdon Hill, Trant Woods, and Burnt Heath. Lucilla fancied the woods. There was a stream, and there would be scarlet toadstools in a clearing.

Miss Marina instantly vetoed woods—"Far, far too damp, my dear." Whereupon Lucilla made a face and joined Ricky in voting for the Roman camp—"And two of us can bicycle, and Sarah can take two more in *The Bomb*."

Miss Marina looked shocked.

"But, my dear, you can have Giles and the Daimler."

Lucilla blew her a kiss across the table.

"Darling, we don't want him. It would be exactly like a personally conducted tour, and if you won't let me go in *The Bomb*—"

"Oh, my dear child—no!"

Lucilla sighed.

"Well, I'd rather bicycle than be conducted by Giles. That's two on the bikes and three in *The Bomb*."

"But what about Miss Hildred?" said Sarah.

Miss Marina explained in tones of horror that she never went for picnics—Mercer wouldn't hear of it for a moment—Mercer didn't really think she ought even to sit out in the garden as late in the year as this—only this morning Mercer had said quite sharply, "After all, ma'am, we're in October, and you oughtn't to forget it."

Sarah turned to Uncle Geoffrey.

"But you're coming—aren't you?"

"Well, I'm afraid not. That call I had just now obliges me to go up to town. I shall have to leave you to get into mischief without me."

"I hope no one will get into mischief at all," said Miss Marina firmly.

Sarah retired into her thoughts again. There was something she wanted to say, but she didn't quite know the best way of getting it said. Bertrand's story about Mr. Brown and his midnight wanderings had given her a lot to think about. She wondered if it was he who had frightened Lucilla. She could imagine no reason why he should have done so. The fact remained that Lucilla was convinced that someone had played a trick to frighten her, and if Mr. Brown was given to mysterious wanderings at night, it might have been he. The mysterious something which had dashed itself against the window might have been an owl, but Sarah wasn't able to feel as certain of this as she would have liked. Lucilla obviously did not believe that it was an owl. She believed that someone was trying to frighten her, and that this someone, having discovered that it was Sarah who was now occupying the blue room, would run no further risks. *But* if this someone—who might be Mr. Brown—could be induced to believe that Lucilla had returned to the blue room, he might make another attempt. Sarah thought she would dearly like to catch him at it. She hadn't forgotten the horrid moment between sleeping and waking when she had heard that clawing on the window-pane.

It was all very well, but how was she going to convey the necessary information to Mr. Brown, or to whoever else the owl might be? She hadn't altogether excluded Ricky from her suspicions, and he was of the age for a practical joke of a rather clumsy kind. You can't just burst into a conversation about plays (this was Uncle Geoffrey, who seemed to have a passion for the theatre), picnics (Ricky, Lucilla, and Ran), and the horrid prevalence of jazz (Aunt Marina)—you can't just burst in on all these things with a bald "I slept in the blue room last night, but Lucilla's going to sleep there to-night."

What made it all the more difficult was that Uncle Geoffrey and Aunt Marina were both addressing their conversation to Mr. Brown, who replied to them alternately. He seemed to be keeping his head, but it was not to be supposed that he could have much attention to spare for any observation that Sarah might make. Yet in the end it was he who gave her her chance. The three-cornered conversation languished.

Uncle Geoffrey was appealed to by Lucilla, and Aunt Marina became occupied with the teapot. Whereupon Mr. Brown turned to Miss Trent and asked her if she were an early riser.

"There was such an uncommonly fine sunrise this morning."

"Ah, that means rain," said Geoffrey Hildred, striking in.

Mr. Brown persisted gently.

"Did you see it? The colours were really wonderful. But perhaps your windows look the wrong way?"

Here was Sarah's chance, but it was offered to her in such a way as to strengthen all her suspicions. She said, smiling sweetly,

"I might have seen it if I'd been awake."

Geoffrey Hildred intervened again.

"Oh, hardly, I think. Your windows—"

"Oh, but I've been sleeping in Lucilla's room, which has a window to the east. I should have seen the sunrise beautifully if I hadn't been asleep. I'm the world's best sleeper, you know."

Miss Marina looked across the table with a worried frown.

"But, my dear, wasn't your own room comfortable?"

"Oh yes, lovely," said Sarah. "We just thought we'd change for a night or two. I'm going back to my own room to-night."

"But, my dear—"

"It was too, too blue," said Lucilla plaintively. "I felt a little pinkness would do me good. I was getting the blues all over—like the mould on a cheese. You know, they always say on the lids of things, 'Mould does not impair contents,' but I don't like it terribly myself."

Miss Marina looked completely bewildered.

"My dear child, *mould*? Are you feeling ill? Would you like me to send for Doctor Drayton?"

Ricky burst out laughing. It was rather a rude laugh. Sarah gave him a black mark for it. She didn't find herself liking Ricky Hildred very much. He mooned about after Lucilla, gave himself possessive airs towards her, and sulked when she snubbed him. It was quite obvious that he had no love for Miss Trent, and Miss Trent, who was unaccustomed to being disliked by young men, found herself a good deal irritated. She also considered him ill-bred, ill-mannered, and a dreep. She conveyed as much of this as it was possible to convey with a pair of finely expressive eyes, and devoted her attention to soothing

Aunt Marina. In this she was ably assisted by Mr. Brown. If it hadn't been for her suspicions, she would have found herself liking him a good deal for his courteous manner and pleasant talk.

When they went up to bed that night, Lucilla came into the pink room with her and said,

"Are you really going to turn me out? I very nearly screamed at tea when you said we had changed rooms and were going to change back again. Why did you?"

"I want to find out who's trying to frighten you," said Sarah.

That bright, strange flush came into Lucilla's face. She looked eagerly at Sarah, opened her mouth as if to speak, and then shut it again. After a moment she said,

"What are you going to do?"

Sarah shook her head.

"I didn't say I was going to do anything. When you're ready for bed, draw back the curtains, and stand up in the window with the light on. If anyone's watching, they'll know that you are there, and then we shall see whether the owl comes again or not."

Lucilla averted her eyes. She was pale again. She said in a small, uneven voice, "It isn't an owl," and ran quickly out of the room.

Sarah sat down and read for half an hour. Then she took off the dress which she had worn for dinner and put on a soft dark brown woolly suit and dark shoes and stockings. She switched off the pink-shaded light, opened the door a little, and looked out.

The passage was dark, but there was a thread of light under Lucilla's door, and when she came to the corner and looked round the turn, there was another bright line under Ricky Hildred's door.

She went back and sat in the dark for the most interminable time. Looking for threads of light is a game that more than one can play. If Ricky was playing tricks, he might want to be sure that she was asleep before he got going.

After what felt like several months Sarah looked out again.

There was no light under Lucilla's door.

There was no light under Ricky's door.

She took her shoes in her hand and went in her stocking feet to the head of the stair. It was as dark as it could be without being pitch dark. She could see the shade of the window that lighted the staircase, and she could discern the black well of the stair. She began to go down with her left hand on the baluster rail, slowly, one step at a time, until she came down into the empty hall. When she had passed the baize door which led to the kitchen premises she breathed more easily. She had planned to get out of the house by way of the servants' sitting-room, because if anyone was playing tricks outside Lucilla's window, she wanted to catch him at it. She only wished she had a better torch. She would have liked the one the burglar had been using at Holme Fallow—a really useful torch. She didn't know whether there would be a moon or not, but if there was one there was, and if there wasn't there wasn't—she couldn't do anything about it.

She groped her way to the door of the servants' room. As soon as she was inside she put on her torch. A warm flavour of cigarette smoke hung upon the air. Sarah wondered whether Mercer smoked, and what on earth Aunt Marina would say if she knew. She tried to picture Mercer with a cigarette, and failed. It simply wouldn't fit in with her neat fussy fronts, her discreet voice, and her air of keeping herself to herself. Watson smoked of course, and probably the cook. She thought Mercer would get a good deal of quiet pleasure out of disapproving of them and telling Miss Marina how much she disapproved. She laughed a little as she opened the window and got out over the ledge.

She drew the sash down to within about an inch of the sill, put her torch in her pocket, and began to make her way round the house.

Chapter Fourteen

THE SERVANTS' WING was screened off by a shrubbery. Sarah blundered into a holly bush and pricked herself. Presently she was clear of the shrubs and moving along the terraced walk between the house and the garden. Uncle Geoffrey's window looked this way. Aunt Marina's windows looked this way, her bedroom first, and then her sitting-room, with the glazed-in balcony which marked the middle of the house. These had been Mrs. Raimond's rooms. She glanced up as she passed. The house stood black above her, and all the windows were blank and dark. A spare room came next, with its dressing-room. Then her own room. Then Lucilla's.

She came to the corner of the house, and hesitated. The window she wanted to watch was round the corner, looking east. There was an open gravelled space with a belt of trees and shrubs beyond. Gravel is the most abominable stuff to walk on if you want to move quietly. This particular gravel was of the malignantly crunchy kind, and she blenched at the idea of crossing it. Instead, she felt her way down the stone steps at the end of the terrace and took a narrow path which led to the back of the shrubbery.

It was while she was standing at the corner of the house making up her mind what to do next that she realized that there was a moon. The sky over the trees showed light, with a dappled mass of cloud banked up almost to the zenith, and she was only half way down the steps, when the cloud-wrack rifted, and the moon came out. The shadow of a tall yew lay black as ink across her way, and the terrace, the upper half of the steps, and she herself were all bathed in moonlight. Sarah jumped three steps, scrambled the rest, and plunged into the shadow of the yew. There must be a wind high up to move the clouds like that. It had been quite dark when she climbed out of the window. It was all rather disconcerting, and she found herself breathing quickly. She could have been seen on the steps from any of the windows which looked this way. Well, who was there to see her? Aunt Marina wouldn't be hanging out of her window at midnight, and Uncle Geoffrey looked as if he would be one of your strong, persevering sleepers. That rosy complexion and that bright blue eye didn't suggest a burning of the midnight oil. The spare room was empty, and there remained only Lucilla's windows and her own.

She began to make her way along the shrubbery path. It was a narrow path, heavily shaded by great mounds of yew, and holly, and laurustinus, but between the shadows there were disconcertingly bright patches. Sarah had to keep reminding herself that there was nothing criminal about walking in the garden at an unorthodox hour. She would really have given anything to run back to her room—"And you're not going to do that, Sarah my girl, so it's not the slightest use bleating."

She pursued the path until she thought she had gone far enough, and then left it to cut through the shrubbery to a point on the edge of the gravel from which she reckoned she would get a good view of the east window of Lucilla's room. She passed between a bush of holly and a bush of bay, and at that moment the moonlight dimmed and went out. Where there had been black shadow and bright light there was only an even gloom. She moved through it with her hands stretched out before her and the oddest feeling that she was wading. It was as if she, and the trees, and the bushes had all been plunged into the sudden depths of some impalpable sea whose dark tides lifted and fell far, far above and out of reach. She could not see at all, she could only feel.

She moved on a step at a time with outstretched hands.

They felt smooth shiny leaves.

They felt rough bark.

They felt twigs.

They felt holly prickles.

They felt the cold, hard contour of a man's cheek.

Sarah stopped dead with the feel of it tingling all up her arm. Her lips parted in a gasp. And immediately before her in the darkness a voice said, "Please don't scream."

Sarah gasped again. She recognized the voice, and she didn't recognize it. It was Mr. John Brown's voice. But Mr. John Brown had an American accent, and this voice had no accent at all. And as she steadied herself, it came to her that she had heard the voice in the dark before, when she had held up a car at the east gate of Holme Fallow and a stranger had let her have a fill-up of petrol for *The Bomb*. The voice said softly but firmly,

"It's all right, Miss Trent."

Sarah was as angry as she had ever been in her life. How dared he lurk? How dared he tell her not to scream? She said in a whisper of passionate rage,

"What are you doing here?"

He had come nearer. He spoke from an inch or two above her left ear. He said,

"I might ask you that."

Sarah was now quite sure that he was Mr. Brown, and almost as sure that he was the stranger whom she had stopped. She thought the American accent was creeping back again. Do you have an accent in a whisper? It wasn't really a whisper; it was a soft, uncarrying tone. Do you take an accent on and off again? Not unless you have something to conceal. If he hadn't something to conceal, why hadn't he said at once that they had met before? He had seen her all right, because she had stood right in the head-lights of his car. These thoughts whirled angrily through her mind. She said, quite low but with evident fury.

"You haven't answered me—and you've got to answer me. What are you doing here at this time of night hiding in the shrubbery?"

"Hiding?" said Mr. Brown.

"Lurking," said Sarah. "And if I had screamed and roused the house, I should like to know what you would have had to say?"

"It would have been awkward," confessed Mr. Brown, but there was no awkwardness in his voice, which sounded frankly amused and quite definitely American. "I'm very glad you didn't scream. You will remember that I asked you not to. I should like to congratulate you on your self-control."

"Thank you," said Sarah. "And now will you please tell me what you were doing here."

There was the slightest of pauses before he said,

"Yes, I think I'll tell you. I think I should have told you to-morrow anyhow if there had been a good opportunity. If you don't mind, I'll begin at the beginning."

"I don't mind where you begin," said Sarah with her chin in the air.

Mr. Brown began to speak in a quiet, serious voice.

"This is Friday. I've been at the Cow and Bush since last Saturday. You, I believe, arrived on the Monday."

"Well?"

"Well, on the Monday evening I was walking through the grounds of this house. Perhaps evening is not quite correct—it was as late as this or a little later."

"What were you doing here?"

"Oh, just walking," said Mr. Brown. "You know I have Mr. Hildred's permission to wander wherever I like."

"I don't suppose he meant the Red House shrubberies at midnight."

"I don't suppose he did. If you really want an explanation, I daresay I could find one, but it would be rather a waste of time. The actual point is that I was here on Monday night. I was standing a little nearer the house on the edge of the drive, when I heard a sound which attracted my attention. It was a sort of thud, and it was followed by a second thud, and by the sound of something scraping or clawing against glass.

I looked up at the house and I saw a large black object moving against the end window of the first floor."

Sarah drew a quick angry breath.

"Wasn't it dark?"

"Fairly."

"Then how could you see in the dark?"

The amusement came back into Mr. Brown's voice.

"Well, that just happens to be one of my accomplishments. It's useful in my job. I just happen to be able to see pretty nearly as well as a cat at night. I couldn't see what the black thing was, but it was a good deal darker than the window, and it moved."

Sarah's voice changed. The anger went out of it. She said quickly, "Was it an owl?"

"No, it wasn't," said Mr. Brown.

"Then what was it?"

He said, "I can't tell you that, but I thought I'd like to find out. By the time I got up to the house it was gone. I waited, and it didn't come back—I waited a good long time. Tuesday night I came again. It was a very dark night. I heard the thud and the scratching sound, but I couldn't see anything to swear to. I came back on Wednesday, and you know what happened then."

Sarah said, "I?"

"Surely," said Mr. Brown. "I saw the thing move, and I heard it all right. I think you heard it too. It banged and scratched, and it went away—moved to the right, away from the window, and I lost it. You know I couldn't see it—I could only see the movement. When it didn't move, it wasn't there so far as I was concerned. I waited to see if it would move again, and then all of a sudden the window was lighted up and I saw you come across it. You were pulling the curtains of the other windows, weren't you?"

"Yes."

"Then you came and stood quite close to the lighted window. You stood there a long time. I heard a clock striking in the house. You pulled the curtain."

"Well?" said Sarah.

"Next night nothing happened. To-night you were going to sleep in your own room. Did you come out because you wanted to see whether the Thing would come again?"

"Yes, I did."

"Did you see anything?"

"Was there anything to see?"

"Oh yes,"

"What?" said Sarah breathlessly.

Mr. Brown laughed a little.

"There was more light to-night."

Sarah could have shaken him.

"What did you see?"

"Nothing very clearly, I'm afraid—just an impression of—" He broke off sharply. "It's a pity you didn't see anything, because of course it's open to you to believe that I'm telling you a tale to cover up my own tracks."

"Yes, you put that very well," said Sarah. She paused, and quite suddenly words rushed to her lips. "Someone's playing tricks on Lucilla."

"Yes," said Mr. Brown—"yes. Oh decidedly. Now what conceivable reason could I have for wanting to scare a child like that?"

"I don't know," said Sarah. "I daresay I could think of a reason if I tried hard enough."

"Well, well," said Mr. John Brown. His tone made Sarah very angry indeed. She came within an ace of stamping her foot as she said,

"If it comes to that, why should anyone else play tricks on her?"

"I don't know," said John Brown—"but I'd like to." His voice became brisk and businesslike. "There are four windows on this side of the house. The one at the end is Lucilla's. Do you mind telling me what the others are?"

"The bathroom comes next," said Sarah. "Then a spare room—there isn't anyone in it at present. And then Ricky's room."

"Ricky's—" said Mr. Brown in a meditative voice. "What do you think of Ricky, Miss Trent?"

"I think he's a dreep," said Sarah with decision.

"A likely practical joker?"

"I shouldn't have thought so." After a moment she added, "He moons about after Lucilla, and sulks when she snubs him. She isn't taking any, I'm glad to say. You wouldn't expect a moony dreep to go playing practical jokes, but you never can tell."

"No," said John Brown, "you never can tell." And then very suddenly he asked, "Is Lucilla frightened?"

"Not now."

"She was at first, but she isn't now?"

"Yes."

"Why?"

Sarah hesitated.

"Please tell me, Miss Trent."

"Mr. Brown—" said Sarah, and then stopped.

"*Please*, Miss Trent."

"There's something horrid about it," said Sarah in a hurrying voice. "It feels horrid—it doesn't feel like a practical joke. I don't know why I'm telling you this, but Lucilla stopped being frightened when she found that I had heard the Thing too. She was afraid—Mr. Brown, don't you see what the child was afraid of? And I've got the most horrible feeling that that's what she was meant to be afraid of." She stopped.

There was a silence. Then John Brown said,

"Thank you, Miss Trent. I think you'd better go in now. I think you'd better change rooms again and let the household know you've done it. Keep that east window latched, and I don't think you'll be bothered. Good-night."

He was gone so silently that she never heard him move.

Her own footsteps sounded unpleasantly loud in her ears as she went back by the way that she had come. The moon was veiled again. The house was like a black rock rising up through a faintly luminous sea. She got in through the window of the servants' room and latched it behind her.

When she reached her own room, Lucilla was curled up in the pink bed reading by the light of the rose-shaded bedside lamp. She raised her eyebrows at Sarah and pursed her lips.

"My *dear* Miss Trent!" The tone was a creditable imitation of Aunt Marina's.

"And what are you doing here?" said Sarah, a good deal relieved.

Lucilla smothered a yawn.

"It banged, so I came to find you. I don't like things that bang. Please, angel darling Sarah, I'd like to stay. And I'd *love* to know where you've been. Assignating with our Mr. Brown in the moonlight, I shouldn't wonder. Oh, Sarah—you blushed! My angel, tell me *all*!"

"Don't be an ass!" said Sarah, laughing.

Chapter Fifteen

THE NEXT DAY came up with a light mist which cleared before eleven and left a sky of cloudless blue. Geoffrey Hildred went off to town with a good-humoured grumble about people who expected to have their business attended to on a Saturday. Miss Marina talked a great deal about the clinging damp, and urged them all individually and collectively to take plenty of wraps, to be sure not to sit on the ground, to avoid wet feet, and on no account to stay out late. Lucilla said "Yes, darling" to everything in a manner which bespoke long practice, Ricky sneered a little, Sarah promised to take the greatest care of everyone, and in the end they got off, Ricky and Lucilla on bicycles, Sarah prepared to drive Bertrand Darnac, Mr. Brown and the lunch in *The Bomb*.

Sarah was wondering a good deal how she would feel when she met John Brown again. Her suspicions had returned upon her in full force, and she simply could not understand why she had talked to him as she had last night. She was quite convinced that the Thing that thudded and scratched upon the window was neither a natural nor a supernatural creature, but some contrivance designed to thud and scratch in order to frighten Lucilla. If you tied a black cushion to the end of a rake or one of those cultivators with curved prongs and climbed to the top of the porch, you could thud and scratch to your heart's content. And who was so conveniently placed for such a performance as Mr. Brown? There was no dog in the house, and on a dark night the chances of detection would be very small. Mr. Brown was abroad. Mr. Brown, by his own admission, was in the grounds of the Red House on five successive nights. Mr. Brown could move as silently as a cat, and the climbing of the porch would be child's play to him. What motive he could possibly have, she did not pretend to guess. She was taken up with her own folly in having spoken to him so freely. She had been full of her suspicions, and she had been full of her anger, and then all at once she had talked to him as if he were a friend. She couldn't imagine why she had talked to him, but it was a certain fact that she had done so. She felt very curious to know what her reactions would be when she met him again.

She stopped for him and Bertrand at the Cow and Bush, and it was he who came out first. He stood by the door of the car and smiled his pleasant smile, and all at once Sarah felt herself pulled in two opposite directions. Her suspicions pulled her one way, and a sense of spontaneous trust and liking pulled her another. She knew just why she had talked to John Brown as a friend. She had talked to him as a friend because there ran between them a very quick, live sense of friendship. All her thoughts suspected him, and all her feelings trusted him. It was extremely confusing. Her colour deepened as though she were angry, and her brows drew together above eyes that were brighter than usual.

John Brown looked on with an admiration which appeared to be tinged with amusement. He seemed to be about to speak, but Bertrand Darnac's sudden appearance stopped the words upon his lips.

They started, with Bertrand and the lunch behind, and Mr. Brown and a map in front.

"And to a certainty we shall lose our way. *Vois tu*, Sarah, it is not at all a clever arrangement that you have made. This Ricky, it is he who should be here with the corners of the lunch-basket running into him whilst he guides you along these roads, which he doubtless knows, as you would say, like the back of your hand."

"I don't say any of these things," said Sarah dispassionately.

"That, *cher ange*, is because you are ignorant of the idiom of your own language. Me, I study to acquire it, and I am already more proficient than you. Beware of jealousy—it is not an amiable trait. It is your favourite uncle, Bertrand surnamed the Wise, who instructs you."

"This is where we turn to the left," remarked Mr. Brown.

The Bomb went as gaily as Bertrand's tongue. They passed Ricky and Lucilla, and in the end, after no more than one wrong turning, found themselves climbing Burdon Hill. It is a very long hill, and quite steep enough. It has been known to be too steep for aged or declining cars, but *The Bomb* took them up it at the top of her form, if with a good deal of noise. They therefore had plenty of time to admire the view and unpack the lunch basket before Ricky and Lucilla arrived, hot with walking their bicycles up the long sunny slope.

You can see a very long way from the top of Burdon Hill. You can see right away across heath, and wood, and valley, and hill to the blue edges of the horizon. There was not a single cloud in the whole expanse of the sky. There was an autumn air and a summer sun. Everything was very good.

They lunched, and then they played games—children's games with forfeits, and Desert Islands, and Stag, which is a most frightfully exhausting game and generally only played by the Very Young. It was Mr. Brown who produced it, and was the first Stag. He promptly caught Lucilla, and hand-in-hand they ran down Bertrand Darnac. Three in a row, they gave chase to Sarah, but Ricky's long legs eluded the chain of four, and they gave him up, panting.

"You really want to play it on a tennis-court, and you want more people," explained John Brown. "We used to—" He broke off abruptly and became absorbed in watching a spider with a round white body and long delicate legs.

They played Consequences after that, a new and frightfully embarrassing sort which would have made Aunt Marina's hair stand bolt upright under her auburn wig.

Lucilla was in the most gay, excited spirits. She sat hatless in the sun with her hair shining like bright pale gold, her eyes a deeper blue than the sky, and a lovely flush in her cheeks. Bertrand Darnac couldn't keep his eyes off her, and Ricky's ill humour became so marked that it surprised none of them when he announced with rudeness that he had had enough of riding a damned second-hand girl's bicycle, and that someone else could push it home—he was for the car.

"Who's going with me?" said Lucilla. "You know, Sarah, you really might call your wretched car something else. Aunt Marina will never let me go in anything called *The Bomb*."

Almost before she had finished her sentence, and before Bertrand Darnac could get his mouth open, John Brown said,

"Will you have me?"

If Lucilla was disappointed, she did not show it. She said,

"Come on, and we'll race them to the bottom of the hill.'

"It's too steep to race. I'm not sure that it isn't too steep to ride."

"Oh, but we always ride it," protested Lucilla. "It's all right if you've got good brakes."

Sarah caught her by the arm.

"Lucilla, you're not to race! No, *really*, I mean. You must promise."

There was a mutinous sparkle in the blue eyes. Then all of a sudden Lucilla laughed.

"You'll get real governessy lines all over your face if you look like that. I've been bicycling since I was six, and what I don't know about Burdon Hill isn't worth knowing, but to please my angel darling Sarah I'll promise not to race."

The Bomb got off first, Ricky behind with the empty basket, and Bertrand Darnac by Sarah in front. The descending slope is a gentle one for about five hundred yards. Then the road turns, steepens, and goes sharply down to a couple of bends. For perhaps a quarter of a mile there is overhanging rock on the left and a nasty drop on the right, after which there is a sheltering bank. *The Bomb* had just reached the steep part of the hill and was in sight of the bends, when Bertrand Darnac cried out and Lucilla flashed past them at a break-neck speed with Mr. Brown following hard behind.

Sarah stared through the wind-screen in a kind of sick horror. Was this the race which Lucilla had promised to forego, or was it something else? She was in bottom gear, going dead slow. If she got into top, she could drive the car down the hill—or she could declutch and coast. But was it any use? Could she reach Lucilla before she came to those horrible bends, or, reaching her, was there anything that she could do? Almost as the choice presented itself, she had declutched. If the pace got too hot, she could always brake and let the clutch in again, praying that *The Bomb* would not blow up. It probably wasn't any use, but she couldn't just crawl behind those flying figures.

"What's up?" said Ricky in a startled voice as they gathered speed.

"*Mon dieu!* Didn't you see them? What can have happened? It is out of control that bicycle!"

"Lucilla's?" said Ricky on a sharp startled note.

"Oh, *mon dieu*—yes! Sarah, it is no good—you cannot catch them!"

Sarah didn't say anything. She felt the speed increase. She felt *The Bomb* buck and sway on the hill. She saw Lucilla's bright hair. She saw her near the first bend at a frightful rate of speed. And the defending wall was no more than a couple of feet in height. If Lucilla struck it anywhere, she would be hurled clear to the drop beyond.

John Brown came into her view. She had not seen him, because it seemed as if she could only see that bright pale hair. She saw John Brown because he passed Lucilla on the outside of the bend between her and the edge. Then she lost them both on the inner curve. And all the while she knew where she was driving. She saw her own road, and made the instinctive movements which a driver must make. She heard Ricky's voice, and Ran's voice, but what they said went past her. There was the road, and there was the straining attention with which she watched the second bend.

Lucilla came into sight again. John Brown came into sight again. They swung the bend together and were gone. Something in Sarah relaxed a little. If they were round the bends, the worst was over—the slope eased and there were banks. She took the first bend with her hands steady on the wheel, and swung the inside curve to the second bend at what was probably the fastest speed ever achieved by *The Bomb*. They were round it and over the worst of the hill. A couple of hundred yards farther on there was an almost level stretch which led to a brief rise. At the crest of this rise two bicycles lay asprawl against the rough earthy bank on the left, and John Brown was picking Lucilla up.

"Brake, Sarah, *brake!*" said Bertrand in her ear.

Sarah nodded. Lucilla wasn't killed, because she was standing. You don't stand if you're killed.

They tore across the level, and as soon as the rise began she jammed on the brakes. *The Bomb* kicked violently. Ricky shot forward and hit her in the back, something smashed in the lunch-basket, and the speedometer needle swung back to forty—thirty—twenty—ten. Sarah spoke for the first time. She said, "Golly! What a joy ride!" and they came to a standstill a yard or two from the bicycles, and Lucilla and Mr. Brown.

They got out of the car. Just for the moment Sarah felt that she had had enough of things that ran on wheels. Your own feet with leather soles on a firm gritty road were good enough. Bicycles and cars were devilish contraptions that ran away.

John Brown had his arm about Lucilla. She was as white as milk, but her eyes shone. She began to shake with laughter as Sarah came up.

"It was a race after all—I didn't break my promise—the blighted thing ran away with me—the brakes are gone—I thought I was gone too—"

"Cilla—are you hurt?" Ricky's sulkiness was gone. He was as pale as Lucilla, and his voice shook.

Lucilla let go of Mr. Brown, whom she had been clutching. She stretched herself cautiously and announced that her bones all seemed to be in the same places as usual.

"You are not hurt at all?" This was Bertrand, very solicitous. "*Mon dieu*, Lucilla, when I saw you go past—"

"Your heart was in your mouth? I know. Where do you suppose mine was?"

John Brown patted her shoulder.

"I'd like to congratulate you on your nerve and on your riding. I didn't think it was possible to clear those bends without brakes."

Lucilla's colour was coming back.

"Oh, I know Burdon Hill like the back of my hand. It wasn't anything really. And it was *fun*!"

"What happened to your brakes?" said Bertrand Darnac.

He picked up the bicycle, and they gathered round.

"The brake, it does not act—no, not at all—neither the front nor the back. They are—how you call it, wash-outs."

"They were all right going," said Ricky in a bewildered voice. "They were, weren't they, Cilla?"

"There's nothing to brake for going. It's level or up hill all the way except for potty little things that don't count."

"The bicycle, it is quite new," said Bertrand.

Mr. Brown had been examining the brake-rods. He spoke now. His voice was still quiet, but under the quietness it rang hard.

"The screws have gone."

"The screws?" said Lucilla. She caught Sarah's arm as she stood beside her.

"The screws that adjust the length of the brake-rods."

"But this is a new bicycle," said Bertrand Darnac in an incredulous voice.

"Cilla, when did you brake last?" said Ricky.

"I don't know. I didn't brake to-day—not at all. We walked up the hill, and anyhow I never brake when I'm getting off."

"But you *must* remember."

"Well, I don't. I suppose it would have been the last time I went to Holme Fallow—that was with Sarah on Tuesday."

Ricky looked relieved.

"They must have been working loose for some time, and this road finished them."

"Both screws—and so exactly at the one time?" Bertrand shrugged his shoulders. "No, no—that is a coincidence for the theatre. For the affairs of ordinary people I find it, as you say, too *steep*!"

Lucilla flushed suddenly and brightly.

"Well, anyhow the screws aren't there. Nobody's dead. And Aunt Marina will have fits if we're not home for tea. I've never used a brake for the rest of the hill in my life, so suppose we get going again."

"I think we will walk down the rest of the hill," said Mr. John Brown.

Chapter Sixteen

THEY WERE RATHER LATE for tea. By common consent, no one mentioned Lucilla's brakes. Miss Marina wondered how they could possibly have sat out of doors for so long, and hoped, with a good deal of anxiety, that no one had taken cold.

"Darling, it was boiling," said Lucilla. "Even when we sat still we boiled—and we didn't sit still, we ran about like hares."

"Stags," said Ricky.

"My *dears*—" Miss Marina pushed her pince-nez quite crooked and looked bewildered—"hares?—stags? Was it a game you were playing?"

Everyone began to explain to her at once—everyone, that is, except John Brown, who sat rather silent. Miss Marina took a great interest in the explanations.

"It sounds very like a game I used to play when I stayed with my cousins the Basildons. There were ten of them—in fact fifteen if you count the children of my Uncle Stephen Basildon's second wife. Yes, fifteen, because he had seven children by his first wife, who was a Miss Gill of Bledstow, and three more by his second wife, who was a widow with five children when he married her. She was a Mrs. Haggard, and not at all handsome like his first, but a very jolly, good-natured, pleasant kind of woman to have in the house and never minded where we played our games or how much noise we made, always provided we didn't get into mischief. We were all very fond of Aunt Maria."

"What games did you play?" said Sarah.

"Well, my dear, there was the game you've been explaining—we used to play that in the garden. And in the house we played all sorts of card games, and round games, and parlour games like General Post, and Nuts and May, and Musical Chairs. But the game we liked best of all was Devil-in-the-dark."

"I know," said Lucilla—"you put out all the lights in a room, and you have a *He*, and the game is to get out of the room without being caught."

Miss Marina shook her head.

"No, my dear, that's not the way we played it. And we couldn't play it very often, because even Aunt Maria drew the line at having all the lights in the house put out at once."

Lucilla's eyes sparkled.

"You played it all over the house? That would be something like!"

"The dining-room was Home," said Miss Marina in a pleased remembering voice. "There was a light in there, of course. Then half of us hid and the other half looked for them, and the game was to get home to the dining-room."

"But there is a game that we can play as soon as it is dark!" said Bertrand. "How soon will it be dark enough?"

"Lovely!" said Lucilla. "I wish there were fifteen of us. Nobody has those nice large families now. I think I'll be a pioneer and have ten children when I marry."

"Lucilla!" said Miss Marina in a horrified voice.

"Darling, it would be rather fun. I'll call the first girl Marina after you. I say—I know what we'll do. We'll go up to Holme Fallow and play Devil-in-the dark."

"Oh no, Lucilla! Oh no, my dear!"

The door opened and Geoffrey Hildred came in.

"Any tea left, Marina?" he said; and then, "Well, how did the picnic go?"

"Lovely," said Lucilla, and stopped at that.

Miss Marina was fidgetting with the teapot.

"Yes, lots of tea. But, Geoffrey, they want to go up to Holme Fallow and play Hide and Seek in the dark, and I don't think—indeed I don't—"

"Now, Aunt Marina, don't be a spoil-sport," said Ricky. "We can—can't we. Father?"

"I don't see any harm," said Geoffrey Hildred benevolently. "Why, Marina, we've all played Hide and Seek in our time. I don't suppose I'll join you, but—"

"Oh, Geoffrey—that great empty house—and no lights—and no one there!"

Geoffrey Hildred laughed.

"Why, they'll all be there," he said. "And for the Lord's sake give me some tea, my dear, for I've been doing business with a most uncommonly obstinate, tiresome fellow, and it's made me very thirsty."

Miss Marina sighed and pursed her lips, and sighed again and poured him out his tea. Dear Geoffrey was not nearly so loud in his voice as her father the admiral, but he had the same straight blue eyes. The admiral's household had never found it possible to argue with him. His daughter had been brought up to do as she was bid. The habit persisted. Dear Geoffrey was always kind, but he sometimes reminded her of poor papa. She said earnestly to Sarah,

"You *will* make them be careful, my dear, won't you? The door to the cellars is locked, or I wouldn't hear of it. But you won't let them do anything foolish, now will you?"

Sarah wondered how it was proposed that she should stop them. She turned to smile at Lucilla, and found her sitting silent and a little pale. She dropped her voice to the child's ear.

"Tired, Lucilla? Would you rather not go?" After all she had had a fright and a shaking.

Her voice had not been low enough, for Ricky struck in.

"She's not tired—she's got cold feet. Always does get cold feet in the dark—don't you, Cilla?"

She threw him a furious glance.

"I don't!"

"Oh, don't you? The trouble is, you're not a stayer. You go off pop with your 'Let's all go and play Devil-in-the-dark at Holme Fallow,' but when it comes to the point you funk."

"I don't!"

"There shall be no need," said Bertrand. "What am I for if it is not to hold the hand? *Ma foi*—that is my *métier*! Sarah will tell you that I have for it a talent truly remarkable—what you say A.I., and beat the band."

"Sarah won't say anything of the sort," said Sarah.

"*Ma foi*—I am sorry for you, Lucilla! If you had asked me, I would have warned you. She has a disposition very unamiable, this Sarah. Perhaps she is jealous!—it is not for me to say." He rolled his eyes and made such a comical grimace that Miss Marina, who had been looking a little scandalised, found herself carried back to the days when sixteen boys and girls had played and chaffed one another under Aunt Maria Basildon's indulgent eye. She glanced at Geoffrey Hildred, saw that he was smiling, and smiled herself.

They walked up to Holme Fallow. There was a short cut across the fields, and it was a much shorter distance than Sarah could have believed possible. They started in a clear dusk, with trees standing up black against a greenish sky. It would be dark enough in the house when they got there. Sarah had put her torch in her pocket.

She found herself walking on the dry field-path with Bertrand Darnac. He slipped a hand inside her arm and slowed the pace so that they fell behind the others. When they were some twenty yards behind, he said,

"Sarah, listen to me. I am very uneasy."

She had fallen back with him, because his touch on her arm had been insistent. She said,

"Why, Ran?"

"You ask me why? You yourself—you are quite easy? Nothing troubles you?"

"What should trouble me?" said Sarah, but the trouble was in her voice.

"What should trouble you? If Lucilla had been killed this afternoon, you would have been troubled—*hein?*"

"Don't, Ran!"

"I am still asking myself why she was not killed. It was a near thing—*hein?* With those screws gone, anyone would have said that she would kill herself on the hill, and I ask myself how it comes that there are two screws that are missing at the one time and from so new a bicycle. I ask myself whether I can believe that they have worked loose as Ricky says, and I find that it is impossible to believe. What do you say?"

Sarah drew in her breath quickly.

"Ran! That's dreadful!"

"*Mon dieu*—yes! I am serious, you understand. I am not playing a fool. I can play him, but I am not playing him now. I am saying someone took out those screws, and when I have said that, I am asking two questions. I ask, 'Who took them out?' I ask, 'Who is Mr. John Brown?'"

Sarah was silent. Her heart beat. A sharp pain went through her at the sound of John Brown's name. After a moment she said coldly,

"Why do you ask that?"

Bertrand stood still, holding her by the arm.

"You ask me why I tell you that someone took out the screws. Was it you—or I—or her cousin—or Lucilla herself? Bah! How can one believe it? There remains this Mr. Brown who comes here from nowhere at all, of whom we know only what he says himself. Why does he come here? Why does he live at the Cow and Bush? It is not an *hotel-de-luxe*, I can tell you that. Why does he get up in the night and go out? Now listen! Last night I followed him. Where did he go, I ask of you. Well, I can tell you that. He went into the gate of the Red House, and into what you call the shrubbery where the trees are thick, and there I lose him. I do not like to go too near. I wait some time. Then I think I will go nearer to the house, and all at once I hear voices. He is there, and he is talking to a woman."

"He was talking to me," said Sarah.

"To *you*?"

"Yes, my child. And it wasn't an assignation, and we weren't planning a burglary."

"What were you doing—*Sarah*?"

"Talking of this and that. Darling Ran, you have too much imagination. I couldn't sleep, so I went for a walk. And I suppose Mr. Brown couldn't sleep either. I bumped into him in the dark. We talked for a few minutes, and then I went in again."

Bertrand took his hand away from her arm.

"Sarah, have you become mad? You find this man walking in the night where he has no business, and you think it is nothing—and you go in and say nothing? What a folly! Do you not ask yourself what this man wants, and who he is?"

"Who do you think he is?" said Sarah in a different voice.

"I have got my ideas," said Bertrand Darnac.

"Ran—what are they?"

"Someone took out those screws. Someone wanted that Lucilla should ride a bicycle without brakes down a hill where it would be very easy for her to be killed. Someone wanted that, and I ask myself why."

"Ran!"

"People do not do such things for nothing. Have you listened to the old lady's histories of the family? She tells them every minute, and they are to make the head go round, but I have asked Lucilla about them, so I get them what you call sorted out. Lucilla's father, he is killed in the war. He has an elder brother who is Henry, and a younger brother who is Maurice."

"Yes, I know."

"Maurice, he is missing in the war. They think he is alive for a long time—the old lady thinks so still. Henry, he dies a few months ago, and Lucilla is the heiress. She would be the heiress even if Maurice were alive. It is Lucilla who tells me that. But figure to yourself—if this Maurice were not dead—if he had lost his memory, perhaps for years, and then suddenly remembered. There have been such cases."

"Someone would recognize him."

"After how long? Seventeen—eighteen years. And he was a boy of perhaps nineteen." He shrugged his shoulders. "It is a very long time, Sarah. Then suppose he comes back. There is no place for him—Lucilla has everything. He has been shell-shocked—his brain it is perhaps not quite right. And so the screws come out of Lucilla's bicycle."

"Oh no!" said Sarah. "Oh no, Ran!"

"If Lucilla is dead, and Maurice is alive, then *vois-tu*, Sarah, there is a very good place for Maurice—there is Holme Fallow, and there is the London property from which the money comes, Lucilla tells me of it. When those screws are gone I look for a motive, and that is where I find one."

"You think he is Maurice Hildred?" said Sarah in a low horrified tone.

"I do not know," said Bertrand Darnac.

Through the dusk Lucilla came flying back to them. "Come along, you two! We can't begin without you."

Chapter Seventeen

THEY WENT UP the west drive all together and in through the side door. It was quite dark in the house. It was almost as dark as it had been on the night when Sarah blundered in upon the burglar. She hadn't told anyone about that. She hadn't told Ran what she and John Brown had talked about in the shrubbery of the Red House last night. She didn't know why she hadn't told him. She hadn't wanted to. If she had told Ran that something came dashing against Lucilla's window in the dark, he would have been quite certain that John Brown was mixed up with it.

Sarah pulled herself up with a jerk. Where were her own suspicions? Had anything happened to allay them? Should they not have been quickened by what had happened this afternoon? Maurice Hildred.... It was absurd. Was it? Such things had happened.

She shuddered violently as they crossed the hall. A hand was laid on her arm, and John Brown's voice said,

"Are you cold?"

Sarah caught her breath.

"How did you know it was me?"

She heard him laugh, and he said quite low in her ear,

"I told you I could see in the dark."

"Why should I be cold?"

"I heard you shiver."

And with that the beam of a torch cut the dark. It was Mr. Brown's torch. It cast a powerful ray which came to rest on the dining-room door.

The dining-room was to be Home. Snagge kept an oil lamp there, so the torch was only a temporary expedient. They must have one lighted room, and the rest of the dark house to play Hide and Seek in.

Lucilla's head and arm came suddenly into the ray. She threw open the dining-room door and turned, laughing and blinking, with the light in her eyes.

"Come along in. Who's got the torch? The lamp ought to be on the sideboard."

Sarah was held back as the others trooped in.

Bertrand whispered, "That Mr. Brown—it is he who has the torch. *Dis donc*, Sarah—how does he know so well which is the right door? Has he been here before?"

Sarah pulled away from him. She was on the threshold, standing where she had stood on that other night when there had been a burglar in the room beyond. She had seen no more of him than the black outline of head, shoulder, and arm as he swung his torch. She stared now at what might have been the same picture. There was the dark room, there was the moving ray, there was the black outline of head, and arm, and hand. Just for a moment the two pictures were the same picture. It was as if something odd had happened to her sense of time, as if it had folded back upon itself, so that this moment was really that other moment ten days ago. She felt so giddy that she caught at the jamb for support.

Then someone struck a match and lamplight filled the room.

Sarah came forward to join the others. The giddiness had passed, but she had a strange shocked feeling. She hoped she didn't look as queer as she felt. She was quite, quite sure that it was Mr. Brown whom she had seen the first time she came to Holme Fallow. There had been a burglary that night. She had seen the burglar. She had seen John Brown. She hadn't seen anyone. She had seen the ray of a torch, and the black outline of a head, a shoulder, and an arm. She had seen what she had just seen again. She had seen a burglar.... Something in her said "No." What had been taken? An old desk had been rummaged. The ray had rested upon the portrait of Lucilla's grandmother.... *What had she seen?* Maurice Hildred looking at his mother's picture? Maurice Hildred haunting his old home like a ghost? Or perhaps someone who would claim to be Maurice Hildred—someone getting up a case—rummaging in an old desk for papers, staring at the family portraits....

Ricky's voice startled her out of these thoughts.

"Sarah's moonstruck. Someone pinch her. What's the matter, Sarah? Have you seen a ghost?"

John Brown was adjusting the lamp, an old-fashioned heavy table-lamp with a round china globe like a harvest moon. He looked over it, met Sarah's eyes, and very slightly smiled.

She said, "I think so."

"What was it like?"

"Sarah darling, you *didn't*!"

Sarah laughed. What a fool to say that. It slipped out. "Oh, my poor Sarah, pull up your socks!" The laugh sounded quite all right. She said, "You all looked like ghosts."

"If anyone talks about ghosts, I won't play," said Lucilla.

Bertrand linked his arm in hers.

"Hand in hand we go. I am of a courage quite extraordinary."

"Who's going to be *He*?" said Ricky.

Lucilla giggled and began to count.

"Eena, meena, mina, mo...

She pointed at each word.

...Eena, meena, mina—*mo*."

The last "Mo" fell on Ricky.

"All right—now we can start. I've mugged it all up from Aunt Marina. Ricky, you've got to count sixty, *slowly*, before you open the door, so as to give us time to get clear. The *He* can stay in the hall, or he can come and look for us. The game is to get back here without being caught. Oh, and I promised we'd stay in this part of the house—not go into the servants' wing. Are you ready? All right—go!"

She ran out of the room with Bertrand. Sarah followed. John Brown brought up the rear, and the door was shut.

Sarah had made up her mind to cross the hall and hide behind the first door she came to. As she slipped in, leaving it ajar, she heard a whispering and a giggling from the stairs. Mr. Brown seemed to have melted into the darkness. She leaned against the wall of what she took to be the drawing-room and waited. She was glad to be alone. The sense of shock was wearing off, but she wasn't quite ready to play. She kept thinking of those two moments which had merged into one moment. Why hadn't she spoken of what she had seen to Lucilla or to Geoffrey Hildred? She ought to have spoken. She certainly couldn't speak now. Couldn't—or wouldn't? She said, "Of course he's not a burglar!" and was surprised at her own certainty. If she hadn't seen a burglar, there wasn't anything to tell. If she hadn't seen a burglar, whom *had* she seen? Maurice Hildred, come back from the dead to find no place in his old home? It all went round in her head, and round again.

A shout from the hall announced that Ricky had caught someone. She was a little surprised, on emerging, to discover that it was Mr. Brown. It had not occurred to her that he would be caught. She found herself wondering if he had wanted to be caught, if he had wanted to be left in the dining-room alone.

They played another round. Mr. Brown was *He*. This time Sarah hid behind the door through which she had come into the hall on that other night. She thought how strange it would be if John Brown were to come across and open the door and put his hand on her in the dark. They had both come that way before. She went over the whole thing in her mind again. It was like some strange recurrent dream which she could not escape. It mesmerized her. And all the time her ears were strained for the sound of a footstep and a touch on the door.

A scream, a scuffle, and a giggle in the hall. She looked through her chink and saw the dining-room door wide open, and John Brown holding Lucilla a yard or two away. Bertrand Darnac was in the lighted room, and even as Sarah looked, Ricky slipped past and joined them. Lucilla was protesting.

"It wasn't fair! I was nearly there! You saw me when Bertrand opened the door!"

"Fair cop!" said Ricky.

Sarah made a dash for it, and got in.

They started out again, leaving Lucilla in the dining-room. This time Sarah made for the stairs. She had had enough of her own thoughts. What was the good of them anyhow? She couldn't do anything about it—it wasn't her affair. Ran had been talking nonsense about the bicycle screws. Screws *did* come out of things. There hadn't been an accident, and nobody was a penny the worse—

She found herself at the top of the stairs in an inky blackness not knowing where to go. She felt her way for about a dozen paces and then stopped to listen. She could hear nothing at all until quite suddenly there was a hand under her elbow and a voice said in her ear, "This way."

It was Mr. Brown's voice, and the extraordinary thing was that it gave her a sense of relief. She didn't really like this groping round in the dark. It might have been different if she had known the house, but as it was, it was rather like the horrid sort of dream in which your sense of direction is gone and you don't know where you are. The touch on her arm brought her back. The dream feeling vanished. It was just a dark house through which she was being guided—very efficiently guided. A door opened and shut again, all with the least possible sound. They stood still. There was a feeling of being in a small enclosed space.

"Where are we?" said Sarah under her breath.

"Where no one will find us unless we talk too loud."

"How do you know?

"I'm very good at guessing."

He had let go of her arm, but he was so near she had the feeling that if she moved she would touch him. She didn't like being very close to anyone, and she couldn't bear being touched. She hadn't minded John Brown's hand upon her arm. All this was rather confusing. She leaned back against what felt like panelling and heard him say,

"You got out of that very cleverly just now."

"Out of what?"

He laughed quite softly.

"*Did* you see a ghost?"

Sarah's heart beat hard. Absurd of it, but she couldn't stop the thing. She said.

"You ought to know."

"I?"

"If you don't, nobody does."

He laughed again.

"Whose ghost do you think it was, Sarah?"

Sarah felt something, she didn't quite know what. It might have been anger, it might have been something else. It made her say,

"Perhaps it was a burglar's ghost."

"Oh, I don't think so," said John Brown.

"Sure?"

"I'd like you to feel sure."

"Why?"

"I'd like it a good deal."

There was a silence—the sort that you want to break, and can't. John Brown broke it, not with words, but with a sigh. And at once Sarah found that she could speak. She not only could, but had to. The words said themselves in a rush.

"Whose ghost was it?"

"Whose do you think?"

"I—don't—know." Then, very quickly, *"Who are you?"*

"A ghost."

"Please."

"If you ask a ghost its name, it's bound to vanish. I'd rather not vanish just yet, you know. You do know that—don't you?"

Sarah's face burned in the dark. She didn't know what she knew, or what she didn't know. She felt she had had all that she could stand. She half turned and groped for the door. The movement brought her against him. She had a feeling that the place was very small, a feeling of being shut in. If she had been ten years younger, she might have screamed. She had learned her self-control in a hard school. She said,

"I want to get out. Where are we? Where's the door?"

"Just here." His voice sounded a little amused, a little tender. "You're not shut in." Then, "This was a powdering-closet—that's why it's so small. Now how will you go? By the stairs?"

"I think so."

"Then I'll just take you to the top. I think we won't go down together."

She thought someone moved near them as they came to the top of the stairs. His hand dropped from her arm. She was left standing alone with a sense of empty space in front of her and below. She didn't want to think any more. She wanted to get down the stairs and into the lighted dining-room without being caught. It would take her all her time, because Lucilla had the advantage of knowing the house.

If she went down holding to the baluster rail, she was much less likely to pull it off than if she gave herself the width of the stair to dodge in. The bother was that she didn't know on which side of the stair she was standing. It came up straight out of the hall and then divided to left and right. She thought they had gone up on the left-hand side, but whether John Brown had brought her back the same way she had no idea. If the baluster rail was on her right, he had. If it was on her left, he hadn't. She groped, found the rail on her right, and began very slowly and cautiously to descend. Even at the risk of being caught, she really couldn't let go of the rail until she was past the turn. She ought to have counted the steps as she went up them.

The steps ceased. Her feet were on the flat, and her hand found a newel-post with a tall carved head. She remembered that there was a railed landing where the stair branched. She remembered that the posts were carved with pineapples. Her hand slid over the pattern, feeling it. Then she let go and went down step by step, keeping to the middle of the stair. At every step she listened, and twice she heard a movement. She could not have said who moved or where. Then she was in the hall, crossing it in the dark as she had crossed it the first time she came to Holme Fallow—only then the dining-room door had been open, and there had been the torchlight to guide her, while now everything was dark and the door was shut.

She did not know how far she had gone, when something made her stop. She did not know why she stopped, but she thought afterwards that she must have heard something behind her and above, because as she stopped, she turned and looked up. And then, before she had time to think, two things happened, not absolutely together, but so near that she could never say which came first. Ricky Hildred cannoned into her, and away above them in the direction of the stairs Lucilla screamed.

The scream might have come first. She didn't know. It was still echoing through the emptiness when Ricky, clutching her, gasped, "What's that?" He had her by the arm, and she was pushing him away, because there was a torch in her pocket and she wanted it badly enough. Had the scream stopped? She didn't know. Her head rang with it. The torch was like a lump of ice and her fingers too cold to feel the switch, yet they must have found it, because suddenly there was light. The stair with its wide shallow steps, its heavy balustrade, and its carved newels, rushed out of the dark. One moment she did not know where she was and had only a sense of space and emptiness, and the next there was the stair quite near, like the overhang of a cliff. She was perhaps four yards from the last step, with the torch in her hand pointing upwards. There was some diffused light, but the ray struck full upon the pale gold of Lucilla's hair. In an instant of confusion and horror she saw that the bright hair hung downwards. Lucilla hung downwards across the balustrade at its highest point where the stair passed out of sight on the right-hand side and where the drop was greatest to the hall below, and above her, leaning over with his hands on her, there was a man—there was John Brown. She hung downwards from the knees, and he leaned over straining with his hands at her waist. It was just for the one moment, but it was like a fixed picture in Sarah's mind—a fixed and most horrible picture. Her eyes felt rigid in her head. The hand which held the torch was rigid on a rigid arm. Her breath seemed to have stopped. She heard Ricky make some horrified exclamation, and with that the picture broke. John Brown straightened himself, lifting Lucilla until he had the weight of her body upon the balustrade. It had all happened outside of any measurement of time. There was, in fact, the briefest possible space between Lucilla's scream and the choking cry with which she sank down half crouching and half sitting on the stair.

At that second sound Sarah came back to life and movement. She ran, and was aware of Ricky running beside her

John Brown was stooping over Lucilla, with a hand on her shoulder. Sarah thrust the torch at him and sat down on the stair.

"Lucilla—what happened? Are you hurt? *Lucilla!*"

After that choking cry Lucilla was silent. The wavering light showed her ashy pale and staring. The hand which Sarah held was deathly cold.

John Brown spoke over her head.

"Ricky, is that you? Go down and open the dining-room door! Bring the lamp out into the hall! Where's Darnac?"

Bertrand was half way up the stairs. He came from the direction of the drawing room. He looked from one to the other and asked no questions. There was a long tense pause while they waited for the lamp.

Chapter Eighteen

THE LAMP SUFFUSED the hall with a warm golden light. In the flickering watery gleam of the torch everything had flickered, wavered, and seemed unreal—a dream resolved from the darkness and dissolving into it again. The lamplight restored an agreeable everyday solidity.

Sarah pulled Lucilla to her feet. The sooner they got down to the ground-floor the better. But as they moved, Bertrand Darnac broke what was for him a most unnatural silence.

"Lucilla—*qu'as tu donc?* What has happened? Are you hurt?"

He darted to her, caught both her hands, and held them in a firm, warm clasp. And to him Lucilla spoke, breaking the silence which had closed her in after that last gasping cry. She looked up at him and said.

"Ran—I fell."

"How did you fall, *chérie*?"

They stood waiting for her answer, John Brown a step above, Sarah beside her, and Ricky halted by the newel-post. He had set the lamp on the hall table and run up the stairs again. He halted now, waiting for what Lucilla would say. They all looked at her, but she did not look at any of them. She looked at Bertrand Darnac, and she said,

"I think—I tripped."

Bertrand held her hands. He said,

"How?"

Lucilla had a little colour. The ashy whiteness was just pallor now. A shadowy pink came and went upon it. She said in a stronger voice,

"I was running. I slipped on the top step. I must have—overbalanced."

"I don't see how you could."

Sarah didn't see either. She turned round and looked with a frowning intensity. The stair came up straight from the hall and then divided, rising by some fifteen steps to meet a corridor on either side. Was it possible that a stumble on the top step could have thrown Lucilla across the stair and on to the balustrade? The stair was wide, the balustrade was low. If she had come running down the passage, bumped into the inside wall, and taken a stumbling fall, could it have happened? She looked, and thought it barely possible. She said suddenly and clearly,

"Mr. Brown, you were there. What happened?"

John Brown answered at once. He was standing on the second step. He had not moved from it. The top step ran to meet a pillar. The step on which he stood was the first to reach the balustrade. He said,

"I was here, by the pillar. Lucilla screamed, and I grabbed her. She was over the edge, and I rather thought she was going to take me with her, but I managed to lift her back. That balustrade ought to be higher."

They all looked at it. Sarah wondered how many of them were thinking what she was thinking. The balustrade was low enough to be dangerous. John Brown was right about that. A plunging fall from the top step might send you crashing over it into the hall below—a break-neck drop. It certainly might. But by no conceivable chance could any fall carry you over the rail at so high a level as the second step. She didn't think it possible that Lucilla could have been thrown against the balustrade any higher up than the fourth step. She would have put it at the fifth or sixth herself, but even at the fourth step John Brown could not have reached her. She must have been on his own level or no more than one step below, or he could not have saved her. The picture she had seen in the beam of her torch came vividly before her mind. The fair hair hanging down. The body hanging down. John Brown bent over the balustrade, with his hands—holding Lucilla? Or pushing her down? What would have happened if her own hands had really been too cold to find the switch? What would have happened if the light had not gone on just when it did? Would Lucilla be standing there, or would she be lying broken on the floor below? She shuddered inwardly. And in a moment Lucilla was talking fast and eagerly with a bright flame of colour in her cheeks.

"It was too frightfully stupid of me—wasn't it? Why are you all staring like owls? I'm not hurt. And it's no use asking me how I did it, because I don't know. I did a sort of a slide and a sort of a wobble, and I tried to save myself, but that beastly balustrade caught me by the knees and over I went. I thought I was gone—and then someone pulled me back again."

"It was Mr. Brown," said Sarah, still in that very clear voice.

No one was prepared for what happened next. Lucilla snatched her hands out of Bertrand's and, whirling round, flung her arms about John Brown and kissed him.

"Noble preserver!" she said; and then, catching Sarah by the arm, "Darling angel Sarah, let's go home."

They went home. There were no stragglers this time. Sarah kept her arm through Lucilla's, and nobody talked very much.

When they had come about half way across the fields, it began to drizzle with rain. Sarah looked up and saw a thick covering of cloud over the whole face of the sky. It gave her a curious sense of some indefinite lapse of time. The sky had been clear when they came; it was cloudy now. They had not been so long, but everything had changed.

They came out of the fields and on to the road. It would have been the natural thing for Bertrand and John Brown to go on into the village to their lodging at the Cow and Bush, but both turned in at the Red House gate and walked with the others up the steep embanked drive. Sarah thought of Lucilla falling suddenly out of the dark into the headlights of *The Bomb*. She might have been killed then. She might have been killed twice over, to-day. You can't, you simply can't, believe in coincidence to that extent.

Miss Marina was dozing on one side of the drawing-room fire when they came in, and Geoffrey Hildred sat reading *The Times* on the other. However warm the day was, Miss Marina liked a fire in the evening. She sat with a cushion behind her shoulders and her feet on a little round stool which had been worked in cross-stitch by Guy Raimond's grandmother about sixty-five years before. The pattern was one of green leaves and fat red roses on a black ground, but the colours were now very pleasantly faded, and no longer contrasted as harshly with the bright yellow maple of the frame as they must have done when they were new. Miss Marina's auburn front was slightly crooked and her mouth a little open. Her knitting was on her lap, but as she had dropped no stitches, it was fairly certain that she had not been trying to knit.

Geoffrey Hildred turned round with a smile as they came in.

"You got tired of your game very soon," he said, and at the sound of his voice Miss Marina woke up with a start.

"It's raining," said Sarah. It was a stupid thing to say, but she said it because she couldn't think of anything else.

Miss Marina blinked a little.

"Raining? Then I must insist that you change your shoes—I must insist that everybody changes."

Her knitting slid off her lap on to the white woolly hearth-rug, and as she stooped to pick it up again, her attention veered to her cousin. He had one foot firmly planted on the white curling wool, and the other crossed upon his knee. It was upon the sole of this foot that Miss Marina gazed with some concern.

"But, my dear Geoffrey, your feet are damp too. Was it raining when you came in? And you have not changed!"

Geoffrey Hildred had been holding *The Times* with both hands. He let the paper slide to the ground and leaned forward to touch the sole of his shoe.

"Nothing to change for," he said. "No, it was fine enough when I came in. I looked out five minutes ago with the idea of taking a stroll, but it was drizzling, so I went no farther."

Miss Marina began to tell a horrifying anecdote illustrating the fearful consequences of sitting in wet shoes. Lucilla sat down on the hearth beside her, and presently took her hand and kissed it.

"Darling, what adventurous lives you had in the nineteenth century—too thrilling, really! Think of the risks if you didn't change your shoes, and wear chest protectors, and respirators, and flannel next the skin! Life must have been one long exciting struggle not to catch cold. *Now* we wear next to nothing, and don't bother about our feet at all. So dull of us—isn't it?"

When John Brown presently took his departure he gave Sarah a small folded slip of paper. It was quite openly given, and his voice was at its usual pitch as he said,

"That's the name of the book you were asking me about. I think you'll find it quite interesting."

Sarah hadn't the least idea what he was talking about, but she could play up if she was given a lead. She laughed a little and said,

"I don't suppose I shall read it really."

Up in her own room, she straightened the paper out. It was a page torn from a note-book with faint blue lines on it. Across the lines John Brown had written:

I want to see you. Same place. Same time.

There was no signature.

She lit a match and burned the sheet to ashes.

She was going to sleep in Lucilla's room, but she dressed and undressed in her own. She had taken off her tweed skirt and jumper, and was hanging them up, when Lucilla came in with her evening dress over her arm. She was still in the black woollen cardigan suit she had worn all day. Sarah thought she looked very pale.

She said, "What is it?" and Lucilla sat down on the bed with her black georgette frock across her knees.

"I did feel to want to dress in here."

"All right—dress. It's about time you did."

Lucilla shook her head with its fair fluff of hair.

"Oh no—lots of time. You've hardly begun yourself, and I dress like a lightning flash."

"Well, get on with it, my child."

Lucilla made no attempt to get on with it. She gazed soulfully at Sarah.

"Angel darling, I want to ask you something."

Sarah was washing at the pink basin. She said, through the sound of the rushing water,

"Ask away."

"Cross your heart and die—you won't tell a lie?"

"I won't if I can help it."

"Oh, Sarah! And you a governess!"

Sarah laughed.

"I really don't tell lies. Get on with it."

"Well then—how passionately do you love Uncle Geoffrey?"

Sarah turned round with a pink linen towel in her hand.

"I could live without him," she said.

"*I'm* serious," said Lucilla. "Nobody ever thinks I'm serious, but I am—sometimes. Do you love him at all?"

"Lucilla, what are you driving at?"

"I asked you a plain question." Lucilla's voice was mournful. "All right, govvy, I won't press for an answer—I'd hate to make you blush. But if you won't respond about Uncle Geoffrey, I would like to know what you feel about Mr. Brown."

Sarah dried her face carefully with the towel, and was glad of it. The most piercingly inquisitive eye cannot see through a yard of pink linen. She said, quite untruthfully,

"I don't think about him at all."

"You ought to think about him," said Lucilla reprovingly. "He's my Noble Preserver. You ought to be palpitating with gratitude, because if he hadn't saved my life you'd be out of a job. You know, I did come most awfully near to being the late Lucilla Hildred."

Sarah put down the towel. Lucilla had her black frock by the shoulders and was dancing it to and fro, making it dip and curtsey. Her face was intent and innocent.

"Lucilla—what *happened*?"

Just for a moment the innocent intentness was broken. Something flickered across it. There was an instant when something wavered. Then all that was gone. Lucilla jumped to her feet with a laugh.

"Nothing happened," she said. "Hadn't you gathered that I was still alive? Now you watch me be a lightning flash!"

She slipped out of her skirt, leaving it on the floor, and peeling off the cardigan, threw it at a chair. It caught on the arm and hung trailing.

Whilst Lucilla washed, Sarah picked up the skirt and reached for the trailing coat, catching it up by the sleeve. She had begun to say, "Untidy child!" but her voice suddenly dried up, because something fell from the pocket of Lucilla's cardigan on to the pink carpet at her feet. To be quite accurate, two things fell. Two little steel screws.

Chapter Nineteen

SARAH LOOKED at the screws. Then she looked at Lucilla, who was drying her hands on the pink towel. She was gay and mischievous. She rolled the towel into a ball, pitched it on to the bed, and began to wriggle into her black georgette frock, which was very tight and slinky, and rather high in the neck. It was the only smart garment she possessed, and it suited her very well.

"Getting into this dress makes me feel exactly like a worm," she said as soon as her mouth was clear. She wriggled a little more, and the black flares swished down to her ankles. With a pirouette she posed before a long tilted mirror. "Moddom is so slim," she murmured, and turned with haughty grace to Sarah. "Moddom's hair, is it not *chic* like this? A new fashion, Miss Trent—especially designed for moddom by Signor Horrifico himself. You see how it stands on end all over the head? That is Signor Horrifico's own secret process. All the famous beauties are on their knees to him for it, but it is moddom whom he has selected to demonstrate this new and *chic* coiffure—What's the *matter*, Sarah?"

Sarah had been standing quite still with Lucilla's skirt in one hand and her cardigan in the other. She let go of them now as if they had suddenly become too heavy to hold. Then she stooped, gathered up the two little screws, and held them out on the palm of her hand. She did not speak, but she looked very intently at Lucilla, who had come to a standstill just out of reach. She saw Lucilla look at the screws, and then she saw the colour come sharply to her face. She knew that colour now. It always meant the same thing—a sudden shock of surprise or fear. She would have given a good deal to know which of the two was sending the blood up to the roots of the fair tumbled hair at this moment.

The moment passed, and the flush was passing too, but as it passed, she met Lucilla's eyes and surprised in them a look which startled her. It was a sick, frightened look—the look which someone might have who has been hit too hard, and is uncertain of being able to rally from the blow.

Yet Lucilla did rally. She made some effort—Sarah was aware that it was a great effort—and she said,

"What have you got there?"

It was not quite her usual voice, but to anyone who did not know her well it would have seemed like her usual voice.

Sarah said in a quiet, measured way,

"Two screws, Lucilla."

Lucilla said, "Yes?"

"Your bicycle screws."

Lucilla said, "Where were they?"

Sarah said, "In the pocket of your cardigan."

And with that the reverberations of the dinner gong came up from the hall below. It was a very large gong slung between two carved posts, and it made a great deal of noise. No one had any excuse for not hearing it, or for being late for dinner. In fact to be late for any meal was an unforgivable offence both to Uncle Geoffrey and to Aunt Marina.

Lucilla took the screws and put them into one of the small drawers of the dressing-table. Then she picked up Sarah's brush, smoothed her hair rapidly, and ran out of the room. On the threshold she looked over her shoulder, to see Sarah half way into her dress.

"Hurry," she said, "or I'll have to say you're dead. It's the only excuse they'll look at."

The excuse was not needed. The gong was still swinging when Sarah caught her on the stairs. They entered the drawing-room together, to find Geoffrey Hildred looking at his watch.

There are some evenings which seem quite interminable. The clock ticks, but the hands seem to get no nearer bed-time. This was one of those evenings. Geoffrey Hildred retired into *The Times*. Ricky sulked over a book whose pages he would either turn three or four at a time or else leave unturned for half an hour. Lucilla produced a canvas strip with a thunder-and-lightning design stamped upon it. A single orange flash was all that she had so far achieved, but it appeared that it was to be a bag. "For my grandchildren," she explained with a small resigned sigh, after which she sat in silence, with a medley of orange and brown wools upon her lap, her needle moving very slowly and carefully, her fair head bent and her attention apparently concentrated upon her work.

Sarah detested needlework and never attempted it. She sat by Miss Marina and heard the thrilling story of how Maurice Hildred had cut four teeth before he was five months old—"A most precocious child, Miss Trent, and so very sweet-tempered. I remember when he was four years old he fell and cut himself very badly indeed upon the arm. It was the gardener's fault, for of course he should not have left the edging-shears lying on the path like that—a piece of gross carelessness, and so I told my cousin John Hildred at the time. And we had to have the doctor to Maurice. It was old Dr. Redman, whom we all liked so much. He died just before the Armistice. He was a widower, and he lost his only son in the war. And of course we like Dr. Drayton very much indeed, and I feel that in some ways he understands me better than Dr. Redman did, but after so many years it was a sad break and very upsetting for all his old patients.... Where was I, my dear?"

Sarah was giving her a most flattering attention. Her eyes were positively sparkling with interest, and her voice thrilled as she said,

"You were telling me about the cut on Maurice's arm. Was it very deep?"

"My dear, it was terrible. The point of the shears went right in. But I can't tell you how good he was, hardly crying at all after the first fright was over. Dr. Redman had to take three stitches, and it left such a scar. I can remember saying to his poor mother, 'Well, my dear, you wanted a girl, but you may be glad that he isn't one, because he'll never lose that scar.' Of course it didn't matter at all for a young man, but it would have looked very bad in evening dress if he had been a girl—a nasty three-cornered jag just above the elbow. And she was most indignant, and declared that she had never wanted a girl at all, but of course she did, and quite natural with two boys already—Henry and Jack were older, you know. But then once Maurice was there, he was such a particularly engaging child that no one could have wished for any change in him."

Miss Marina dropped half a dozen stitches and let her knitting fall. She began to fumble in a black velvet bag with an oxidised silver handle for the handkerchief which she always needed when she talked about Maurice. Her sandy lashes were wet, and half a dozen round tears rolled down her plump, pale cheeks.

Sarah found the handkerchief and picked up the knitting. Then she had to pick up the stitches too. Geoffrey Hildred looked over the top of *The Times*, cleared his throat as if he was going to say something, but thought better of it and went back to an article on Debt Settlement.

Miss Marina said, "Thank you, my dear. It is stupid of me to talk about Maurice, because it always makes me cry. You see, I remember him as such a very dear little boy. I suppose he was eighteen when he went out to the war, but I had hardly seen him for some years before that. I used to visit his mother a good deal, but she died and he went to school, so I always think of him as the little boy I knew, and it seems so dreadful to think of him—*missing*." She dabbed her eyes as she spoke. "Henry and Jack were older—it doesn't seem so dreadful for them. And Henry always had rather an aloof disposition. I remember someone saying once that he looked as if no one was quite good enough for him to speak to."

Sarah had had a question burning her tongue for the last five minutes. She got it out now.

"Were they tall? Lucilla's tall, and Mr. Hildred, and Ricky."

Miss Marina dropped another stitch.

"Oh, my dear, if you wouldn't mind—I think these polished needles are to blame. I really like the old bone ones better, but they are so unreliable since the war. What was it you asked me? Oh well, Henry was about an inch shorter than Geoffrey, and he was the tallest of the three boys, but I believe he got to stoop very much. And I always think Maurice would have grown—he was still so young. Now let me see ... Geoffrey is five foot eleven—so that would make Henry five foot ten—and last time I saw Jack and Maurice they were certainly not quite so tall, but there wasn't a great deal of difference."

She continued to talk, but Sarah was no longer listening. She therefore missed hearing how Henry had been thrown by the pony that he would ride, and that Jack had had a passion for black currant jam. She was wholly occupied in wondering how she could get John Brown to roll up his sleeve above the elbow. It would have been quite easy if it had been August instead of October. They could have bathed somewhere, and she would have been able to see whether he had an old jagged scar on either of his arms. If he was Maurice Hildred, the scar would be there. If there wasn't any scar, he wasn't Maurice Hildred. A line came between her brows and she tried to see him standing by Geoffrey Hildred. He was not as tall—she was quite sure of that—but she had an idea that there wasn't much in it. Geoffrey Hildred looked taller than he really was.

The evening came to an end at last. Lucilla had completed two more orange zigzags and had begun on something that looked like a dark brown thundercloud. The finished bag would undoubtedly be quite extraordinarily ugly, but on the other hand it was so improbable that it ever would be finished that it really didn't matter very much. When the clock struck ten, Miss Marina put away her knitting, yawned in a ladylike manner behind her white plump hand, and got up, letting her handkerchief fall upon the hearth-rug. This happened every night. Sometimes the knitting fell too, but to-night there was only the hem-stitched linen handkerchief with its scent of *eau-de-Cologne* for Sarah to retrieve. After which Miss Marina kissed her cousin on the cheek, patted Ricky's shoulder with a "Good-night, dear boy," and offered her own cheek to Lucilla. Everybody said good-night to everyone else.

At the top of the stairs Miss Marina turned to the right, and Sarah and Lucilla to the left. By the door of the pink room Sarah took Lucilla by the arm, and was met by a very reproachful gaze.

"I'm asleep, Sarah—really I am. If you don't let me go and undress before I'm right off, I'll never get out of this frock. It really would be a pity if they had to cut it off me."

Sarah pulled her inside the room and shut the door.

"No, you don't, my child! We're going to have this out. If you're asleep, you've got to wake up. How did those screws get into the pocket of your cardigan?"

Lucilla yawned without any polite screening hand. She had very white and perfect teeth.

"Darling Sarah, how do I know? I suppose someone put them there."

"They are the screws from your bicycle, aren't they?"

Lucilla yawned again.

"Can you answer questions about screws when you're asleep? I can't."

"Lucilla, be serious. Who took those screws out of your bicycle, and who put them in your pocket?"

Lucilla drooped against the door.

"What did you say, darling?"

Sarah took her by the shoulders and gave her a shake.

"You won't get off that way! Those are your screws."

"One of mine was called Edward, and the other one Clementina. I don't *know* that these are Edward and Clementina. Such large families and all twins, you know, and *exactly* alike. I wasn't ever, ever quite sure which was Edward and which was Clementina. Have you ever tried saying 'I wasn't ever, ever quite sure' ten times really quickly? I believe it's most *frightfully* difficult."

Sarah shook her quite hard.

"Lucilla, those screws didn't come out by themselves."

Lucilla looked at her mournfully.

"Edward is Exceptionally Enterprising and Energetic, and Clementina *will* always do what he does."

"Lucilla—did you take those screws out yourself?"

Lucilla winced. Not with her body—Sarah had her hands on her and there was no movement—it was her eyes that winced. There was a look which gave Sarah a sick feeling. She had meant to startle but not to hurt like this. The look was one of a suffering momentarily too acute to be under control. It was horrible to have hurt someone as much as that. She took her hands away and said,

"Lucilla—what *is* it?"

But the moment had passed. Lucilla was rubbing her eyes with her knuckles like a sleepy baby and saying in a small strangled voice between yawns,

"Angel darling Sarah—I do hate talking in my sleep. I just want to tumble into your darling pink bed and go into a lovely pink dream. A real angel would peel me out of this blighted dress."

Sarah peeled her out of it, and put her to bed very much as if she had been five years old. She snuggled down on the pink pillow with the rose-coloured eiderdown tucked about her. A sleepy blue eye looked up at Sarah. A sleepy voice said,

"Would you like to kiss me good-night?"

Chapter Twenty

SARAH WENT INTO the blue room and shut the door. She had at the very least an hour and a half to put in before it would be safe to assume that everyone else in the house was asleep. She might or might not go and meet John Brown; she hadn't made up her mind. But whether she went to meet him or not, she wanted time to think, to straighten things out, to plan what she would say to him when they did meet, whether it was to-night or to-morrow. She locked the door, took off her evening dress, and put on a dressing-gown. Then she sat down in a very comfortable armchair covered in the same blue and white stuff as the curtains and began to try and straighten out her thoughts.

"Golly! What a day!" she said to herself. The picnic seemed to have receded into the week before last, but it really did belong to this horrible mixed bag of a day. She began to tabulate the things that had happened. She had a very clear and logical mind. The untidy odds and ends of things which had been happening filled her with anger and with a determination to get them cleared up.

They had picnicked. They had played games. Someone had taken the screws out of Lucilla's bicycle. The brakes being out of action, Lucilla had had the narrowest possible shave of being killed on Burdon Hill. No one could have expected her to survive that hill without brakes. Well, who had taken out the screws? It was Ricky who suggested that they had fallen out. If they had fallen out, they wouldn't have been in the pocket of Lucilla's cardigan. Someone had taken them out and put them in the cardigan pocket.

Who? And *when?*

As to who had taken them out, it lay between Lucilla herself and any one of half a dozen other people. Had Lucilla taken them out herself? It looked as if she had. But had she? To take them out, and then to ride the hill was tantamount to suicide. But if Lucilla had wanted to go over the edge, she could have done so anywhere on the bends. Only an unshakable nerve and courage had taken her safely through. If someone else had removed the screws, it amounted to an attempt on Lucilla's life—an attempt that was to look like an accident. Any one of the picnic party would have had the opportunity of tampering with the bicycle. But the screws might have been taken out before they ever started for the picnic. There was nothing to brake for on the outward journey—only a road that ran along the flat or climbed a rolling down, and then the long ascent of Burdon Hill.

Sarah frowned impatiently. It might have been Lucilla, or it might have been anyone else, and at any time that day. But the screws— something flashed into her mind about the screws. If someone else had put them in Lucilla's pocket, she thought she could guess when it was done. Not before that horrible ride down the hill without brakes, because that was to look like an accident. No one would have worried about a couple of screws if Lucilla and the bicycle had been smashed, as they might have been smashed, on the rocks below the bends, but when the attempt had failed, when the loss of the screws had been noticed, then they might have been slipped into Lucilla's cardigan pocket....

Sarah counted over the people who could have put those screws into Lucilla's pocket. Herself—Ricky—Bertrand Darnac—John Brown—and, after their return to the Red House, Aunt Marina and Uncle Geoffrey. She and Lucilla had gone upstairs together and come down together. She was quite sure that no one else had been within touching distance. No one else—unless there had been someone in the dark at Holme Fallow.... There might have been.... She couldn't get farther than that— there might have been ... But then this unknown person must have had the opportunity of removing the screws, and must have known that they were going up to Holme Fallow to play Devil-in-the-dark. But they had gone up to Holme Fallow on a sudden impulse. Lucilla had suggested it herself. There were no servants in the room. That narrowed the list again to Aunt Marina and Uncle Geoffrey, Ricky, Bertrand, herself, and John Brown.

Which of them had tried to kill Lucilla?

She recoiled from the thought with a shudder. Had Lucilla tried to kill herself? Frankly, Sarah did not believe it. She remembered Geoffrey Hildred's story of the fires in Lucilla's room at school. She remembered Lucilla plunging down from the bank in front of *The Bomb*. And still she didn't believe it. To believe it involved believing that Lucilla was mentally unbalanced. Sarah's mind closed sharply against the thought. Lucilla was as sane as she was herself. She considered a comforting alternative. Were all the things that had happened a succession of daredevil practical jokes? The jump from the bank, the sensational ride without brakes, and a pretended stumble over the low baluster rail at Holme Fallow. It was a comforting theory, but it wasn't a true one. She didn't believe it, because she couldn't believe it. She had seen the sick terror in Lucilla's eyes. The practical joke theory went by the board.

Except for the one moment when she had been considering that theory, Sarah had kept her thoughts away from what had happened at Holme Fallow. She must see John Brown before she let herself think about it. She knew by now that she was going to meet him. She put her face in her hands to shut out the sham blue moonlight and stayed quite still for a long time. There were sounds in the house, and with one part of her mind she was conscious of them—Geoffrey Hildred and Ricky coming upstairs—Ricky coming along the passage to his room—then the house settling into silence, going to sleep—time going by—Sarah herself a long, long way off—thinking her own thoughts— new, strange thoughts—

She came back at last, and got up. It was a quarter to twelve. She put on the dark woollen suit which she had worn the night before and went down. It wasn't like the first time. It was odd. She felt as if she had done it a hundred times before, and she wasn't afraid that anyone would wake. She knew they wouldn't.

She got out of the window, and found that the rain had stopped. She had not thought about it till now, but when she dropped from the window ledge she remembered that it had been raining when they came back from Holme Fallow. The sky was cloudy, and the air was very damp and mild. It was much darker than it had been the night before. She followed the same path as she had done then, skirting the house and descending the steps at the corner of the terrace. The path that led into the shrubbery turned off to the left at the bottom of the steps. It was very dark indeed under the trees. She moved slowly with her hands stretched out before her. There were tall blocks of holly and yew. She pricked her hands. It got darker all the time. She went on for half a dozen steps, and then stood still. She wasn't going to walk into a holly-bush and scratch her eyes out for any John Brown in the world. (Miss Marina at breakfast: "My dear, what singular scratches! How did you get them?") The game wasn't worth the candle. If John Brown could see in the dark, let him get on with it and come and find her. Sarah Trent had done as much as she was going to do, and a good deal more than she had ever done for anyone else. Sarah Trent was respectable. Sarah Trent had a job to hold on to. Midnight assignations were not in her line at all. She stood in the dark and told Sarah Trent just what kind of a fool she thought her.

Then, without any sound at all, a hand came out of the dark and took her by the arm. John Brown's voice said,

"Nice of you to come."

Sarah didn't jump, because she didn't let herself jump. A tingling ran from her shoulder to her fingertips. She said in a furious whisper,

"You call this *nice*?"

She thought he laughed. There wasn't any sound; there was just the feeling that he was laughing at her.

Then he said, "We can't talk here," and began to walk her along the path, moving as quickly and easily as if it were noon instead of black midnight.

After a moment Sarah stopped expecting to run into a holly-bush and let herself be taken along. For some unexplained reason she no longer minded the dark. She felt exhilarated. She told herself that it was an adventure, and that she liked adventures.

They came out into the drive. She knew it was the drive by the gravel under their feet, but she couldn't see a thing for high banks, overhanging trees, and general murk.

"Where are we going?"

"To my car. It's just down the road. We can't talk here."

"I thought your car was crocked."

"It was to be ready to-day. I walked into Ledlington and fetched it. I want to talk to you. That young fool Darnac follows me round at night—he's probably somewhere about now."

Sarah hoped he wasn't. She kept quiet and walked faster. They reached the car, and she felt a good deal relieved. A scene with Ran would put the lid on everything.

The car moved off. She said again,

"Where are we going?"

"Just up on to the heath."

When they were there, he ran off the road and switched out the lights, leaving only the glimmer on the dash-board.

"And now," he said, "we can talk."

Sarah sat back in her corner half turned to face him, and what she saw was a black shadow that reminded her of the burglar's shadow at Holme Fallow. She said quickly,

"Which of us is going to talk first?"

"You can if you like."

Sarah did like. She was bursting with things that wanted saying. They crowded in her mind and jostled one another for first place. This made her rather breathless as she said,

"There's such a lot—I don't know where to begin. I oughtn't to be here, but I've *got* to talk to someone."

"You can talk to me, Sarah."

She took him up in a flash.

"You mean I can trust you?"

"Yes."

She found herself giving a shaky laugh.

"I can't think why I should, John Brown."

"*Do* you?"

She evaded that.

"I'm going to talk to you—I've got to. These things that keep happening—what do they mean? Do you know what they mean?"

There was a pause. Then he said,

"Go on. I'll talk presently."

Sarah had one knee over the other. She clasped her hands tight upon it and said,

"What happened this afternoon?"

"You mean about the bicycle?"

"No, I mean at Holme Fallow. *What happened?*"

"You want to take that first?"

"Please."

"All right."

"What happened?"

John Brown said, "I told you. What I said was quite true. I can add a little to it, but not very much. I was on the second step, by the pillar, touching the balustrade with my knee. Lucilla wasn't telling the truth when she said she was running and tripped on the top step. She came down the passage walking, and on the top step she stood and listened. Then she came on to the second step, and the third—I could hear every time she moved. She was the width of the steps away from me, by the wall. She certainly didn't trip. When she was on the third step, she moved along it to get to the balustrade. She didn't know I was there. If she had moved in my direction she would have touched me. She leaned over the balustrade and looked down into the hall. Then she screamed and went over. I caught her. Your light went on. And fortunately I was able to lift her back. I was only just able. It was a very near thing."

Sarah sat silent and thought about what he had said. She was quite sure that he was telling the truth. Lucilla's story of a running stumble had exonerated him from suspicion. He said Lucilla's story wasn't true. His own story positively invited suspicion. Why should he tell a story like that if it wasn't true?

"Is that all?" she said.

"Not quite."

"Tell me."

"It's a thing I can say, but it isn't a thing I can prove."

"Do you mean—that she threw herself over?" Her voice went down into horrified depths.

"No, I don't mean that. I mean that there was someone else on the stair—I think."

"*Who?*" The word came suddenly loud, but it didn't sound loud to Sarah, because the beating of her heart drowned it.

"There you have me," said John Brown.

"Did you see anything? What did you see?"

"Nothing at all. Sarah, I don't know anything—I'm guessing. I'm guessing there was someone below Lucilla on the stair. I heard something. Nothing to swear to, you know, but—something. There could have been someone there, crouching down so as to keep below the balustrade. If there *was* someone there like that, he could have taken Lucilla by the ankles and tipped her over. You didn't see anything when your light came on?"

"No, I only saw Lucilla—and you."

John Brown nodded.

"He would get away at once, probably down to the landing and up the other side. He must have got a fright all the same—he wasn't expecting that torch."

Sarah leaned towards him.

"But who—*who?*" she said. And then, as he didn't answer, "Ran was in the drawing-room, and Ricky had just run into me in the hall."

John Brown remained silent.

After a moment Sarah leaned back.

"It makes me sick."

John Brown nodded again.

Sarah went on in a shaken voice.

"People don't do that sort of thing without a motive. What is the motive?"

"I suppose Holme Fallow might be the motive, Sarah—Holme Fallow and what goes with it."

Sarah asked a question.

"Who would get all that—if Lucilla died?"

She asked the question, but how should John Brown be able to answer it?

He did answer it, and at once.

"Marina—she's an old woman—then Geoffrey and his son."

Sarah felt as if her breath was going to choke her. She held both hands hard against her breast. She made herself say,

"Supposing—Maurice—was—alive—" She choked, and got her breath again. "Maurice Hildred."

She saw John Brown's hand lift and fall again upon his knee, a shadow moving in the faint glimmer from the dash-board. He said in his quiet voice,

"Maurice Hildred is dead."

Chapter Twenty-One

AFTER A SILENCE John Brown said,

"What put that into your head, Sarah? What made you think of Maurice Hildred?"

"They don't think he's dead."

"Who don't?"

"Miss Marina and Mr. Hildred."

He made a short contemptuous sound that wasn't quite a laugh.

"Oh, Marina? Poor old dear. But Geoffrey—I'm quite sure Geoffrey doesn't believe that Maurice is alive."

"If he *were*, he would get Holme Fallow if anything happened to Lucilla. He would, wouldn't he?"

"He would—certainly." This time he did laugh. "So that's the game, is it? Maurice is alive, and Lucilla's in his way, so he's trying to remove her! I suppose he took the screws out of her bicycle this afternoon! It's all very ingenious. Was it your idea, or Darnac's— or Geoffrey's? Wanted, a murderer with a motive, so it has to be Maurice, who's been dead for fifteen years! And I suppose I'm cast for the part!" There was an extraordinary bitterness in the voice which was usually so quiet and pleasant.

Sarah said, "Don't, John—*please*," and didn't know that she had spoken until she heard herself saying his name. *Was* it his name? She didn't know. She only knew she couldn't bear that bitter sound in his voice.

He said, "Did you think I was Maurice?"

"I thought—you might be. Just that—not anything else."

"And why that?"

Sarah took hold of herself with both hands. These currents of emotion frightened her. They'd got to be practical and sensible. She sat as far back in her corner as she could and tried for a steady, friendly voice. It wasn't as steady as she would have liked it to be.

"You were at Holme Fallow the night I came down to be interviewed. I was late because of Mr. Hildred. I ran out of petrol by the east drive, and I came up to the house to try and get some. The side door was open and I came in. You were in the dining-room. You turned your torch on Mrs. Hildred's picture. It was so like Lucilla that it startled me and I ran away. You see, I'd just had a very narrow shave of running over Lucilla—I'll tell you about it presently. I didn't know it was you I had seen until this evening. You were in the same place and doing the same things. Then I knew it was you the first time. Ran thought you were Maurice, but I didn't think so till then. You don't expect me to believe that you're a burglar?"

"I see. Did you know that I followed you up to town?

"You?"

"I was the obliging stranger with the petrol. Didn't you know?"

"Of course I didn't. Why on earth did you follow me?"

"I wonder—" said John Brown.

There was a pause. It lasted until Sarah could have screamed. Why couldn't he say why he had followed her? He was not the first, and he certainly wouldn't be the last. Sarah had a short and shattering way with followers. She ought to be saying some of the things which as a rule came so trippingly from her tongue. The only thing she wanted to say was his name. She managed not to say it.

In the end he said in a different voice, "Why did you nearly run over Lucilla?"

Sarah answered him with relief.

"She came plunging down off one of those banks in the Red House drive. She said she fell."

"She falls rather a lot, doesn't she?"

"Look here," said Sarah, "I'm going to tell you the whole thing from the beginning."

"Isn't that the beginning?"

"I think," said Sarah—"I think that Henry Hildred's death is really the beginning. All these other things have happened since then—since Lucilla came into Holme Fallow."

"What things?"

"Mr. Hildred told me that he was asked to take Lucilla away from school because on two separate occasions her room was found to be on fire. They thought she had done it herself, and they asked him to take her away. Miss Marina doesn't know."

"I see. Go on."

"Then there's this business of her falling in front of *The Bomb*. If I hadn't braked like mad and driven into the bank, I'd have been over her. Then there's the thing that flapped and scratched at her window. It's stopped now that I'm sleeping in the room."

"I can tell you how that was done. I went upstairs after tea and looked out of the bathroom window. It was done from there. Quite easy. You lock the door, you lean out of the window with a light rake or cultivator which has something dark and soft tied on to it, and you can tap and scratch and dash at Lucilla's window till all is blue. Or, if I'm the villain of the piece, I could have climbed on to the top of the porch and done it from there. I think that would be Darnac's explanation."

Sarah said, "It's not mine," and thought that she had said it a little too quickly. She went on more quickly still. "That's *how* it was done. But *why*? That's what I want to know—*why*? It doesn't seem to fit in with the other things. You see, the fall from the bank, and the bicycle affair, and the fall over the balustrade, they are one sort of thing. They might be Lucilla's doing or someone else's. Either she has tried to kill herself or someone is trying to kill her. Now this dashing, scratching thing is different—it's more like a practical joke. And the fires—I can't make up my mind about them. They might be meant to be dangerous, or they might be meant to make her appear hysterical or—queer."

John Brown said in a meditative voice, "I don't think there's any discrepancy really. We've got to assume something. I'm assuming that Lucilla is being attacked. I don't think the fires would be meant seriously. If they created an impression that she was unbalanced, they would serve their turn and be remembered later. You may call the thing that dashed against the window a practical joke, but if it had sent Lucilla into hysterics or induced her to tell a wild unbelievable tale, that would have been more evidence as to her being—queer. It must have been a disappointment when she held her tongue. Of course when you heard the Thing too, it lost its value."

Sarah said, "Yes—I see." And then, quickly, "But why did she hold her tongue? That's what I can't understand—she won't say anything. She must know things, but she won't tell what she knows. She's sick with fright one moment, and making a joke about it the next. I want to know *why*."

"She's plucky," said John Brown with rather an odd tone in his voice.

"Of course she's plucky. But you see, there are some things she *must* know. She must know whether she set fire to those curtains in her room at school. She must know whether she was pushed off the bank. And she must know whether somebody tried to throw her over the balustrade. I've never spoken to her about the fires—she doesn't know I know about them. But when I'd nearly run over her, and almost before she got her breath, she was saying she had fallen. And at Holme Fallow this evening you heard her yourself—she was as quick as lightning with that lie about having tripped on the top step."

"Yes—it wasn't true."

"But why?" said Sarah. She bent towards him, leaning on her hand. "Can you tell me why? Is she shielding someone? Do you go on shielding someone who goes on attempting your life? It isn't reasonable, John— it isn't reasonable." She stopped herself, and then went on in a lower voice. "I'd better tell you—there's something you don't know. Those screws that were missing from Lucilla's bicycle—they dropped out of the pocket of her cardigan when she was dressing this evening."

"What?" said John Brown.

"They dropped out of the pocket of her cardigan when she was dressing for dinner."

"What did she say?"

"She looked—*sick* with fright. She didn't say anything. The dinner bell rang, and it's the eighth deadly sin to be late, so we went down. Afterwards she made a joke of it. She talked a lot of nonsense. Well, there you are. What does it mean?"

John Brown sat silent for about a minute and a half. Then he said.

"There's one explanation that covers everything. It's the only one that does. I don't like it, and you won't like it. I don't believe it, but I don't think we can just turn our backs on it."

Sarah knew what was coming, but she said,

"What do you mean?"

He must say it himself. She wasn't going to meet him half way.

"We assumed just now that Lucilla was being attacked. Now we've got to assume that she herself is at the bottom of all these things that have been happening. She set light to her own curtains, and she played a practical joke to frighten you after getting you to change rooms."

Sarah gave a sharp involuntary exclamation.

"She couldn't!"

"Sarah, she could. Just think for a moment, and you will see that she could. She gets you to change rooms with her, and she goes into the bathroom, leans out, and bangs and scratches on that end window with a rake and a cushion, or something like that."

"She was frightened," said Sarah. "I'll swear she was frightened. And, John, I'll tell you why she was frightened—she thought she'd been hearing something that wasn't there to hear. As soon as she knew I'd heard it too she wasn't frightened any more."

John Brown made some kind of movement with his hand.

"On our present assumption, that would be acting. She'd played her trick and lost interest in it. We're assuming that she's unbalanced. She threw herself in front of your car. She took the screws out of her bicycle. And she tried to fling herself over the balustrade."

"No!" said Sarah. "John, I don't believe it!"

"I don't say I believe it. But, as an explanation, you will admit that it covers all the facts. You said it was unreasonable that she should screen anyone who continued to attempt her life. It stops being unreasonable if the person she is screening is herself. Then there's another point of view, which makes this explanation easier to believe. The attempts may not have been very serious ones. You say you nearly ran over her, but it was bound to seem a nearer shave to you than it really was. She may have left herself a margin of safety. She may have known that she could ride that hill without brakes—I could have done it at her age. And she may have known that I was on the step above her when she tipped over the balustrade at Holme Fallow."

"She couldn't have counted on your catching her."

"No. But she may have overbalanced—intended to play a trick, and gone farther than she meant. There's a thing they call exhibitionism, you know. It's a form of hysteria. People who've got it must be in the limelight somehow." He gave a sudden short laugh. "The good old-fashioned name for it was showing off."

Some of the horror cleared from Sarah's mind.

"You think it might be that?"

"It might."

She felt as if an intolerably heavy weight had been lifted. A naughty child playing tricks—a naughty child showing off. What a relief! *If she could believe it.*

There came a sudden sighing wind across the heath. It was the first outside thing that Sarah had noticed since they had driven off the road. They had been shut in together, just the two of them, out of the world, talking with as close an intimacy as if they had been familiar friends. Only a few hours ago, and her thoughts of him had been dark with suspicion, yet, outside all reason, she had trusted him frankly and told him what she had told to no one else. She had told him what she had not told Ran—what she would not tell Ran. She felt a little cold reaction. If she was going to talk to anyone about Lucilla, it was to Geoffrey Hildred that she should have talked. Something shut down close in her mind. She couldn't possibly talk about Lucilla to Geoffrey Hildred. The gulf which separates the generations was wide and dark between them.

The wind came again. It ruffled her hair and left a little damp upon her cheek. The window on her side was open, and there was a smell of rain in the air. She said quickly,

"I must go back."

"All in a hurry like that?" said John Brown.

Sarah made an impatient movement.

"What's the good of talking? We don't get anywhere. I oughtn't to have come."

"Are you sorry you came?"

"I shall be if I get the sack."

"I'll take you back in a minute. I don't think you'll get the sack."

"It wouldn't matter to you if I did, but it would matter damnably to me. This sort of job isn't so easy to get. I'm not trained, and I've no certificates or qualifications. I'd like to go back now if you don't mind."

John Brown took no notice. He said,

"I wanted to talk about what we're going to do next."

"I don't see there's anything we can do."

"I don't—know—"

She had put away the idea of Geoffrey Hildred, but it came back insistently. Gulf or no gulf, he was the person ultimately responsible. He was Lucilla's guardian. She found herself saying,

"I suppose we could tell Mr. Hildred."

"And what makes you suppose he doesn't know already? You haven't told me about that. Lucilla had two very narrow shaves. Hasn't anyone told Geoffrey—Ricky—you—Lucilla?"

"*I* didn't," said Sarah. "And I'm sure Lucilla didn't. I don't know what Ricky did, but no one would say anything in front of Miss Marina. We spent one of the gloomier family evenings. Nobody uttered except Aunt Marina, and she never stopped. She talked about the boys, as she calls them. She talked a lot about Maurice. She loves him awfully. I suppose that's why she doesn't believe he's dead."

"I suppose so." His voice was even and noncommittal.

He began to start the car, and as they got back on to the road and went past the pillars of the east drive, Sarah found herself most unreasonably angry. She had demanded to be taken back. She was being taken back. But when she had made her demand he had taken no notice. It was only when she began to talk about Maurice Hildred that John Brown had remembered that she wanted to go home.

They stopped a couple of hundred yards from the gate, and he walked with her up the dark drive and through the shrubbery to where the path came out below the steps which led to the terrace. Neither of them said a single word until then. They stood a moment there, and Sarah's anger died. A deeply troubled feeling took its place. They were in darkness, and she could not see his face. She was afraid of what had been spoken between them. She was afraid to go in. There was a burden of fear upon the night, and upon the day that would follow it.

His hand came on her shoulder with a quiet pressure.

"Don't worry, Sarah."

And with that he was gone.

She went up the steps and along the terrace, and in through the window which she had left ajar. The house was heavy and drowsy with sleep. Her feet were like lead as she climbed the stairs.

She got into bed and fell very deeply asleep.

Chapter Twenty-Two

NEXT DAY WAS SUNDAY. Breakfast was at half-past nine instead of nine o'clock, and there were sausages at one end of the table and boiled eggs at the other. Miss Marina, in a formidable black brocade and a brooch which contained the admiral's hair and her mother's neatly interlaced within a border of pale chased gold and small rose diamonds, narrated with extraordinary zest the story of the curate's egg—"And he said, 'Excellent in parts, my lord—excellent in parts.' I suppose he was shy, poor young man. Curates used to be shy, and I suppose the egg was really not what you would call new-laid. These, I hope, are quite trustworthy. We get them from Olivia Bennett, our late Vicar's daughter, who has started a small chicken-farm on the Ledlington road. Lucilla, my dear, if you do not eat your breakfast, I cannot possibly allow you to go to church. *Either* an egg, *or* a sausage."

Lucilla flushed, took the sausage, finished it, and then had toast and marmalade.

When they came out of the dining-room, Geoffrey Hildred put a hand on Sarah's arm.

"If I could speak to you just for a moment in my study—"

But when they were there, he walked to the window and stood looking out, whilst Sarah's guilty heart sank lower and lower. She was going to be taxed with getting out of the window and having a midnight assignation. She was going to be told that her services could be dispensed with. What an ass she had been—what an absolute and complete chump!

Geoffrey Hildred stood for a moment looking out at the mildly misty sky and the damp green of the grass and the trees. When he turned round, he was frowning and his ruddy face had an expression of concern. She thought he looked more like a farmer than ever—perhaps a farmer whose hay crop had just been spoilt by rain.

"I wanted to speak to you about Lucilla," he said, and immediately Sarah's heart bounded up.

"Never, never, *never* again," she said to herself. Aloud she murmured, "Yes, Mr. Hildred?"

Geoffrey Hildred's frown deepened.

"Ricky tells me that Lucilla had a very narrow escape of a bad accident yesterday."

"Yes, she did." Sarah was wondering which particular escape was being referred to. Her tone was perhaps a little dry.

Geoffrey Hildred said quickly,

"In fact two escapes."

"Yes, Mr. Hildred."

He came a little nearer.

"My dear, won't you help me out a little? I'm—very much distressed. I suppose Ricky wasn't—exaggerating?"

"I don't know what he said. Lucilla's bicycle ran away with her down Burdon Hill, and afterwards, when we were playing Devil-in-the-dark up at Holme Fallow, she nearly fell over the balustrade at the top of the stairs. She would have fallen if Mr. Brown hadn't caught her."

"Good heavens! So Ricky said. But I can't understand it. The bicycle was new."

"The screws that hold the brake-rods were gone."

"Yes, yes—he said so. But I can't understand it at all—a perfectly new bicycle. What could possibly have happened to the screws?"

It was at this moment that Sarah should most undoubtedly have told Lucilla's guardian what she had already told Mr. John Brown. Lucilla's guardian was enquiring what had happened to the screws. They were in the left-hand drawer of the dressing-table in the pink bedroom. She had watched Lucilla put them there after they had fallen out of the pocket of her black cardigan and Sarah had picked them up Doubtless Uncle Geoffrey's question was a rhetorical one. He did not really expect Sarah to have any answer to it. Or did he? She rushed into a pause which had lasted a little longer than was comfortable.

"I don't know what happened. She gave us all a most horrible fright."

"Yes—yes—" said Geoffrey Hildred. He walked to the window and back again. "Miss Trent, I am very much concerned about these two accidents. As to the second one, Ricky says she tripped on the top step. Is that correct?"

"That is Lucilla's own account, Mr. Hildred."

"I see, I see. But when you put your torch on—would you mind telling me exactly what you saw when you put your torch on?" He was anxious enough for her answer. There were beads of sweat at his temples. His eyes looked hard into hers.

Sarah answered steadily.

"Lucilla was hanging head downwards over the balustrade. Mr. Brown had hold of her. That's what I saw when the light went on. She was hanging downwards from the knees, and he was bending right over. He managed to lift her back. She said she had tripped on the top step."

"And where did she go over—at what level?"

"The second or third step," said Sarah without any expression in her voice.

Geoffrey Hildred made a sudden startled movement.

"But that's not possible, Miss Trent. If she had tripped on the top step, she would have pitched down. She couldn't possibly have slid across to the balustrade as high up as the second step—it's quite impossible."

Sarah said nothing. She knew that it was impossible, but she said nothing.

"Where was Brown?" said Geoffrey Hildred in a louder voice. There was a tinge of anger in the loudness and his florid colour had deepened.

"On the second step, by the pillar—near enough to catch her."

"Or to push—No, no, I oughtn't to say that—there's no proof. Forget it. I'm too upset to think what I'm saying. It must have been an accident. She must have tripped—not on the top step—that's impossible—but it was dark—she didn't know where she was—and she tripped. That's the explanation. She couldn't have meant to—No, no, what am I saying? My dear, you must forgive me for having so little command of myself, but Lucilla, she means a great deal to *us*. I daresay I'm over anxious. I don't think she's been leading a very normal life. Losing her parents like that. And then Marina and myself—too old for her altogether. That's where we count on you. She wants brightening up, taking out of herself. I'd like to get her out of those black clothes. It doesn't seem right to see a young girl in black. Not colours of course, but surely she could wear grey, and in the evening white. What do you think?"

"I think it would be a very good idea."

He looked pleased.

"Well then, my dear, I'll tell you my little plan. I want to carry you and Lucilla off to town. There's a quiet family hotel we've always stayed at—Millington's. I don't think there could be any objection to your staying there. They've known us all, well, I should say for the last fifty years. I remember Marina stayed there for the old Queen's first jubilee."

"Golly—what a riot!" said Sarah to herself.

"What do you think?" asked Geoffrey Hildred anxiously.

What did she think? She didn't know. It would be pleasant to go shopping with Lucilla. The hotel sounded like *the* ultimate Arctic frost. There was a pringle of fear down in the depths of her. She had to say something.

She said, "I think it would be a very good thing," and at once he was beaming with delighted kindness.

"Well, there we are—we have our little jaunt! I'll let you into a secret. I got theatre tickets yesterday—two lots—a musical show for the afternoon, and a play for the evening. And I've booked the rooms at the hotel for next Tuesday. I thought just our four selves for the evening—you, and I, and Ricky, and Lucilla—but I got six tickets for the afternoon. I thought it would please Lucilla if we invited young Darnac, and then it seemed a little discourteous to leave Mr. Brown out. I had, in fact, mentioned the project to him, but now I'm inclined to wish—but no, no, there's nothing to go upon—nothing—nothing at all. There, I won't keep you any longer—I don't want to deprive Lucilla."

Sarah turned to go with relief, but at the door he called to her.

"Miss Trent, you won't mention those accidents—No, no, thank heaven they were not accidents really—but you won't mention them to Miss Hildred?"

"Of course not."

She had her hand on the door knob, when his voice came again, a little hesitant.

"Miss Trent—with whom was Lucilla bicycling when the screws were missed? I don't think Ricky mentioned. Who was with her?"

"Mr. Brown," said Sarah, and got out of the room.

Chapter Twenty-Three

THEY ALL WENT to church, and sat in the squire's pew, a great square box furnished with red cushions and very fat hassocks. The pew faced sideways to the rest of the congregation, so that when the parson came in and they stood up they could see exactly who had come to church and who had stayed at home. Mr. John Brown sat half way down on the left of the aisle, Mr. Bertrand Darnac a little higher up. He caught Lucilla's eye, but retained an admirable gravity. Presently an old man preached about the law of kindness. And then they all came out into the October sunshine.

Lucilla hung back and talked to Bertrand. When she caught Sarah up she had a bright colour and a sparkle in her eye.

John Brown joined them in the road.

"Bertrand and I are going for a walk," said Lucilla. "After lunch, you know—to walk it off. Roast beef, Yorkshire pudding, potatoes, Brussels sprouts, and horse-radish sauce, also apple pie—and Aunt Marina thinks you're going to die, if you don't eat it all. What are you and Sarah going to do?"

"I am going to sketch by the lower pool," said John Brown.

"That's what I call hogging it. Anyhow Sarah doesn't sketch."

"She can watch me if she likes," said John Brown kindly. He looked at Sarah and his eyes crinkled at the corners. The smile in them said, "Come."

Sarah bit her lip and said she was going to write letters.

"Which means going to sleep," said Lucilla. "My angel darling, if you go to sleep after Yorkshire pudding and apple pie and all the rest of it, you'll be the same size as Aunt Marina before you know what's happening to you. She has written letters on Sunday afternoon for years and years and years. You'd much better go and watch Mr. Brown sketch. It's half a mile to the lower pool and uphill all the way back, which is so slimming. Ran and I, being young and active, will probably go at least a quarter of a mile farther."

Ricky was apparently not included in anyone's plans for the afternoon. He had stayed away from church, and appeared at lunch to be in what Lucilla characterised as a foul temper. After lunch Miss Marina retired to her room and Geoffrey Hildred to his study. Ricky, after bickering with Lucilla, took out his father's car and made off in it, whereupon Lucilla put on her hat and went down to the gate to meet Bertrand. Sarah caught her up at the turn, and was received without enthusiasm.

"Did we ask you to come too?" said Lucilla.

"I'm not coming too—I'm only going to see you start."

Lucilla pulled a face.

"Give handy to Nanna and walk nicely, and take care you don't fall and spoil your nice Sunday dress," she said in a mincing voice.

Sarah looked at her straight.

"Well, you did fall here once, Lucilla," she said. "And after yesterday—I'll see you start with Ran."

"A good, trustworthy young man." Lucilla's voice was meek, but there was a gleam in her eye.

"He'd hate to hear you say so. But I think he is—really."

Lucilla insisted on holding Sarah's hand to the bottom of the drive, where they found Bertrand waiting. She went off with him in high spirits.

Sarah watched them out of sight and considered what she would do next. She had not said that she would go down to the lower pool, but she went. It was in the Holme Fallow grounds, but the road lay between it and the house. There was a stile which shortened the distance, and a path which ran down hill through the fields and skirted an orchard. A few late apples showed among the leaves, which were yellowing too. A gate led into the orchard, and the path went on dropping until it left the trees behind. There were two pools, fed by the tiny trickle of a stream which ran through the middle of the orchard. Lucilla called them Penny Plain and Twopence Coloured. Penny Plain was used for watering the cattle on the grazing land, but Twopence Coloured was given up to water forget-me-not, and tall yellow flags, with a very old crooked willow-tree standing on the east side, where it only kept the early morning sun off the water. The yellow irises were out of bloom long ago, their tall sword-like leaves beginning to turn, but the forget-me-not still bloomed with careless profusion.

John Brown was not merely sketching the forget-me-not. He was drawing the portrait of a very large and brilliant dragon-fly which hung above the water. He had a long pale green body tipped with blue, poised motionless amid the unceasing and almost invisible motion of four gauzy wings. Every now and then he darted here, there, away, and back again, and at every turn there was a faint clang as the wings touched. The portrait was a very faithful one. Sarah stood looking at it.

"But you can't paint that stillness in the midst of movement," said John Brown regretfully. "Look how his wings go—and he keeps it up all the time."

"He's awfully like an aeroplane," said Sarah.

John Brown looked over his shoulder laughing.

"That's putting the cart before the horse, isn't it?"

Sarah laughed too.

"But you know what I mean. Isn't it awfully late for dragon-flies?"

He nodded.

"That's why I wanted to catch this gentleman. They only show up when it's sunny."

The dragon-fly dropped suddenly to the point of a dipping iris leaf, hovered a moment, and settled. For the first time the bewildering misty motion of the wings ceased. They stood out straight and stiff, clear as the wings of a gnat but with a bronzy iridescence. The weight of the apple-green body brought the leaf's sword-point down and down until it almost touched the drift of forget-me-not. Turquoise of the flowers, bright pale green and metallic blue of the dragon-fly, green and yellow iris leaves, and all the water colours of the pool, glowed together in the very clear, thin gold of the October sunlight. Sarah caught her breath at the sheer beauty. It stayed like that between that one caught breath and the next. Then the creature was off again, fanning the air with almost invisible wings, now poised, now darting.

"Well?" said John Brown, still with a smile in his eyes. "Are you glad you came, Sarah?"

Sarah nodded. Just for the moment everything was quite simple, and clear, and happy. There were no problems. It was a nice world, with green and blue dragon-flies, and a crooked willow tree, and a fine Sunday afternoon. Sunday afternoons ought always to be fine.

She sat down on the bank above the pool and said,

"Why can't things be just like this always?"

"You like this?" He had a little the air of being in his own house and pleased with the pleasure of a guest.

She nodded without speaking.

"Do you feel at home here?"

She nodded again. There was a half smile on her lips, but no words. And then he said,

"Where are you really at home, Sarah? Tell me about your own people."

And with that the charm broke.

He saw her flinch and lose colour, and at once she was angry because he had taken her unawares. Her voice was clear and hard as she answered him.

"I haven't any people."

"Then you're like me," said John Brown.

"I don't think so," said Sarah. "I should think I'm unique." She laughed a little. "I've got a mother, but I never see her, and I've got a father, but he never sees me. I'm an entirely independent woman, and sometimes I'm particularly thankful for it, and sometimes it's a bit bleak—when you haven't got a job and wonder how long the cash is going to last. Frankly, that's the only thing that stops me packing up and lighting out of here to-morrow."

Sarah was not really being frank at all. The consciousness of this made her put her chin in the air and look defiantly at John Brown. He said,

"I don't think that's true. I think you're fond of Lucilla."

Sarah's colour rose becomingly.

"I don't get fond of people," she said, still in that clear, hard tone.

He looked at her with the faint air of amusement which always made her angry.

"Is that because of your icy disposition, or because you find us—" He paused for a word, and then said, "unlovable?" He said it quite gravely, and her colour rose again.

"I don't let myself got fond of people," she said. "It doesn't pay. They let you down, and it hurts—too much."

They were so near that he could have touched her, but he did not move, only looked at her and said,

"Poor Sarah."

Sarah looked away across the pool.

"Do you know what happened to me when I was ten years old? My father divorced my mother. I don't blame him in the least—he had plenty of reasons for it. But he said I wasn't his child, and he pushed me out too. He found some old letters and he just turned me out. And we'd been friends. It nearly killed me, and I made up my mind that I'd never love anyone again. It hurts too much."

John Brown put out his hand and covered one of hers.

"Poor little Sarah," he said.

She flashed round on him with wet eyes and an unsteady smile.

"Yes—I'm sorry for her too. She was only ten. I don't believe you can break your heart as badly afterwards as you do when you're ten years old. You see, there was nothing left. I had a pony, and a dog— they went too. It was just outer darkness. I'd always hated my mother, and she'd always hated me. We dragged about together for seven years, and then she married the most completely awful of the men who had dragged about after us. I don't know what would have happened to me if it hadn't been for a heavenly American woman who was in the same hotel. She had a cripple child, and she took me on to talk French and German to the poor kid. That was my first job, and when she went back to America she got me another—the same sort of thing. And then I went to the Manifolds. And now I'm here, and if I wasn't an absolute cast-iron fool, I'd leave to-morrow."

John Brown's hand closed on hers very hard. Just when the pressure became unbearable it relaxed again and he lifted the hand to his lips and held it there.

"I wouldn't let you down, Sarah," he said.

She felt the words against her palm. He kissed them there, and lifted his head and said them again with just a change of tense.

"Sarah, I won't let you down."

Tears were running down her face. She felt as if they were taking her pride with them. She dragged her hand away and said,

"You'll never have the chance!" Her voice was rough and angry. No one would have recognised it.

John Brown said quietly, "You're trying to hurt me because you've been hurt yourself. That's not quite fair."

Sarah dabbed at her eyes.

"You made me—make a fool of myself. I never cry. You made me cry. I've been babbling like a lunatic. I really do hate you a good deal, John!"

He smiled again.

"Well, that will do for a start. It's quite a good start really. I'd like to tell you about following you up to town. You see, it was this way—I didn't see you when you walked in on me the night I was burgling Holme Fallow."

Sarah stopped wanting to cry. She passionately desired to know why he had been burgling Holme Fallow. Was he Maurice Hildred? He had said he wasn't—but was he?

"What were you burgling?" she asked rather breathlessly.

"Some letters and photographs," said John Brown. "Never mind about that—I'll tell you some day soon. Well, I heard you run away and I turned the torch on you, but you were too quick for me. By the time I reached the dining-room door you were through the passage door across the hall—I only got a bit of brown tweed skirt. Then I thought I had stayed long enough, so I went away by the west drive and round by Miller's Lane to cut back on to the London road, and when I got round the corner, there you were in the middle of it—" He stopped.

Sarah said, "Well?"

John Brown laughed a little.

"My dear, you had me all mixed up. I was frightfully angry with you for standing out in the road like that, and I could see your brown tweed in the headlights, so I knew you had just come from Holme Fallow. What I didn't know was whether you'd seen enough of me to recognise, and I thought I'd better find out whether you were heading for the nearest police-station."

"Is that why you followed me?" said Sarah. It was rather a damping sort of reason.

"Probably. Do you believe in love at first sight?"

Sarah said "No" in a little too much of a hurry.

"Well, you needn't call it that—it doesn't matter. But there's something. I felt as if I knew you very well indeed—well enough to scold, you know. And that's a very odd, upsetting feeling to have about someone you've never seen before. It was absolutely necessary to find out who you were and where you lived, so I followed you to town and watched outside the garage until you came out and went into the Lizard. Then I parked my own car and sat down at the next table."

"Oh?" said Sarah.

John Brown nodded.

"I'm afraid I listened to your conversation with Darnac."

Sarah's second "Oh" was a very indignant one.

"I know, my dear—really shameless behaviour. No gentleman would dream of doing such a thing. I'm not even ashamed of it. I learned quite a lot about you before we'd all finished supper." His eyes crinkled at the corners. "I heard you say you were going to marry Geoffrey. You know, I shouldn't if I were you."

Sarah burst out laughing.

"*Really*, John!"

"Yes, really. It was a very interesting evening. You did something to me, Sarah, whilst I sat there watching you. It's so difficult to get these things into words. I've had quite a good sort of life—friends, work, knocking about all over the world, jobs that interested me—but I'd been feeling a bit drab since I came back to England. I don't think burglary's my line—I felt pretty mouldy after it. You know how it is when the colour is out of everything and you don't know why you were born or why you go on living. It was like that. But all the time I was sitting there eavesdropping the colour was coming back. Not just ordinary everyday colour either, but the sort you get when there's a tremendous sunrise— you know, lashins and lavins. Well, that's the way it was. Everything got so interesting that I just grudged going to sleep and losing touch with it. That's what made me go walking in the night. But I wasn't walking alone. I tell you, my dear, you walked with me every step of the way. You were there so plainly that when you came into the shrubbery two nights ago it seemed the most natural thing in the world. When I put out my hand and touched you, it was like having a dream come true. Now wouldn't you call that falling in love?"

"I shall never fall in love with anyone," said Sarah in the firmest voice she could command.

"Oh, but I wasn't talking about you," said John Brown—"I was talking about me. I thought you might be interested in a genuine case of what is called love at first sight. I should certainly never have expected it to happen to me, but so far as I can make out it has. I don't see how it could be anything else. Do you?"

Sarah's eyes stung suddenly. She felt a hot anger and a cold fear. She felt defenceless and young. She said in the voice of a vexed child,

"You're laughing at me."

"Because I love you, Sarah," said John Brown. He added, *"Very much,"* and took her hand and kissed it again.

Chapter Twenty-Four

BERTRAND AND LUCILLA walked in the High Woods. There was a bridle path under the trees. The oaks were still green, but beech and chestnut had begun to put on tints of gold and russet. No leaves had fallen yet. Emerald moss and grey lichen showed here and there. They sat down presently on a fallen tree in an open glade. The sunlight made a shining about them. It was warm, and very still. Lucilla was bare-headed, and her hair was like pale flame in the sun. She looked at Bertrand with a gay impudence in her blue eyes.

"Well, Ran?" she said.

Bertrand gazed at her with admiration.

"What is that 'well,' Lucilla? If it is that you are very well here, then so am I—very well indeed—what you call at the top of the hole."

Lucilla giggled.

"I suppose you mean top-hole."

"That is what I said."

She kissed two fingers at him and said in a mocking tone.

"Why didn't you ask Sarah to go for a walk with you?"

"Sarah does not want to walk with me."

Lucilla flushed.

"Did you ask her? Did she say no? Is that why you asked me?" she said all in a breath.

"To the first question, no. And to the second, no. And to the third, no again."

Lucilla was sitting on one of the branches of the fallen tree. She could make it move up and down by touching her foot to the ground. Bertrand sat facing her on the trunk. She swung her branch and said,

"You came down here to see Sarah."

"That is true," said Bertrand. "Sarah and I are very good friends."

"Oh—friends?" Lucilla made a face. "Don't you make love to her?"

He burst out laughing.

"Lucilla, you are an *enfant terrible*. Does one ask that sort of question?"

"I do," said Lucilla calmly. "Sarah says you make love to every girl you meet. She said you would make love to me, but you don't. Why don't you?"

"Because I am a very good boy," said Mr. Darnac virtuously.

Lucilla made her branch swing again. She said in a pretty, soft voice, "Don't be silly, Ran. I would like you to make love to me—really."

"Would you, Lucilla?"

"Sarah says you do it very well. She says you've had lots of practice. Nobody has ever made love to me except Ricky, and he doesn't count."

"This poor Ricky!"

"He's not. Don't let's talk about him. Show me how you do it. How do you begin?"

A fleeting grin left Bertrand's agreeable ugliness free to assume a sentimental aspect. He gazed at Lucilla in a mournful and devoted manner.

"First of all I look—*comme ça*."

Lucilla giggled.

"Why?"

"To soften the heart."

"Did it soften Sarah's?"

A gleam of animation dispelled the melancholy.

"*Ma foi*—no! I have even wondered whether she has a heart at all."

Lucilla giggled again.

"Mine's like a feather bed, it's so soft. Go on."

"There are different ways. For me, I generally say that she has the most interesting eyes I have ever seen."

She made a face.

"Interesting?"

He nodded.

"One must strike out a new line. You see, she has already been told her eyes are beautiful—a hundred times, perhaps a thousand."

"But I haven't."

"And you would like me to tell you that?"

"Are they beautiful, Ran?"

"Ravishingly beautiful."

She gave a pleased sigh.

"Oh, Ran—go on."

"They are like the very young blue spring sky. And your hair is like the sunshine that there is then—all young, with nothing to spoil it." He leaned forward suddenly and caught her hand. "Lucilla—No, I cannot! That was a game you play with me, but I cannot play at making love to you. It is to me all real, all serious. It is not a game at all. I am in so great a trouble for you that I cannot speak pretty words and play with them. It is yesterday which has shown me that. How do you think that I felt when I saw you go past on your bicycle and I thought that you would be killed?"

"How did you feel?" said Lucilla in an interested voice.

He sprang to his feet, pulling her up with him.

"Ah, you laugh at me! And you say your heart is soft! I did not know that I could suffer as I did in that moment—I did not know that it was possible to suffer like that. In one moment to know that I loved you, and to know that you were going to die, and that there was nothing— nothing that I could do to save you! Oh, *mon dieu*—what a torment!" He had his arms round her. The words came pouring out.

As his clasp tightened, she could feel the beating of his heart. She put up her lips to be kissed, and in a moment he was kissing her, murmuring French love-words, holding her tight. When, half sobbing, he released her, she sat down again on her branch. Her hands gripped it. She looked down at the bright moss and the bare ground. Then, as Bertrand fell on his knees beside her, she met his agitated gaze with a clear look and said in a small, steady voice,

"You did that very well, Ran."

"Lucilla!"

There was such pain in his voice that she flinched. Her grip on the bough tightened.

"Lucilla! Did you think that I was playing? I told you it was real! When I kissed you, could you not feel it was real?

"I don't know how kisses feel. I haven't ever kissed anyone like that before."

He had the flash of a tender smile for her.

"Dieu merci!" he said.

The clear gaze had not left him. The eyes were blue in a very white face.

"I wanted to know what it was like."

"Lucilla! My darling!"

"It's so dull to die before you've had anything, Ran."

Her voice was still steady, but the words only just reached him. Under the shock of their impact his emotion died. She saw his face change and harden. He remained kneeling beside her, but it was about a minute before he said,

"What do you mean by that, Lucilla?"

He kept himself in hand until he reached her name, but then a shudder went over him. It shook Lucilla too as he leaned against her knee. He was aware of that, and aware that she was stiffening herself against it, using a force which somehow horrified him. He stared up at her in great uncertainty of mind, his thoughts racing confusedly. Such a young girl. So much control. If she wept, it would be natural. "Is it her tears that she controls like this?" And all the time, deeply and persistently, his heart called her name: "*Lucilla—Lucilla—Lucilla!*" He had seen her face change as he stared up at her. It was like a little, set mask in the sunlight, with eyes that were like shallow blue pools. He repeated his question very urgently.

"*Mon dieu*—what do you mean by that?"

Lucilla's tight pale mouth opened. The lips parted and stretched into a smile. He had the feeling that some horrible force was being used, that without it she could not have moved her lips at all. She said in a small toneless voice,

"I—nearly—died—yesterday—Ran."

He put his arms about her as he knelt. The bough swung a little.

"Why, Lucilla—*why?*"

It was then that she looked down at him and he saw in her eyes what Sarah had once seen there—fear, naked and shuddering.

"Lucilla, *qu'a tu*—what is it?"

In a flash it was gone. She bent towards him.

"Kiss me, Ran—kiss me again!"

She kissed him back this time, pressing against him, but without relaxing at all. Then in a minute she leaned back, pushing him away.

"Don't kiss me any more! Tell me you love me! Say all the things people say when they're in love! I want to know them all!"

Bertrand steadied himself.

"Lucilla, what is all this? You talk about death—*mon dieu*, I cannot bear it. What do you mean? You say too much, and not enough. You are afraid—I see it in your eyes. What are you afraid of? What are you hiding?"

She smiled again. This time her lips moved easily.

"Do you call that making love?"

"I am not making love. I am tormented about you. It is true that yesterday you were so near death that when I think about it I shudder. And not only once but twice. Will you tell me now that we are alone why it is that you fall on the stairs at Holme Fallow?"

"I told you," said Lucilla, drawing away.

"What you told us, it was not true. It was a lie, and it was not even a clever lie, my darling. You see, you had not time to think. You had to make up a story all in a hurry, and the one you made up, it had not the common sense. *Vois tu*, my little angel, if you had fallen as you said, you would have gone down five, six steps before you could hit the balustrade. But you are on the third step when I come up, and I ask Mr. Brown and he tells me that is where you fall over, and he is on the second step, by the pillar, and he catches you. And I say—*I*—that it is not possible. No—*jamais de la vie*—as you would say, not on your life!"

"Take your arms away, Ran. If you're not going to make love to me, I don't want them there."

"My darling, tell me what happened! See, Lucilla, I love you with all my heart, and I ask you to tell me—just me, your Ran who loves you!"

Her smile flickered and went.

"What do you think?"

"I think he pushed you." His arms were still round her, and he felt her faint movement as she said,

"Who?"

"That *sacré* Brown."

And all at once Lucilla laughed. She took her hands off the branch and set them on Bertrand's arms.

"Oh, Ran—you silly boy! Mr. Brown is my Noble Preserver."

"Lucilla—someone pushed you. Who was there to push you except this Brown? And who was it who fetched your bicycle before it ran away with you down the hill? I saw him fetch it, and the one who fetched it was the one who removed those screws. I say that he has tried to kill you twice, and I have my own idea why it is that he tries to kill you."

Lucilla pushed him away with sudden vehemence and slipped down from the branch. As he got on his feet, she went back a pace or two, the colour bright in her cheeks.

"Oh, Ran, how silly you are! Why should he try to kill me?"

"Because he is Maurice Hildred."

Lucilla's eyes opened like those of a startled kitten.

"My goodness gracious me, Ran—are you mad?"

"*I?* No, no! But perhaps he is mad—I do not know."

"But Uncle Maurice—Ran, he's *dead*!"

"He was not dead—he was missing. I think that he has come back and found that there is no place for him. And see, Lucilla, if you were not here, he would have everything. And perhaps he is mad—how do I know? Only I am sure that he is Maurice Hildred. I tell you I have watched him, and I have seen in him something that comes and goes— something of all of you—of Mr. Hildred—of Miss Marina—even of Ricky, and of you. And when we were at Holme Fallow and he thought that he was alone in that dining-room with the portraits—when we all went out and left him there—I tell you I turned back and I looked at him, when the door was a little open."

"What did he do?"

"He looked at the pictures."

Lucilla burst out laughing.

"Oh, Ran!"

"Wait a little. He looks at the old man's picture, and he says something under his breath. I do not hear what he says, but I see his face. It is, how shall I say, *émotionné*—it is not the face with which one looks at the portrait of a stranger. It is his grandfather he looks at, and whilst he is looking I see the likeness very strong and clear. I tell you that he is Maurice Hildred, and that he is dangerous."

Lucilla brought her hands together. She held one with the other. She held it hard. She said in a little clear voice,

"That is nonsense, Ran."

"And I say that it is not nonsense. It is the truth."

"Someone is trying to kill me?"

"I say that this Brown has tried to kill you."

"Do you know what they say if you think people are trying to kill you?" Her voice dropped to a breathless whisper. "They say you're mad. Ran, they say you're mad."

"Lucilla!"

She lifted the hands that were holding one another so hard and pressed them against her breast. There was a kind of desperate, quivering tenseness about the whole of her. He had the feeling of something strung to the limit, and it came to him that only at this pitch could she have said what she was saying now. The words came with a rush, yet with hardly any sound. It was as if all her effort went to say them quickly, lest they should not be said at all.

"Do you know what they do to mad people, Ran? *They shut them up.* Do you know what they do if they think you're mad? They bring two doctors to see you and then they can shut you up. If I said that someone was trying to kill me, they would say I was mad. They would say I had tried to kill myself, and they would shut me up. And I'd rather be dead than shut up. Do you hear, Ran? I'd *much* rather be dead. Do you hear? You're to leave me alone—you're not to do anything—you're not to interfere. It's my game, and I'm going to play it my own way. You're not to butt in. Do you hear?"

"I am to stand by and see you in danger and do nothing? Is that what you are telling me?

"Yes—yes—*yes!*"

"But, Lucilla—"

"What can you do? You can't do anything. I've kept alive for three months." She suddenly unlocked her hands and flung them out towards him. "Three months—and it will go on for three years unless they get me first! It will go on till I'm twenty-one, and that's more than three years. I don't know if it will stop then, but I should be able to go away."

He tried to take her hands, but she pulled away from him.

"Lucilla, what is this? What do you know?"

There was a change. She relaxed. Her hands went up to her hair and pushed it back—the age-old gesture of the tired woman. Her voice came slow and hesitating.

"That's just it—I don't know anything."

He put an arm round her and made her sit beside him on the tree trunk. She was quite docile and gentle, letting him hold her, letting him stroke her hair and kiss her hands whilst she leaned against him and drew long sighing breaths.

Presently he said in a coaxing voice,

"Lucilla—little one—tell me—tell your Ran! I will be very clever indeed—very discreet. But you are afraid without cause, my little one. See then, we can all speak for what happened at Holme Fallow—Sarah, Ricky, I myself. It is true that I did not see you fall, but I came so soon afterwards and heard at once what Sarah and Ricky said. And about the affair of the bicycle—the screws they were gone. They did not remove themselves. How can your uncle not believe if we tell him these things? It is to him that we should address ourselves. It is he who is your guardian, your protector."

Still leaning against him, Lucilla began to shake with laughter.

"Darling angel Ran!" she said, and kissed his cheek and went on laughing. There was no hysteria in the laughter. The unnatural strain seemed to have passed.

Mr. Darnac was not amused. With his arm about her shoulders, he shook her a little and said in an annoyed tone,

"It seems that I amuse you."

"Very much," said Lucilla, and kissed his cheek again.

He let his arm fall and moved away along the trunk.

"You are laughing at me!"

"Yes, darling."

"Why do you laugh at me?"

"Because you are very, very funny, Ran."

"And why am I funny?" Offence stared at her out of his dark eyes.

"Funny—and nice."

"You laugh at me—you mock yourself of me! Perhaps all the time you have been laughing at me—you have been mocking yourself of me! Is that it?"

Lucilla tilted her head sideways. Her lips still smiled. Her eyes were blue and wary. She said with a bubble of laughter in her voice,

"Perhaps."

"All this time you have been laughing at me—you have been playing a scene of the theatre!"

"Perhaps I have."

He sprang up, his face convulsed with anger and pain.

"*Mon dieu*, Lucilla! And you dare to tell me that!"

The blue eyes gazed at him innocently.

"How cross you are."

"Cross? It is to tear the heart! You throw back my love, my faith!" His voice choked on the words. "And you say I am cross! It is all a trick then—that you love me—that you are afraid—that you are in danger! There is nothing true about it from the beginning to the end! Is that what you would tell me? Perhaps it is a trick that you play on us at Holme Fallow that you pretend to fall—and a trick with your bicycle when you ride down the hill? Answer me, then! Were these things a trick?"

Lucilla continued to gaze at him. The wariness had gone. Her look was one of admiration tinged with awe.

The young man's voice became thunderous.

"Answer me, Lucilla!

Lucilla got up. She drooped a little. She said in a bashful voice,

"Do you know where the screws were, Ran?"

Mr. Darnac started. He had been about to declaim some fine rolling reproaches. Her question checked them. He found himself saying instead,

"The screws of your bicycle?"

Lucilla gave a little schoolgirl nod.

"Yes, Ran. Do you know where they were?"

"I? How should I know? Do you think it was I who took them out?"

She looked down at the emerald moss. She said,

"Oh, no, Ran." Then, after a little pause, "They were in my pocket. Sarah found them there."

Chapter Twenty-Five

JOHN BROWN had finished the portrait of his dragon-fly. While he put the final touches to it he talked pleasantly to Sarah on the unemotional topic of protective colouring in insects and birds. Having kissed her hand and informed her that he loved her—very much—he had resumed his painting.

Sarah found her rather agitated declaration of indifference falling a little flat. While she explained with more heat than she intended that she hadn't ever been in love, wasn't in love, and never meant to be in love, Mr. Brown was mixing his colours and did not appear to be very much interested in what she was saying. This goaded her into an amplification of her remarks, and if by the time she had finished he had not gathered that if she ever did fall in love it would not be with him, it certainly was not Sarah's fault. She derived a good deal of angry pleasure from making herself perfectly clear on this point.

John Brown preserved an amiable silence until she had finished. Then he turned his head, smiled into her eyes as if she had just been saying something very delightful, and inquired in his pleasant voice whether she had ever seen a stick-insect.

"They pretend to be sticks. There are some very large ones in Brazil. Protective colouring, you know. You wouldn't believe they were not just dry twigs. I can show you some drawings if you're interested. There's no end to the things that creatures will pretend. It's a very interesting subject. Of course you get wise to it, and then it doesn't take you in—much." There was an amused flicker in his eyes as he went back to his drawing.

All at once Sarah said abruptly,

"We're going to town on Tuesday—but you know that."

John Brown nodded. He was washing his brushes preparatory to putting them away.

"Yes, I know. I don't want you to go, Sarah."

His tone was too serious to be taken personally. She frowned and said,

"I don't see how you can help it."

"Nor do I. But I don't want you to go."

"Why not?"

He closed his paint-box and slipped it into the old brown satchel. He said,

"Too many chances, Sarah."

"You mean—for Lucilla?"

"Yes."

"But I shall be there—I shall be with her all the time. What could happen?"

He was shutting his sketching-book now. He held the page to the light to see if it was dry. The dragonfly gleamed like a jewel in the sun. Then the board came down on it and the satchel covered all.

"What *could* happen?" said Sarah impatiently.

She had felt when he spoke as if a single drop of very cold water was trickling down her spine, and it irked her. She had an intense longing to get out of this place, to be in London, to get away, to be in brightly lighted restaurants, theatres, shops, to spend money, to be surrounded by people, to have no time to think. That was it—here in Holme there was a great deal too much time to think.

She repeated, with that irked sound in her voice,

"What could possibly happen?"

John Brown answered her very seriously,

"I don't know, Sarah—any one of a number of things."

"Well, we're going anyhow. Mr. Hildred has arranged it all. It will be very good for Lucilla—she's getting morbid here."

He nodded.

"I suppose you're staying at Millington's?"

"Yes. Did Mr. Hildred tell you?"

"No—but they always do."

"How do you know?" said Sarah quickly.

She thought his colour rose a little, but he laughed.

"I know quite a lot of things. That's one of them. Now look here, Sarah, I want you to promise me that you'll stick to Lucilla like glue. Don't leave her alone for a moment. Don't let her stir a yard by herself. Either you or I have got to be there all the time. I'd like you to share a room with her. I think you might stick out about that—tell Geoffrey it looks better—something of that sort. But I don't think there's any real risk at night." He looked away from her, frowning deeply. "It's the day we've got to be careful about—the hundred and one chances of something that would look like an accident. You see what I mean? Don't cross a road till the policeman stops the traffic—that's the sort of thing. Do you know, I've wondered sometimes how many road accidents really weren't accidents at all. It's rather a horrifying thought."

A second drop seemed to be trickling down her spine after the first. She shivered and said vaguely,

"Oh—accidents—" Then she put up her hand and yawned. "My dear John, I can't spend the rest of my life clamping on to Lucilla like a dog with a bone."

John Brown laughed.

"You won't have to. If you can stick it out till the end of the week, we'll be all right. If we can keep Lucilla safe to the end of the week, she'll be safe for good and all. But whatever is due to happen will be comfortably dressed up as an accident—of that I'm quite sure—so we've not got to take any risks that way."

Sarah had turned rather pale.

"Why will Lucilla be all right at the end of the week?"

John Brown seemed to hesitate. He may have been considering what to say, he may have been regretting that he had said so much. He looked past Sarah up the hill and saw Lucilla coming across the fields on the far side of the orchard. There was a trace of relief in his voice as he said,

"There's Lucilla. I'll tell you some other time."

He stood up and waved, and Lucilla waved back at him. Then she began to run towards them down the hill, coming up with bright blown hair and a changing colour, to drop on the grass between them.

She leaned her elbows on the grass and said in a little mournful voice,

"I've quarrelled with Ran."

"Why on earth?"

"Oh, just because—Don't you ever quarrel with people, angel darling? It's a frightfully good way of getting to know them, really." She sat up and began to speak with more animation. "You see, when they boil over, all the nice company manners go and the real things come bubbling up all hot and hot. Ran boiled like anything. I came away because he'd got to the point where English wasn't any good to him, and I didn't know what sort of French words he was saying. I expect some of them weren't a bit proper, and I didn't think Aunt Marina would like me to go on listening to them, so I came away."

"Why did you quarrel?" said Sarah again.

Lucilla sighed.

"We were having a lovely time before it began. Do you know what he said about my eyes?"

"No—and I don't want to."

Lucilla threw a saintly look upwards.

"Governesses always are jealous," she murmured. Then, with a sudden twist of her slim length, she faced John Brown. "I shall tell my Noble Preserver. He said the most thrilling things. Don't take any notice of Sarah—she's just a govvy. If I could make a face with the back of my head, I'd be making one at her."

John Brown laughed.

"Come along then—what did he say?"

Lucilla gazed up at him, but her expression had changed. It was obvious that her attention had wandered from Mr. Darnac's pretty speeches. She frowned a little, and said in a confidential voice,

"I partly quarrelled with Ran because he said you were Uncle Maurice. It would be lovely if you were."

"Would it?"

"Lovely. *Are* you?"

John Brown laughed.

"Why should anyone think I was?"

Beyond Lucilla he saw Sarah looking at him. Her expression puzzled him. It distracted his attention for a moment. Then he heard Lucilla say,

"Ran thinks you're like us—all of us—even Aunt Marina." She giggled. "Talk about compliments—there's one for you!"

"Am I like Ricky? Have a heart, Lucilla!"

She sat right up, shook back her hair, and stared at him. It was the solemn, unwinking stare of a very young child.

Sarah moved so that she could see them both. She had a feeling that something might be going to happen, she didn't know what. She watched them both—Lucilla with that solemn stare, and John Brown sitting carelessly with the old brown satchel across his knees and that air of being quietly amused.

Lucilla spoke at last.

"You're not like Ricky—but I know what Ran means. There's a sort of a kind of a family look, the sort you can't pin down. When you look for it, it isn't there, and when you're not thinking about it, it gets up and hits you in the eye. *Are* you Uncle Maurice?"

He shook his head very slightly and answered as he had answered Sarah.

"No, Lucilla. Maurice is dead."

Lucilla sighed.

"What a pity—it would be so romantic. You see—" she drew up her heels and hugged her knees—"you see, Ran's got it all mapped out. You're Maurice, and you've come here on purpose to get Holme Fallow out of my clutches. Well, the only way you can do that is by making me have a fatal accident, so that's why my bicycle ran away with me and I nearly took a header over the balustrade when we were playing Devil-in-the-dark. Ran's got the *mos'* melodramatic mind. I'm sure he ought to be writing scenarios for Hollywood instead of learning to be an *avocat*."

Sarah's eyes were sparkling.

"Lucilla, you really ought *not* to talk such nonsense."

Lucilla looked innocent.

"It's not my nonsense, but Ran's. And I quarrelled with him—I told you I did. I'm afraid you weren't attending, darling. I told you the very first thing of all that I'd quarrelled with Ran. Only I didn't tell you why, but it was really because of him saying that Mr. Brown was a Secret Assassin, and my saying that he was my Noble Preserver. And then he got into a fresh rage, and I came away all calm and dignified with my nose in the air."

"Darnac's an ass," said John Brown.

Lucilla nodded.

"That's what I told him. I said, 'I don't suppose you can help it any more than red hair or a squint, but you needn't be a *silly* ass.' But it didn't seem to soothe him at all."

Sarah got the curious impression that all this was according to plan. It was more than an impression, it was a conviction. Lucilla had not just strayed here by chance. She had come here of set purpose because there was something she wanted to say. All this nonsense was her way of getting it said.

John Brown had made some laughing reply. Lucilla did not laugh. It struck Sarah suddenly that she was very pale. She said,

"Ran went right off the deep end when I told him about the screws."

Sarah knew what was coming now, but John Brown did not.

"Don't, Lucilla!" said Sarah quickly, but all she got was a mournful shake of the head.

"Must. Can't have people saying that the Noble Preserver is a Secret Assassin."

"Lucilla, what on earth are you talking about?" said John Brown.

"Hasn't Sarah told you where she found the screws? I thought she told you *everything*. You know—the screws that came out of my bicycle. She found them in the pocket of my cardigan when we were dressing for dinner. Didn't you, darling?"

John Brown looked quickly at Sarah, and as quickly away again. He too found Lucilla pale—dreadfully pale. She essayed an impudent laugh.

"I put it across you all pretty well, didn't I? You were all scared stiff, weren't you? There wasn't any danger really. I could ride that old hill in my sleep."

"I see," said John Brown—" it was a trick."

Lucilla nodded.

"And the fall from the balustrade—was that a trick too?"

Lucilla nodded again.

"Perhaps you'll tell us how you managed it, or rather how you would have managed it if I hadn't caught you."

She jerked up her chin and looked at him defiantly.

"I knew you were there. I screamed first and then tipped over. I was going to hang by my knees until someone caught me. It was just a trick. It's quite easy if you know how."

"I see—" said John Brown gravely.

Sarah was looking at Lucilla's hands. They were still locked about her knees. They were locked as if the world and all hung on their grip. The knuckles were as white as bone, the fingers straining. What effort was she making, and at what cost? Why?

At John Brown's quietly spoken words the grip relaxed. It seemed as if the effort had spent itself.

"I frightened you all—didn't I?" said Lucilla.

"Very much."

There was a silence. A sunny stillness with a weight upon it. Lucilla broke it with an exclamation.

"Oh! Just then you did look like someone—you really did!"

"Who did I look like?" said John Brown.

Lucilla unlocked her hands in an excited gesture.

"You looked like my Eleanor grandmamma in the picture at Holme Fallow! You saw it there—in the dining-room, opposite the door as you come in. And that's a compliment if you like, because she's frightfully lovely. She must be of course, because she's like me." She paused, staring hard, and then went on again. "She was Maurice's mother. Are you sure you're not Maurice?"

John Brown tossed the old brown satchel on to the grass and got up.

"Quite sure," he said in a tone of finality.

Chapter Twenty-Six

SARAH FELT AS IF it had been rather a long day. The nasal singing of the village choir and the sermon on kindness appeared to be quite incredibly removed from the moment when they all said good night and went upstairs. There had been Sunday tea. There had been Sunday supper. Aunt Marina had talked about the family. Uncle Geoffrey had talked about porcelain.

As a matter of fact Uncle Geoffrey had been quite interesting. He had opened the cabinets at the end of the drawing-room and shown her a number of very beautiful things, all of which were Lucilla's property. There was a mandarin's supper set in four tiers, each tier a different colour—egg-shell blue, egg-shell green, rose-pink, and primrose-yellow—each with its own tracery of pæony and pomegranate. On one side of the lid a single wary grasshopper stared at them across four hundred years. There was a collection of snuff-bottles—rose quartz, with a green jade frog for a stopper; lapis, with a blood-red fruit; mutton-fat jade; deep red lacquer. There were about a hundred of them, and every one a very perfect work of art—amber, crystal, onyx, malachite, in the shape of fruit or gourd, the stopper delicately fashioned in a contrasting colour. An eighteenth-century Hildred had brought them back from China.

"Lucilla doesn't care for them," said Geoffrey Hildred regretfully. "But I hope she will some day."

Lucilla did not look up from her book.

She followed Sarah into her room when they went upstairs, and Sarah turned on her.

"Now look here, Lucilla, you're not going to stay here and talk. You can sleep in whichever room you like, but you must just pack along and undress."

"How harsh you are," said Lucilla plaintively.

"I feel harsh. Go and undress! This day has lasted about a century and a half already."

Lucilla giggled.

"Aren't you funny? Such a nice day too—no nasty rough accidents and things. And I'm sure I've been a Perfect Pattern of Piety. Ungrateful—that's what I call you, Sarah Trent."

"Lucilla, will you go to bed!"

"Presently, darling. I've got something awfully important to say to you. You don't want me to go to bed without saying it?"

Sarah took off her dress and hung it up.

"I don't suppose it's important at all."

"'M—it is—thrillingly important."

"Then for goodness sake say it!"

Lucilla leaned against the end of the bed, gazed at the cornice, and recited in a voice modelled on the most nasal of the choir-boys, "Under the harsh and un-sym-pathet-ic treat-ment of her cru-el gov-er-ness the un-hap-py gy-url quick-ly with-ered a-way."

"Lucilla, I'll pour cold water over you if you don't stop."

"Her cru-el-ties—No, angel darling Sarah, I've stopped—I've quite stopped."

Sarah put down the water-bottle.

"You're a perfect pest," she said. "*What* do you want to say?"

"It's about Mr. Brown," said Lucilla in a bubbling voice. "No, Sarah—do listen. I'm in deadly earnest—I really am. You know, he swears he isn't Uncle Maurice, and I'd simply love him to be, because I do think he's a pet besides being my Noble Preserver, but there really was a sort of truthful gleam in his eye when he said he was quite sure he wasn't, especially at the end. Don't you think so?"

Sarah was brushing her hair. She brushed it all over her face and said in the voice of a person who is bored to extinction,

"I don't think, and I won't be made to think."

"Dull," said Lucilla. "Besides, it's not true. Your brain's waving quite brightly really. But you mustn't keep interrupting, because what I was going to say was this. He swears he isn't Uncle Maurice, and I think the gleam really *was* a truthful one, though of course you never can tell, men being deceivers ever, and all that sort of thing."

"You're talking exactly like Aunt Marina," said Sarah in a vicious voice.

Lucilla clutched her side with a long-drawn moan of anguish.

"O-oh! What a *stab!* And it's all your fault if I don't get on. Now do be an angel and just listen for a minute—curb the tongue, you know, and all that sort of thing. A snare, my dear Miss Trent—a terrible snare. No, Sarah! Not cold water! I'll scream if you don't put that bottle down—I really will! Angel darling, I'm as good as gold. Butter isn't melting in my mouth. And what I've been trying to say is that if the Noble Preserver isn't Uncle Maurice, perhaps—*perhaps*, I say—"

"Well?" said Sarah. She had tossed back her hair and still held the water-bottle poised.

Lucilla screwed up her face mysteriously, dropped her voice to a thrilling whisper, and said,

"Why shouldn't he be Uncle Henry?"

Sarah put the bottle down slowly and carefully. What fantastic nonsense. She found the last word saying itself quite loudly and emphatically—*"Nonsense."*

Lucilla nodded.

"Of course, angel. But then, it's all nonsense. Can you put your hand on your heart and say one single sensible thing has happened since you got here? You can't. It's nonsense for him to say he's John Brown, and be able to find his way in the dark all over Holme Fallow. There's that little step down going through to the back of the hall. I sometimes trip over it myself if I'm not thinking. But he didn't. I hid down there when he was *He*, and he came along in the dark and never stumbled. He knew it was there. Isn't that nonsense? And isn't it nonsense for him to look like my Eleanor grandmother? *And he did*—down there by the pool." She changed her voice suddenly. "Sarah, you don't *know* what a feeling I've got about his being Uncle Henry."

Sarah's cheeks were burning. She made her voice quiet.

"When did Henry Hildred die?"

"He was supposed to have died about six months ago. I wish he hadn't. Oh, how I do wish he hadn't!"

"Where?"

"Some Pacific island sort of place. I never can remember its name. You know, it could quite easily have been a fake, Sarah. He just travelled, and travelled, and travelled with a servant who'd been with him for ages. Nobody ever saw him, and he never came home. Well, suppose he thought he'd like to come back like a sort of ghost without anyone knowing who he was—"

"Why should he pretend to be dead?" said Sarah.

"I dunno. What's the good of asking silly questions like that?" She pointed solemnly at the ceiling and made her voice deep and quavery. "'It's a mad world, my masters.' Don't I know a lovely lot of Shakespeare, govvy darling? I think my Uncle Henry ought to be very, very proud of me—don't you? And Holme Fallow belongs to him and not to me—oh cheers! And—and we all live happy ever afterwards. Oh, I do, do, *do* hope he's Uncle Henry!"

A very bright, lovely colour came into Sarah's cheeks.

"What does it matter who he is?" she said.

"Oh, *Sarah*! As far gone as all that!" She clasped her hands and looked upwards in round-eyed adoration. "*Oh, John—a cottage with you!*"

Sarah took her by the shoulders and shook her.

"Lucilla, you're a brat. Now I give you fair warning—if you're not out of this room by the time I've counted five, I'll come in the middle of the night when you're asleep and pour cold water slowly down the back of your neck."

Lucilla uttered a muffled shriek, wrenched herself free, and fled. But a moment later she put her head round the door again and murmured,

"Please, darling, where am I to sleep?"

"Wherever you like."

"Oh, I like sleeping in here. The pinkness soaks right down into me and does me a lot of good."

"Beat it!" said Sarah.

Lucilla put out her tongue and shut the door.

When they had changed over and Sarah was alone in the blue room, she found herself no longer in the least sleepy, but quite extraordinarily wide awake. She went and looked at herself in the glass, and was startled at a reflection all bloom, and colour, and shining eyes. Not Maurice, but Henry.... Was it possible? A sardonic voice in her own mind asserted that anything was possible, but that some things were so unlikely that they didn't happen.

If John Brown was Henry Hildred, he had been offering her Holme Fallow, down by the lower pool. Holme Fallow and Sarah Trent.... And she had blushed like a schoolgirl in front of Lucilla and said it didn't matter who he was.... Was it true that it didn't matter? If he was just John Brown, making an up and down living with his sketches and his articles on insects and birds, if he was plain John Brown, rather poor and never likely to be anything else, would she take a risk with him and let herself care? As sure as you care you get hurt. She had kept that in mind all these years, and it had kept her light-hearted and safe. Other people had got hurt, but not Sarah Trent. Was she going to risk being hurt because John Brown could put something into his voice that made her feel glad and sorry, or because the corners of his eyes crinkled when he smiled? She shook her head and spoke very firmly indeed to the radiant image in the glass. "Sarah, my girl, you're a fool," she said. And with that she turned away and snapped off the light, blotting out the image and its follies.

The glowing bulb faded into the surrounding darkness. It really was a relief to get rid of all that pale blue, but she wasn't in the least bit sleepy. She heard Ricky pass the door and go along to his own room. Uncle Geoffrey was the one who sat up late. It was only that afternoon that she had told John how early they all went to bed, and how drugged with sleep they were by ten o'clock. "Mr. Hildred sits up till about midnight as a rule. He says his brain works best at night. Mine's boiled long before the evening's over." She had said that. And John had said—no, she couldn't remember what John had said, though she could remember how he looked when he was saying it.

"Sarah, you're potty," she said sternly. And as much to break her thoughts as anything else she went over to the east window and looked out.

At first she couldn't see anything at all. She dropped the curtain behind her, opened the lower sash and leaned out with her elbows on the sill. The air was warm and dark. She could distinguish the black line of the trees against the sky, which was not black, but a deep colourless grey. It was still, but there are always sounds in the stillness of the night. Sarah listened to these sounds and was soothed by them—the stirring of a sleepy bird, the falling of a leaf to other leaves which are fallen and withered.

She had begun to feel sleepy again, when she heard another sound, and immediately was awake. Someone had come up the drive and was crossing the gravel. There was no attempt at concealment. It was a man by the sound of the footsteps. He walked with a quick, light tread. She heard him pass under Ricky's window and go round to the front of the house.

Sarah's heart beat hard. She could have sworn that the footsteps were John Brown's, but what in the world could be bringing him up to the Red House at this time of night, she simply could not imagine. It must be close on eleven o'clock, and he knew how early they went to bed. There was an answer to that, but Sarah didn't like the answer. He knew that Geoffrey Hildred usually sat up late. Sarah didn't like the answer at all. Why should he want to see Geoffrey Hildred?

She crossed her room in the dark and opened the door. Opposite the pink room there was an empty guest chamber whose windows looked out at the front of the house. She slipped across the passage, shut the door of this room behind her, and made her way to the windows, all in the dark. She got one of them open and put her head out, and as she did so, she heard a sound of knocking on the window below.

"What on earth?" said Sarah to herself. She leaned out as far as she could. She couldn't see anything at all, but the knocking was repeated.

This room was over the study. John Brown was knocking on the study window. It was a long French window, opening like a door.

And all at once it was open. The curtain must have been drawn back on the inner side, for a bright slanting rectangle appeared suddenly upon the gravel. The window opened, and there was a low murmur of voices. A man came into the light, stood there a moment, and then passed in at the open window and out of sight. The bright rectangle moved, narrowing quickly until it was gone. There was a faint thud as the glass door fell to. Sarah remained staring down into the darkness.

And then one of those little unexpected things happened. Upon the darkness there crept the faintest, narrowest streak of light. And this streak was not stationary. It moved. Sarah stared at it. It went on moving. A bare inch one way—and back again. A bare inch the other way—and back again.

She drew in her head and straightened up. The moving streak could only mean one thing—the French window was not quite shut. It had closed with that little thud and started again. It was now open, perhaps an inch, perhaps a little more, and the slight draught which came through the crack was moving the curtain gently, rhythmically, and so releasing that moving streak of light.

Sarah has never been very proud of what she did next. In the far away days before the crash she had been taught by her excellent and respectable nurse that there were a number of things which little ladies didn't do. Little ladies didn't bite their nails. Little ladies didn't tell lies. Little ladies didn't listen at doors. Sarah still retained a distaste for people who transgressed this nursery code. She was now, however, about to transgress it herself. Her only excuse is, and always has been, that she simply had to know what John Brown was saying to Geoffrey Hildred.

She went quickly back into the blue room. She could not go eavesdropping out of doors barefoot and in her night-gown, a mere wisp of yellow *crêpe-de-chine*. Her own clothes being next door, she had to fall back upon Lucilla's. She found a pair of dark stockings and the black cardigan suit and put them on. The stockings would probably get cut to pieces on the gravel, but she couldn't risk the noise that shoes would make. And she would have to get out of the house and go round, because the opening of one of the drawing-room windows might be heard, and of course the front door was out of the question.

She climbed out of the window of the servants' sitting-room and made her way along the back of the house. Miss Marina's light was out, but Lucilla's still burned, throwing a faint rosy glow through the pink curtains.

She turned the corner. Three dark windows here, her own, the bathroom, the spare room, and then one lighted one. Ricky wasn't in bed yet.

She came round the corner to the front of the house and saw the streak of light which she had seen from above. She must go very very quietly now. The gravel hurt her feet. She remembered the story of the pilgrim and the peas. You can't boil gravel.

She came very slowly and cautiously to a level with the nearer hinges of the French window. Two stone steps led up to the sill. The window had two leaves. It was the farther one that stood ajar, and through the glass she could see an inch-wide gap in the heavy crimson curtains which hung within.

Sarah got off the gravel on to the first step. She could not hear a sound of any sort from the room. She had not heard a sound of any sort since she had turned the corner. The silence made her feel cold. There were two men in that room. There must be two men there. She had heard one of them knock, and she had seen the window open to admit him. She had seen John Brown go into the room. If he had gone away, the window would have been shut and locked again. She began to be afraid, and more afraid, and her fear took her up on to the top step and set her right hand on the leaf that was ajar. She pulled it a little and leaned towards the gap in the curtains.

And as she leaned, she heard John Brown say,

"Well, Geoffrey?"

It was John Brown speaking, but it was not quite the John Brown she knew. The gentle, amused tone was gone from his voice. It was quiet, but it rang hard.

There was no answer. There went on being no answer for such a long time that Sarah began to feel quite giddy with the strain. Her thoughts rocked. Who was John Brown that he called Geoffrey Hildred

"Geoffrey"? There were two answers that would fit. Either Henry or Maurice Hildred would say Geoffrey, as cousin to cousin.

John Brown spoke again. He used the same words. He said,

"Well, Geoffrey?"

And this time there was an answer. Geoffrey Hildred spoke in a laboured voice. It sounded as if he had his work cut out to speak at all. He said in that hard-come voice,

"I don't recognize you." And then, "You're a stranger to me—a complete stranger."

There was a pause. There was the sound of something being poured into a glass. The gap in the curtains was no more than an inch. Sarah leaned very near, and saw a handsbreadth of the writing-table, the corner of a silver ink-stand, and beyond it a couple of inches of whisky in the bottom of a tumbler. The whisky was neat. The fingers of Geoffrey Hildred's right hand came above it on the glass and lifted it out of sight. She could hear that he drank. And then the tumbler came down again empty. The hand withdrew. Geoffrey Hildred must be sitting at the writing-table. She could not see John Brown at all, but his voice had come from her right. It came from there now.

"Feeling better?"

It was obvious that Geoffrey Hildred was feeling better. Whatever shock he had had, he was getting himself in hand again. He spoke rather heavily, but with self-command.

"You know, Brown, this is a most astonishing claim."

"You seemed to be rather more than astonished."

"I was very much astonished. I cannot believe that you are serious. And I would like to say that if this is a practical joke, I consider—"

John Brown interrupted him.

"You needn't consider anything at all. I'm not joking. You won't find it a joke, I'm afraid."

"And what do you mean by that?" said Geoffrey Hildred.

The other man laughed.

"Pretty much what you'd expect me to mean," he said.

There was the sound of a chair being pushed back. Geoffrey Hildred's voice came louder.

"The whole thing is preposterous! After all these years! Do you imagine for an instant that you could make out a case? This sort of thing has been tried on before. You may have heard of the Tichborne case. Do you happen to remember that the plaintiff got fourteen years for perjury? *Pour encourager les autres*, Mr. Brown. If you're hankering after an opportunity of acquiring first-hand knowledge of English prison life, I advise you to take this claim of yours into court."

John Brown laughed again very quietly.

"Oh, I don't think it'll ever come into court. There will be an amicable settlement. Think it over and you'll see that that will be best for us all. Joyous reunion, happy family party, and all the rest of it."

"Take care," said Geoffrey Hildred. "Take care, Brown." His voice had thickened. "I'm warning you—that you're on dangerous ground. The whole thing is preposterous—the whole thing! What's your case? Where are your witnesses? They're all dead, I tell you! That's convenient for an impostor, isn't it? Old John Hildred is dead, and Lucy is dead—Lucy Raimond—and the doctor, and the parson. They're all dead. And it's fifteen years since the war came to an end. You're fifteen years after the fair, Mr. Brown. And you can put that in your pipe and smoke it!"

"Thank you. Now just for a moment I would like you to listen to me. I've got something to say, and I really think you had better let me say it."

Geoffrey Hildred's right arm came into view—his hand, his right arm, and a bit of his shoulder. He had pulled his chair in again and leaned forward with his elbow on the table. The hand went out of sight. Sarah guessed at it supporting his chin, perhaps covering the line of the mouth. He said with a composure that was now complete,

"Oh, say anything you like. It won't be the first tall tale I've heard, or the last either."

"What I want to say is this. It is a pity to take a tone which is bound to make things more difficult all round. When I came over here I wasn't sure whether I would stay or not—I wasn't sure whether I wanted to stay. I thought I would just come over and see how I felt about it all. When I walked into your office I was quite prepared for you to recognize me. Are you quite sure you didn't?"

Geoffrey Hildred laughed briefly.

"How should I recognize a man I'd never set eyes on before?"

"Well, well," said John Brown—"that's what you say. I've never felt sure about it myself. Sometimes I could have sworn you had recognized me, and sometimes I didn't know whether you had or not."

The shoulder which Sarah was watching went up in a shrug.

"I do not admit that there was anything to recognize."

"Well, as it happens, there is. I want you to understand that I can prove who I am. I can prove my case right up to the hilt. I think you will remember Eversley—Ronald Eversley.... Yes, I see you do. Well, I've been in touch with him all along. He has always known where I was and what I was doing. We corresponded quite regularly. I saw him in Philadelphia just before I came over—in fact he came there to see me. He said it was time I came home, and—well, I came. He had other business in the States, so I didn't wait for him. He's due in London at the end of this week. You see, I'm putting my cards on the table. Eversley's an unassailable witness. When you didn't seem to recognize me, I thought I'd wait till he arrived."

Sarah, watching all she could see of Geoffrey Hildred, received an impression of rigidity. His voice came hard from a dry throat.

"And you are not waiting. May I ask why?"

"I don't think I should," said John Brown.

"Don't you? What do you mean by that?"

"I shouldn't ask that either, Geoffrey. Let us say that when I first came over I hadn't made up my mind, and that now I have. It might have suited me to stay dead, but since I came down here I have decided against it. I naturally hasten to inform you of my decision—as Lucilla's guardian, *and in Lucilla's interests.*" He stressed the last words so sharply that Sarah's pulses leapt.

Geoffrey Hildred made a movement which took him out of her field of vision. She thought he leaned forward. She heard him repeat the words that had been so stressed.

"Lucilla's interests?" His voice was smooth again. The thought came to her that it was too smooth.

"Oh yes," said John Brown. "Lucilla's interests must of course be your first concern—and mine. You may trust me to safeguard them in every possible way. It is on this account that I thought it would be best to have an informal talk with you now, instead of waiting till Ronald Eversley arrives at the end of the week. In order to satisfy you personally of my identity I want to ask you to carry your mind back to the holiday we all spent at Woolacombe in 1913. We were all there. Ricky was a baby of three. Do you remember the little Jap we used to call Koko, and how people were tumbling over each other to be tattooed by him? He was a wonderful artist.... Ah, I see you remember him. You had a butterfly done on your left arm just above the elbow. We boys couldn't run to butterflies, but each of us had his initial done on the fore-arm. Here's mine, Geoffrey—and I think you'll admit that it's evidence."

Sarah would have given almost anything she possessed to have been able to see through the curtain. She couldn't see, but she could hear—and how inadequate it is to hear when you want to see. The rustle of cloth—a sleeve being pulled up. A rustle of paper—Geoffrey Hildred bent forward, straining across the table, crumpling some bill or letter. A step on the carpet, a forward step—John Brown coming forward with his bare arm held out. She made that much of it. And then Geoffrey Hildred came suddenly into sight. He had sprung up. She heard his chair go over with a crash. She saw a narrow strip of his face between the crimson of the curtains, and what she saw was almost as darkly red. The angle of the brow, the eye cheek and chin were all blood-shot and suffused. The glimpse horrified her and was gone. In the silence which followed he spoke in a voice of controlled rage.

"Evidence? A faked initial! The easiest fake in the world! You'll have to do better than that, Mr. Brown."

John Brown laughed a little.

"Why, so I can—a great deal better. I told you that was just for your private edification. It edifies you all right—doesn't it? Now listen to me, Geoffrey. I've given you what is proof to yourself. You know it, and I know it. And you know why I've come forward to give it you now. If you don't, sit down and think it out, and then get hold of this. I have no desire to wash the family linen in public. I am considering Lucilla's interests, and I should like you to conclude that they are your interests too. Goodnight."

He came straight to the window. Sarah, leaning there, one hand on the frame of the open leaf, was off her balance and off her guard. She had to straighten up, swing round, and spring aside. She reached the lower step as the red curtain lifted and the light came past her in a broad shining beam. John Brown came out with the light. It shone past him and he was black against it. She could see his face like a silhouette. She did not dare to move, or breathe, or think, lest he should be aware of her. The curtain dropped. The light went out. The window was banged and harshly locked from within.

Chapter Twenty-Seven

JOHN BROWN CAME down the two steps on to the gravel before the house. He passed Sarah on the second step, passed her within a foot where she stood as still as a bit of stone and very nearly as cold. There was no feeling in her hands and feet, there was no feeling in her whole body, and she had stopped being able to breathe. But he had passed her. He had stepped down on to the gravel. She heard it grate under his foot as he stepped forward. And then she heard it grate again as he swung round. He had an arm about her before she knew that she was discovered, and if she had not been so set and rigid, she might have cried out. As it was, she caught the breath which she had not been able to draw, and the arm came about her hard and strong, jumped her down from the step, and marched her along to the corner of the house and around it.

Ricky's windows were lighted still.

He took her along the side of the house, down the steps at the end of the terrace, and into the shrubbery, all without a single word. When they were in amongst the bushes, he swung her about, put his other arm round her too, and said,

"Eavesdropping, Sarah?"

Sarah had nothing to say. She had transgressed her own code. She was ashamed. And she would have done it again next minute. She simply hadn't got anything to say.

John Brown shook her a little.

"Well? How much did you hear?" There was the old amusement in his voice.

Sarah had an answer to that. It wasn't a very brilliant one. She said, "I don't know."

"Well now, how do you mean you don't know?"

She plucked up a little spirit.

"I don't know how much I missed."

This time he laughed outright.

"You shameless creature! How did you know I was there?"

"I was looking out of my window—I mean the blue room window, the one that looks this way—and I heard you coming across the gravel."

"How did you know it was me?"

"I thought it was."

"And you came down and eavesdropped on the chance?"

"No, I didn't. I went into the room over the study—it's an empty bedroom—and looked out, and I heard you knock on the study window just beneath me. Then Mr. Hildred opened it and I saw you go in. And then I just had to come down."

"I see. You had to come down. And just how far had we got when you came down?"

Sarah leaned back against the hands that were holding her. She was neither frightened nor cold any more. She had the feeling that they were both being carried down the rushing current of a stream which was taking them fast and far. She abandoned herself to its flow. She heard John Brown repeat the question.

"How far had we got?"

"The door was open," said Sarah.

"Yes, I noticed that. Where had we got to when you arrived? What were we saying?"

"You were saying, 'Well, Geoffrey?'"

"And what did he say?"

"He said he didn't recognize you." She laid her hands suddenly against his breast. "Who was he to recognize? John—won't you tell me?"

He paused, laughed, tightened his hold upon her.

"Oh, you didn't hear that?"

"No, I didn't."

"But you heard all the rest?"

"Yes." Her head lifted. "I could hear very well." Then, with a pressure of her hands upon him. "*Who* are you?"

John Brown used a new voice. She had never heard it before. It touched something that lay deep in her—the cold, hurt place which was afraid of loving because it was afraid of being hurt again.

The new voice said, "Sarah—" very gently. And then, "Sarah—" again. And then, "Does it really matter?"

And Sarah said, "No," and somehow or other she found that her arms were round his neck and that they were kissing each other.

It was all very confused and incoherent after that. She found that she was crying, and this surprised her very much, partly because she never cried, and partly because it was completely insensate to cry when the most wonderful thing in the world had just happened. And the wonderful thing was not that John loved her, or even that she loved John, but that she wasn't any longer afraid of loving. The cold, sore place was gone and she wasn't afraid of it any more. Wonderful to feel all light, and warm, and whole again. Completely and absolutely idiotic to cry.

There was an interval. John comforted her. She had never had anyone to comfort her since she was ten years old. John did it beautifully.

The interlude lasted rather a long time. Presently Sarah said,

"Aren't you going to tell me who you are? It doesn't matter, of course, but I *would* rather like to know."

"Who do you think I am?" said John Brown.

"I thought you might be Maurice, but—"

"I told you Maurice was dead."

"Yes, I know. But you did say in the study that you hadn't made up your mind whether you would stay dead or come alive again."

"I'm not Maurice, Sarah. Guess again."

She laughed a little, her head against his shoulder.

"Well, to-night Lucilla was quite sure you were Henry. She was awfully glad, because if you were, she'd get rid of Holme Fallow and all the rest of it."

His voice came quick and pleased.

"Did she say that? I'm glad."

"Yes. Are you—are you Henry?"

"No, my dear, I'm not."

"John, aren't you going to tell me who you are?"

He said "Yes." And then, "Not here. Will you be cold if we go down to the seat by the tennis court? I'd like to get away from the house and the drive.

Cold? She was springing with warm life. There was no such thing as cold. She said with a laugh in her voice,

"Oh no, I shan't be cold."

They went down to the tennis court under a clear night sky that was bright with stars. The grass court looked like dark water. They found the seat and sat down upon it. He took both her hands and held them. They could not see each other except as shadows, but their hands clung and were warm. He said,

"Sarah, why did you or anyone else think that I belonged here? Why did you think I was Maurice, or Henry? Why did you think I was a Hildred at all?"

Sarah's heart beat hard. Her voice sounded low and confused.

"I don't know. You were in Holme Fallow that night. I couldn't believe you were a burglar. I saw you looking at Mrs. Hildred's picture. And then Ran said he had seen you looking at the pictures too. He said you were like the Hildreds, and he was sure you were Maurice. You know Miss Marina talks about them all until you can't help thinking about them by their Christian names."

"And why did Lucilla think I was Henry?"

Sarah laughed.

"I've stopped asking why Lucilla does anything. She said she thought you were speaking the truth about not being Maurice, and she said you were like Eleanor Hildred, her grandmother."

"I see. But why Henry? Eleanor Hildred had three sons, Sarah,"

Sarah caught her breath.

"Three—yes. But you—"

"I'm Jack."

"John!"

"Yes—John Hildred—Jack—Lucilla's father."

Sarah said something quite inarticulate. And then her hands were being kissed.

"Sarah—you don't mind? It won't make any difference? It's pretty awful to have a daughter who's nearly eighteen. Do you mind it very much?"

"Silly!" said Sarah in rather a choked voice. "Oh, John, don't! I want you to tell me—I don't understand."

"My darling, I am telling you. It makes me feel much too old for you, having a grown-up daughter."

"I'm twenty-eight," said Sarah. "I'm not really young at all."

"And I'm thirty-eight, so what about me?"

Sarah said, "Just right."

There was another interlude.

When it was over, she drew away as far as his arm would let her and said,

"You haven't told me very much yet—have you?"

He answered her with a grave "No," and paused upon it. He had not been Jack Hildred for seventeen years. Seventeen years is a long gap to bridge. On the other side of it there was the boy not much older than Lucilla was now—eager, young, undeveloped. No wonder he paused. It wasn't easy to think back and be Jack Hildred again. He wondered if Sarah was going to understand.

She waited, leaning against him, and presently he began to speak, so quietly that no one could have guessed at the effort he was making.

"There were the three of us—you know that—Henry, myself, and Maurice. My father was killed out hunting when we were children, I can just remember it. My mother died two years before the war. We lived at Holme Fallow with my grandfather."

Sarah drew away a little. She didn't belong to those years. She thought it would be easier for him to tell her if she were not touching him.

He went on as if he had not noticed her withdrawal.

"I was nineteen when the war broke out. I was just going up to Cambridge. I had a fancy for the bar." He laughed a little. "You never can tell—can you? I got a commission instead—Kitchener's Army—Tenth Sandshires. We went out in May 1915, and a week before I went I was married to Lucy Hill. Wickedly unfair of course, but everyone was doing it and the old man pushed it on. Henry was in France already, and he wanted to feel sure that Holme Fallow wouldn't go to Geoffrey. He always hated Geoffrey like poison, though he left all his affairs in his hands. Well, there it was, Sarah. I was twenty, and she was eighteen. She was an orphan. She used to come and stay with cousins at Burdon. We fell in love. If it hadn't been for the war, we should have had to fall out of it again. As it was, we married amidst public applause, and

Lucilla was born at the end of January 1916. In July I was blown up. I can't tell you how it happened, because I've never remembered. I suppose it was a mine. Anyhow I was reported killed, though I didn't find that out till afterwards. When I came round I was in a German hospital, and I hadn't the faintest idea who I was or how I'd got there. There was a J. tattooed on my arm, and there was an identification disc knocking about which said I was Private John Brown, 12th East Yorks."

"Why?" said Sarah.

"Well, I've often tried to figure it out. I was stark naked when they picked me up—one of the orderlies told me that. I can only suppose that the identity disc was there, and that someone thought it belonged to me. I couldn't contradict them, because my memory was clean gone. I was quite sane and I wasn't badly damaged, and presently they drafted me off to a German prison camp, and there I was for the best part of two years."

The grimly compressed narrative gave Sarah a feeling of horror. War. The things that happen in war. The blowing up of a mine. "I was stark naked." "The identity disc happened to be there." And the man to whom it had belonged—the real John Brown.... She shuddered away from the pictures which floated on that dark background of horror.

He went on speaking.

"That's where I met the man I've been working with all this time. He was an American bug-hunter who'd enlisted in our army quite early on. He said it was because he wanted to study insect life in France, and as there were a lot of armies messing about all over the map just where he wanted to go, he thought the best way of getting there was to enlist. He'd been about a month in the camp when I came along, and we palled up at once. His name was George Eckhard and he is one of the very best. I'd always been keen on birds and beasts and insects, and he got me a lot keener. He said if the war ever did come to an end, we'd go round the world together and write a book. He was pretty useful with a camera, but he couldn't draw a line. When he found that I wasn't a bad hand with a pencil and brush, he got frightfully keen. We used to yarn away about it for hours and plan where we'd go. It made the time pass. I'm telling you this so that you'll understand what happened afterwards."

"Two years—" said Sarah. "How awful!"

"Oh, it wasn't a bad camp as camps went. We were treated quite decently. But of course prison is prison, and we didn't want to stay there. I escaped once, and George escaped once. He got shot in the ankle, and I didn't get very far. After that we thought we'd make a try at it together, but we had to wait for his ankle to get right, and it took a long time. We got away in the end and over the Dutch frontier—I'll tell you about it another time. We got back to England. It was August 1918, and we both got pushed off to France before we had time to turn round, George to some umpteenth battalion of his regiment, and I to mine—to John Brown's. I needn't go into all that. I was in a lot of scrapping, but I never got a scratch, and I went on being John Brown."

"You didn't remember anything?"

"Not a thing. My memory began in that German hospital. That identity disc said I was John Brown, and the J. on my arm bore it out. I don't think I bothered about it. Well, the Armistice came along. After that we were waiting to be demobbed. In January I ran into George Eckhard again. He reminded me about going round the world with him and gave me an address in London that would always find him. We fixed to meet there when we got out of the army. I got out in May." He paused. A long minute went by.

Sarah said, "When did you remember?"

"In London, when I got back. It was awfully odd—there I was in a suit of civvies walking along Piccadilly. I'd written to George, and we were going to meet next day. Meanwhile I was at a loose end. I didn't know a soul, and I hadn't got anyone in the world belonging to me, so far as I knew. I was thinking about that, but not really worrying about it. And then I don't think I was thinking at all. I must have had a sort of lapse of memory, because the next thing I knew I was walking up the steps of the Junior Services Club. It all felt quite natural and clear, and I knew that I was Jack Hildred. I used to go there a lot with Henry before we went out to France. I'd got into the hall before I remembered about John Brown. Well, it made me feel a bit giddy. I went into the writing-room and sat there in the darkest corner I could find. When I'd got my mind straightened out again, I could remember everything that had happened to me both as Jack Hildred and as John Brown, except the bit round about being blown up—that's never come back. I realized that I had been dead for just on three years. I supposed that they would have thought that I was dead. When I'd got it all sorted out I went into a telephone-box and rang up Holme Fallow. That's where I got my first jar. They said the house wasn't on the telephone any longer—it was shut up. I thought a bit, and I asked them to put me on to the Vicarage. The girl in the Holme post-office was very chatty. She told me the old Vicar was dead, and there was a new man, and would he do? I said yes, because I was getting pretty desperate. Well, I got the new man, very pleasant and willing to oblige. I didn't want to spring my resurrection on a stranger, so I said I was a friend of the Hildreds just demobbed, and that I would be very glad to have news of them all. He asked my name, and I said John Brown. And then he got going. My grandfather was dead—I guessed that when I heard the house was shut up. Maurice was dead—missing since August '17. Henry had been badly shell-shocked. He was in a private hospital on the Riviera." He stopped speaking.

Sarah could not see his face. She loved him very much. She wanted to comfort him, if he needed comforting. He must have needed it then, but there hadn't been anyone to comfort him, no one at all. It hurt her so much that she didn't know how to bear it.

He went on, his voice a little harder.

"I left asking about Lucy to the last. He told me Jack Hildred was killed in July '16. He remembered the date because it was just before the old Vicar died and he came to Holme. I got to Lucy at last. She had married Guy Raimond a month before, and they were on their honeymoon in Devonshire."

"Oh, John!"

"It was a bit of a landslide—wasn't it? There didn't seem to be anything left. I rang off and tried to think what I'd better do. As I came out of the telephone-box, I walked right into Ronald Eversley. He recognized me at once, and we went round to his rooms and I told him the whole story. Well, telling him helped me to make up my mind. He wanted me to come back, but I pointed out that the mess was quite bad enough without my making it any worse. You see, I did really feel most awfully sorry for Lucy. She'd had an absolutely rotten show—a week's honeymoon, a war-baby, and three years of being a widow. She'd just got reputably and respectably married to Guy Raimond, who was quite a good fellow in his way, and here I was, coming back to smash up her life all over again. I don't want you to think it was pure altruism either. I *was* frightfully sorry for her, but there was my own side of it too. It seemed ages and ages ago since our marriage. It seemed as if it had happened to quite different people. I suppose I ought to have thought about Lucilla, but a baby I'd never seen didn't seem to mean very much to me. I told Ronald Eversley that I was going to stay dead. I told him I was seeing George Eckhard next day, and that we were going to fix up to go round the world together and write a book. I told him I should just go on being John Brown. In the end he saw it was the best thing I could do, and he swore he'd hold his tongue. The only stipulation he made was that I should keep in touch with him, so that if anything unforeseen happened, he could let me know."

Sarah put out a hand and found his. He said,

"Don't be harrowed, darling. I've liked my life a good deal."

"I'm not being sorry for *you*." Her voice was rather choky. "You don't need being sorry for. You've got me and—and Lucilla. I'm sorry for that poor boy who hadn't got anyone."

John Hildred kissed her.

"You're rather a nice person," he said, and Sarah laughed.

"Aren't you lucky?"

"*Frightfully* lucky."

She leaned against his shoulder. It was much more comfortable than sitting yards away, but she hadn't wanted to be too near whilst he told her about Lucy. Not easy for either of them. But it was over now. The rest was hers.

She said, "Go on," and he told her about going round the world with George Eckhard.

"I enjoyed it awfully, and we wrote our book and made quite a lot of money out of it. Then we did a lecture tour in the States. Then more travels, and more books. I've made some good friends, and I've liked it all. We'll go off round the world some day. I'd like to show you everything."

Sarah laughed happily.

"It sounds awfully grand," she said—"as if it belonged to you—John Hildred's world."

"Well, it is in a way. When you know things and are keen on them, they do belong to you."

"What made you come back?"

She felt his arm tighten a little.

"Eversley. When Henry died, he wrote to me very urgently about coming home. He said I ought to, and that in the circumstances I could get a divorce from Lucy without it hurting her—her reputation, or position, or anything. She and Raimond could marry, and I could take over Holme Fallow and Lucilla. It wasn't as if there were any other children. He wrote very strongly. He said Raimond hadn't any use for Lucilla and it wasn't being fair to her."

"What did you do?"

"Nothing. I couldn't. I told him I felt bound to stand by what I'd done." He paused for a minute.

"And then?"

"You know. Lucy and Raimond were killed in a motor smash, and that altered everything. Eversley turned up one day in Philadelphia and told me I'd got to come home. I'm going to tell you what he told me, Sarah, but it's between the two of us. Eversley's on the Stock Exchange and he knows a lot of people—contacts all over the place. He told me he had heard very disquieting rumours about Geoffrey Hildred. Geoffrey had been plunging, and Geoffrey was supposed to be pretty heavily dipped. He said I ought to come home and look into things. You see, Henry never had come home, and Geoffrey had had everything to play with for years. I'm very much afraid that there are going to be shocks all round when I do go into things. Fortunately, the London leases are all due to fall in in the next year or two, and he can't very well have played old Harry with them."

"So you came home?"

"Yes. I wondered if Geoffrey would recognize me when I walked into his office, but he didn't—I think he really didn't. I got him to do a spot of business for me and then came down here as his client."

"Why did you burgle Holme Fallow?"

He laughed a little.

"I wanted some photographs—my father and mother, and the old man. They were in my old desk, and I broke it open to get them."

"I thought it was something like that—only I thought you were Maurice."

"And Darnac thought I was trying to kill Lucilla. You know, Sarah, that business was a most awful jar. I knew there was some dirty work going on, and I guessed Geoffrey was in a hole, but even now—"

"*Mr. Hildred?* Oh, John!"

"Who else, Sarah? Who else has anything to gain? If Lucilla was out of the way, the property would go to Marina. She's an old woman, and Geoffrey must come next. He could raise as much as he wanted on his expectations. Do you see?"

"He wasn't at the picnic—he was away all Saturday."

"I know. But either the screws were taken out of Lucilla's bicycle before she started, or else Ricky took them. There was nothing to brake for on the way out, so they may have been gone then. Either Ricky or Geoffrey could have put the screws in her pocket. Then, as regards the business up at Holme Fallow, you will remember that Geoffrey had got back from town before we started. He could have cut across the field-path and got into the house without anyone knowing. If he bumped into anyone—well, he'd changed his mind and come after us. There was really very little risk. I believe he was on the stair below Lucilla just before she fell. He got away, but that shower came on before he reached the Red House. His shoes were wet."

Sarah sat up straight.

"But Lucilla," she said—"*Lucilla.* If it's the way you say, Lucilla *knows.* And if she knows, why doesn't she speak? She swears it was all a trick. And she must know. It's quite impossible that she shouldn't know."

"Yes, she knows," said John Hildred.

"Then why, John?"

"I don't know, but I think I can guess. There's something she's afraid of."

"Yes, I've seen that," said Sarah

"She's plucky, but she's afraid. I'm going to find out what she's afraid of. Meanwhile she ought to be safe from any more *accidents.* It wouldn't help Geoffrey to get her out of the way now that he knows that I'm alive. He does know it, though he wouldn't admit it just now. He knows I'm Jack Hildred all right, and because he knows it Lucilla will be quite safe. That's why I had to see him to-night. Eversley will be back by the end of the week, but I didn't dare wait for him. Lucilla will be all right now."

A cold shiver passed over Sarah and shook her. Lucilla would be all right....

"What about you, John?" she said in a quick shaken voice.

Chapter Twenty-Eight

SARAH LAY AWAKE so long that she thought she would not sleep at all. Her mind was like some brilliantly lighted hall hung with vivid, arresting pictures that filled the eye and filled the imagination. The pictures were pictures of the things which had happened in her life and in John Hildred's life. In a place by themselves the things that had happened to them together.

She could not have said at what point this waking fantasy passed into a dream. There must have been a moment when she crossed the dividing line, but she could not have said when it was. She was walking down a long flight of marble steps into a dark forest. The white marble glimmered strangely beneath the black trees. There was some light, but it did not come from sun or moon, and it got fainter and fainter until she was walking in thick darkness. Her feet had left the marble and went softly upon moss. They went too softly, for the moss clung to them and all at once she knew that she was walking into some deep bog that would hold her, and draw her down, and drown her. She tried to run, but the bog held her feet and she began to sink in it, down, and down, and down, until at last when she opened her mouth to scream the mud flowed in and choked her.

She woke with the bed-clothes over her face. It was still dark, but not far off the dawn. She hoped that she had not screamed. She decided that she would not go to sleep again, turned on the light, and read till Annie brought her tea.

Lucilla was in a silent mood at breakfast. Sarah looked at Geoffrey Hildred and wondered. He was in his most benignant humour—the comfortable, florid countryman to the life, with polite attentions for Miss Marina, an affectionate kiss for Lucilla's pale indifferent cheek, and a gallant compliment for Sarah Trent.

Sarah herself felt as if behind the front which she presented to the family breakfast-table some queer division had taken place, leaving, as it were, a façade and two flats. The façade alone was familiar. It showed the Sarah Trent to whom she and everyone else was accustomed. This Sarah Trent talked, smiled, helped herself to marmalade, and asked for another lump of sugar in her tea. In the two flats behind the façade there were two quite different Sarahs. They appeared to have moved in overnight, and she hadn't got accustomed to either of them. One of them was the wildly, unbelievably happy Sarah was who going to marry John Hildred and be mistress of Holme Fallow. She had the sun streaming in at every window, and sometimes she shouted for joy, and sometimes she went down on her knees and said her prayers. A very upheaved, disturbed, unadjusted Sarah. In the other flat the blinds were all down. There was a Sarah here who was afraid. She had the doors locked and the curtains drawn, and she was afraid. She wanted to run away and stay away. A despicable coward of a Sarah.

Very confusing being three people at once.

Probably everyone except Miss Marina was glad when breakfast was over. Miss Marina liked to linger chattily over her second cup of tea. She told them that Mercer had had a letter from her sister—not the one in Canada, but the one who had married her school-friend's widower two years ago—"Such an extremely disagreeable man, and they were two such nice women, but she seems quite happy. And now she's a step-grandmother, because his eldest daughter who married a young man in the mercantile marine last November has just had twins, a boy and a girl. And Mercer says ..."

They did get away at last. Lucilla dragged Sarah upstairs, shut the door of the pink room upon them both, and said,

"Grab your hat, grab anything you want, and come along out! I shall start screaming if I don't get right away for at least three hours. Let's go up to the High Woods and scream together. I don't mind talking the Noble Preserver if you want him to play with."

They were half way down the garden, when Lucilla began to giggle.

"This isn't the way to the High Woods."

"It's the way to the lower pool." Sarah's voice was deep and smooth. Her colour stood high.

"Is the Preserver at the pool? I say, that goes rather well—doesn't it?"

"He might be," said Sarah, who was wondering whether there was any chance that Lucilla would believe that their meeting with John Brown was a fortuitous one.

Lucilla giggled again.

"For a chaperone, my angel, you do go it a bit, don't you?" She linked her arm in Sarah's, breathed another giggle into her ear, and said in a piercing dramatic whisper,

"What were you doing last night?"

"I was asleep," said Sarah with commendable calm. "Weren't you?"

"Asleep? No, no—not while my Sarah was in peril. I wandered in just to see if her angel eyes were closed in slumber. As a matter of fact I'd thought of a simply clinching reason for the Preserver being Uncle Henry, and when I rushed to tell you about it you weren't there. And hours, and hours, and hours afterwards I heard your guilty footsteps pass my door. Nice goings on, I don't think! Govvy, you're blushing! And you were perfectly right—the Preserver *is* down at the pool. I believe you had an assignation."

Sarah said "Yes" in an absent voice. She was trying to control the happy and still unadjusted Sarah who was waving flags out of the window and calling to John Hildred in an extremely forward way.

Lucilla saw the flags at once. Indeed she could hardly have missed them, they flew so bright in Sarah's cheeks. John Hildred saw them too as he came up from the pool to meet them. He looked from one to the other, saw the mischief in Lucilla's eyes, and putting his arm around Sarah, enquired,

"Have you told her?"

Lucilla instantly uttered a shriek of joy, clutched them both, and kissed first Sarah and then John. She continued to hold on to them, laughing and chattering.

"Have you told anyone else? I'll never forgive you if you have, because of course I've seen it coming. You cannot deceive your Aunt Lucilla. Now was it really really truly love at first sight? Because if it was, I must write at once and collect ten bob from Angela Marsden. She said no one ever did fall in love at first sight, and I said they did, and we had ten bob on it. If I couldn't collect a first-hand, authentic, word-ofhonour case within the year, she won, but if I got one, I did. So you'll be careful, won't you, because I shall have to put my hand on my heart and swear it's a genuine case."

John Hildred laughed.

"You can collect your ten bob all right. I'm the genuine article."

"Glory!" said Lucilla.

They went up across the fields to the High Woods. When they came under the trees Lucilla drifted away from them. John Hildred looked after her and said quickly,

"She mustn't go far—I'm not taking risks. But look at this. Geoffrey sent it down by hand first thing this morning." He handed her a note, and as she straightened it out, he put his arm round her again and held her close. It was the first time since she was ten years old that she had known the strength of a certain love, something to lean against and be safe. The sense of it came deeply and quietly into the depths of her consciousness and stayed there. She felt steadied and calmed. She was very happy.

She read what Geoffrey Hildred had written:

My dear Brown,

With reference to our conversation last night, I would ask you to realize that you took me very much by surprise, and that I feel quite unable to arrive at any conclusion. You say that Mr. Eversley will reach London towards the end of the week. I suggest that we await his arrival and meanwhile revert to the status quo ante. *I hope that you will agree that our relations have been of a very pleasant character. When I say this, I am speaking not only for myself, but for the rest of the household. I should like these friendly relations to continue undisturbed. I hope very much that you will join us to-morrow as arranged. Lucilla would, I know, be much disappointed if you were to secede from her party.*

Yours very sincerely,

Geoffrey Hildred.

"Well—" said Sarah. And then, before she could stop herself, "You won't go?" She heard the words, and didn't know why she had spoken them. It was the other Sarah who had said them really, the Sarah who was frightened. She stood in her dark room behind her locked doors and was frightened. She didn't know exactly why she was frightened. She was listening all the time for something that would frighten her if she could hear it. It was this Sarah who had spoken.

John Hildred took the note from her, folded it up again, and put it in his pocket.

"Don't you want me to come to the theatre with you? I've been rather looking forward to it myself."

"Why does he want you to come?" said Sarah-who-was-afraid.

He laughed a little, looked round the empty woodland, and kissed her.

"Oh, Geoffrey's playing for safety. He wants to keep friends."

"Why?" said Sarah, and then *"Why?"* again. The thing she was listening for seemed nearer. She didn't know what it was, but it frightened her terribly.

John Hildred did not laugh this time. He said rather seriously,

"Geoffrey's bound to keep friends with me. If he's got himself into a mess, I'm the only person who can help him out of it. If he's overstepped the law, he's got to reckon on my not wanting to wash the family linen in public." It was the phrase he had already used to Geoffrey Hildred. He went on speaking. "He's in a mess all right. He'd not be so conciliatory if he weren't. But I'm very glad he wrote, because the whole thing is going to be a lot easier if he doesn't stir up trouble—also I'd like to come to the theatre, and I was being rather worried because I didn't quite see how I was going to manage it."

"Is Ran coming?" said Sarah.

"Oh, I suppose so. Why?"

"He and Lucilla have quarrelled."

"Well, I shouldn't break my heart about that. I don't want a French son-in-law."

"Oh—a son-in-law?" Sarah laughed. "Lucilla isn't breaking her heart either. She's a great deal too young to think about being married. But Ran's rather a darling all the same. John, are you going to tell her about you?"

"Not yet—not till Eversley comes. Better not."

She nodded, then lifted her voice and called,

"Lucilla-a-a—!"

A faint "Coo-ee!" answered, and presently Lucilla came running.

"Don't you call me a tactful chaperone? But I thought you wouldn't want me for simply ages. Do you know, I think I must be growing a halo, because if I hadn't a simply saintly disposition, I'd be hating the Preserver like poison for taking my angel Sarah away.

"'I never loved a gazelle of a govvy

To glad me with its bright black eye,

But when I came to know it well

And love it, it was sure to get married.'

"Original *vers libre* by Miss Lucilla Hildred, one of the most daring exponents of the New Realism!"

"Would you like to come and live with us?" said John Hildred lightly.

Lucilla had her arm through his. She drew away a little and with her other hand caught Sarah's fingers and squeezed them, desperately hard. Then she said in a flat tone,

"That's not kind."

Sarah said, "Oh!" and John said, "Why not?"

"Because you don't mean it," said Lucilla slowly.

"I wouldn't say it if I didn't mean it."

Her colour ran up brightly and then faded again.

"They wouldn't let me," she said, her eyes on his face.

"Well, I think they would. Would you like it?"

Lucilla let go of him. She let go of Sarah, stepped back a pace, and stood there staring blankly. All of a sudden her face twisted as if she were in pain. She gave a queer little choking cry and ran away from them down the path.

Chapter Twenty-Nine

THE LUNCH PARTY before the play was not the complete success which it might have been a week earlier. Geoffrey Hildred, it is true, made a most charming host. His slightly old-fashioned geniality never flagged, and he had certainly not spared expense. But Lucilla alone responded with a flow of spirits equal to his own. She looked brilliantly pretty in the new grey frock and squirrel coat which she and Sarah had chosen before lunch. Fifty pounds to spend, and everything new, would go to the head of most girls of eighteen. Lucilla talked, laughed, and sparkled as if she had just come alive and was enjoying it giddily.

But of the others Ricky looked ill and, beyond that, morose and disgruntled to the last degree. Once, half way through lunch, Sarah saw him looking at Lucilla and felt that curious sharp jerk of the muscles with which one sometimes starts awake. She didn't like the boy, but the look she surprised made her pity him a little. It had a sort of savage misery such as she had sometimes seen in the eyes of a bad-tempered dog. And then she thought, "If I saw a dog look like that, I should say he was dangerous," and with that a light shiver went over her, and Lucilla said, "Somebody's walking over your grave." The Sarah who was afraid became suddenly much more afraid.

Bertrand Darnac was being offended and polite. He and Lucilla had not made up their quarrel, and he would have been very glad to be anywhere else. Lucilla's excitement, her heightened prettiness, and her new clothes all plunged him into an angry despair, but the angrier and the more despairing he became, the more assiduously he produced his politest social small talk. Sarah could have laughed if it had not been for the curious weight upon her mind which took the spring out of everything. She couldn't laugh, and she couldn't really talk. She said things, because you cannot sit quite silently beside a genial host, but the words seemed as empty and mechanical as the words of a gramophone record, and even as they sounded in her ears, she was listening for the thing she was afraid of, and knew that it was coming nearer.

John Hildred was really the most normal member of the party. He talked quietly and pleasantly in his pleasant quiet voice. No one would have supposed from his manner that he had any serious preoccupations, yet that he was very much on the alert Sarah was aware.

They had come up to town in the two cars, Geoffrey Hildred driving Ricky, and the rest of them in the Daimler with the elderly chauffeur, who was pledged by Miss Marina on no account to exceed twenty-five miles an hour. Geoffrey had to look in at his office. Bertrand had business of his own, or said he had. But John Hildred accompanied Sarah and Lucilla through their orgy of shopping, displaying a sort of abstracted patience which Sarah found funny and rather touching. He explained that if you went in for photographing birds and insects, you often had to wait for hours without moving hand or foot. Knowing that he was there, and knowing that he would continue to be there, prevented the weight on Sarah's mind from becoming intolerable. The odd thing was that her personal happiness was quite undisturbed. There were still two Sarahs, the one who was happy and the one who was afraid, but they didn't seem to have very much to do with each other, though they both lived in her house.

When Lucilla's shopping was done, John Hildred wanted Sarah to choose her engagement ring. The sharpness of her own recoil surprised her a good deal. She hoped he didn't see how sharp it was, because how could she explain that this wasn't their day at all? This was a day that had to be got through somehow before they could think about themselves. It wasn't a day to be getting their betrothal ring. She was glad that he didn't seem to be hurt. He just said "Why?" and smiled at her as if her vehemence amused him. And all she had to say was, "It isn't that sort of day." At which he laughed outright and said, "When it's the right kind of day, which would you rather have, an emerald, or a ruby? You'd better be thinking about it." And Lucilla giggled and said, "In one of Miss Yonge's books which Aunt Marina made me read there's a girl called Robina who won't have any engagement ring except a lock of her young man's hair—all plaited up, you know. He was a red-haired parson with green eyes, and I'm not making it up—it's in the *Pillars of the House*. Now that's what I call romantic—much more *loving* than emeralds and rubies. Only the Preserver would have to grow his hair for months, and months, and months before you could get enough to plait into a ring."

They had all met for lunch, and all except Lucilla were glad when lunch was over. The play was much easier. It was light and amusing, and the intervals were commendably short. Lucilla seemed to be enjoying herself very much. Bertrand's gloom relaxed a little. In the last interval he had become definitely less polite, but as they emerged from the theatre, Lucilla hanging on John Hildred's arm and talking nineteen to the dozen, he had a sudden relapse and made the most formal and courteous of adieux. Lucilla sparkled a little less brightly when he was gone.

Sarah found herself walking with Geoffrey Hildred. Ricky seemed to have disappeared. They were making for the Tube station. It was a cooler evening than they had had, and the daylight had that peculiar flat and chilly tone which disconcerts eyes accustomed to the warm glow of the footlights. The chill was reflected in Sarah's mood. She looked at the kindly florid face of her host and wondered if its kindness and geniality were all "theatre." Was it possible that he had attempted Lucilla's life? Wasn't there some explanation which would exonerate him? In this cold daylight the thing just didn't seem possible to her.

They turned in at the Tube station and went down in a fairly crowded lift. John Hildred and Lucilla kept ahead in the passages and on the steps, but they all came out on to the platform together. John looked round and smiled at Sarah, and she came up on his other side.

"Where's Ricky?" said Lucilla over her shoulder, and when no one answered her she began to chatter again, leaning across to talk to Sarah. "Isn't it noble of it to be cold to-day, so that I can wear my furry coat? You said I'd be boiled, but I haven't been a bit. It's the nicest, cosiest thing and as light as light. I wouldn't know I'd got it on if it wasn't so pussy warm. The Preserver says I look nice in it, but he can't tell me whether my hat's right or not."

"It isn't straight," said John Hildred deprecatingly.

"It isn't meant to be straight, darling, but it has to be the right sort of crooked. Sarah my angel?"

Sarah laughed.

"Just right," she said.

And John Hildred said, "Keep back a bit, Lucilla—here's the train."

And then it all happened, and so quickly that thought seemed suspended. There were a good many people on the platform. They themselves were in the front row, and Lucilla was leaning across John Hildred with her left hand still resting lightly on his arm. The train came out of the low, dark tunnel on their right, and just before it reached them Lucilla took a stumbling plunge forward and over the edge. She screamed, and a woman in the crowd screamed too on a very high, sharp note. It all passed between one thudding heart-beat and the next. Lucilla was over the edge. John, snatching at her, was off his balance. And Sarah, clutching desperately at his arm, felt the world rock and go black. She didn't know what had happened in that black moment. The train went by and stopped. The wind of it passed her, and the noise. She could see again and feel. She was still gripping John's left arm. His right was about Lucilla, whose face was hidden against his shoulder. But he was not looking at either of them. He was looking behind him, looking at the crowd, and Sarah knew very well what he was looking for. He was looking for Geoffrey Hildred.

And Geoffrey Hildred was far back in the crowd. There were at least three rows of people between him and them. The whole thing had been too quick for him to have changed his place. There hadn't been time. John had caught Lucilla as she slipped. He felt his balance go as her weight dragged on him, felt Sarah catch at him and throw herself back, and in the next instant he had got his balance again and swung Lucilla up.

And Geoffrey Hildred stood three rows back in the crowd.

Lucilla lifted her head and said, "I slipped," and with that they were all getting into the train.

Geoffrey Hildred wore a look of worry and distress. He found a seat immediately opposite the other three, and kept on regarding Lucilla with an air of anxious concern. Once or twice he seemed as if he were going to speak, then he checked himself and leaned back frowning. When they emerged upon the platform again, he came up to Lucilla and said,

"What happened? What happened, my child?"

The little grey cap and the grey squirrel coat, which had been so becoming at lunch, now accentuated Lucilla's ghastly pallor. She said without looking at him,

"I slipped."

And John Hildred said, "We won't discuss it here, Geoffrey." After which no one spoke at all until they reached the hotel.

Millington's Hotel is a relic of the Victorian age. It has what might be described as an hereditary clientele. It stands in a small secluded square, and it is as respectable as the Victoria and Albert Museum. Until a year or two before the war it had no electric light. Rumour says that a gas globe or two still haunt the top landing, and it is sober truth that there is a gas fire in every bedroom.

Geoffrey Hildred was received with a sort of decorous enthusiasm rather suggestive of a welcome from loyal retainers. He had a pleasant word for everyone, and inscribed the names of his party in the register with a pleasing return of his usual geniality.

As he laid down the pen, John Hildred took it up. There was a moment when both men stood there with the register between them. Geoffrey Hildred looked sideways, and saw a face more sternly set than he had seen it yet. He looked away again.

"But I did not know you were staying here too," he said.

John Hildred's eyebrows went up a little.

"Didn't you?" he said. And then he pulled the book towards him and leaned down and wrote his name—"John Hildred." And in the space for the address—"Holme Fallow."

Chapter Thirty

SARAH AND LUCILLA went upstairs together. Two single rooms had been booked for them, and in reply to Sarah's enquiry the stout grey-haired chambermaid was sorry but they had no double room available.— We're that full, miss. But there—you're ever so close together. Mr. Hildred was most particular about that—asked special for these two rooms he did. They're what Miss Hildred and her maid always had, and we've kept them special. Here you are, miss—29 and 30, with just the bathroom between you. Miss Hildred she always says it's so good as having her own private bath."

The rooms were small but comfortable. The luggage was already there, the chauffeur having deposited it earlier in the day. The two bedrooms and the bathroom had communicating doors, the bathroom being obviously a converted bedroom. Sarah tried both doors and found them locked. She went into the bathroom and had a look from that side. There was no sign of a key anywhere. The chambermaid said, no, miss, there wasn't a key—"and you won't find it only a step to go round." And with that she went away and shut the door.

Lucilla had been standing at the window with her back to the room, but as the latch clicked she turned round and laughed. The sound struck Sarah's heart and jarred it. She said involuntarily, "Don't!" and immediately Lucilla laughed again.

"My angel Sarah—if you could see your face! *Grim!*"

Sarah came up to her and took her hand.

"Lucilla—how did you fall?"

"It seems as if you were always asking me that. Sort of habit, isn't it? Bad habit, I think. Don't you?"

"Yes."

"I slipped, my angel."

"Why did you slip?"

"Just did. Dunno why."

Sarah let go her hand and stepped back.

"Why don't you tell me the truth?"

Lucilla's face worked for a moment. Then she went to the wash-stand and began to pour hot water into the basin. The hot-water can was brown picked out with black, and the basin an immense and solid affair wreathed in brightly painted roses.

Lucilla plunged her hands into the hot water with a little shriek.

"Boiling I Absolutely boiling! Darling, don't you simply love putting your hands in water that's just not quite boiling enough to scorch your skin off? I can feel it squirling right down to my toe-nails and up to the roots of my hair. It's lovely!"

Sarah stood irresolute. That cold doubt which had come to her once or twice before just touched her again. She had hoped for something that would exonerate Geoffrey Hildred. Had she found it?... She recoiled, as she had always recoiled. Yet whatever there was to know, Lucilla must know it. Then why didn't she speak? John said she was afraid. Afraid of what? She risked death by remaining silent. And she had courage.

Sarah went out of the room and into her own room and shut the door. Presently there came a knock on it. John Hildred stood there.

"I want to speak to you. Where can we talk?"

She said, "I don't know—not here, I suppose."

He shook his head.

"They'd have a fit. There used to be a little hole of a sitting-room along here. We can see if it's empty."

Empty it was—a small gloomy room, with heavy maroon curtains, a drab carpet, and the more unyielding kind of Victorian chair. A debilitated electric bulb shed a kind of wan twilight in the contract-ed space.

John shut the door and took her as far from it as possible.

"What does she say?" he asked.

Sarah made a gesture of despair.

"What does she ever say? Just nothing."

"You asked her?"

"Of course I asked her. She said she slipped. She said she didn't know how."

He was silent for a moment. Then he said,

"She slipped. And Geoffrey was three rows back in the crowd—wedged. I saw him."

"Yes, I saw him too."

"There was no general push forward—it wasn't done that way. I wasn't pushed at all. It was her weight that nearly took me over. Sarah, he's damned clever. If you hadn't held on just long enough to give me time to get my balance, we'd have been gone and out of his way—both of us, Lucilla and I. Do you realize that?"

Sarah looked at him steadily. Her eyes were dark and her face very pale. She said,

"Yes, John." And then, "How did he do it?"

"I think I know, but knowing isn't proving. If we'd gone under the train, it would have been an accident or—or suicide—and the way all nice and clear for Geoffrey. I think it was done with his stick. I think he was watching for a chance, and he got it. That stick he always carries would have done the trick. One good hard shove would be enough. Everyone was looking at the train—"

Sarah was paler still.

"Then why doesn't she say so? She must know. John, that's what defeats me—she must know."

"Yes, she knows. But she's afraid. She can't prove anything, and she's afraid he'll try to make out she's mad."

"John!"

"I'm sure of it. I'm sure he's threatened her with a lunatic asylum. And she'd rather face death—my poor plucky girl! Don't you see, there's no proof—there's never been any proof. If she talked, he'd have the doctor in and make out a case for persecution-mania. I guessed at something of the sort when they played that damnable trick to frighten her—the Thing dashing at her window. It would have suited their book remarkably well if she had run screaming through the house, but they dropped it like a hot brick as soon as they knew you had changed rooms. It wouldn't have suited them to have Lucilla's story corroborated."

"She said it would stop when I'd seen it." Sarah's lips were stiff on the words.

John Hildred nodded.

"Yes—she knew. She's been playing a lone hand ever since Henry died. Do you happen to know whether she's refused Ricky lately?"

"I don't know. I shouldn't wonder—he's looked so sulky."

"I think that's been the alternative. Now they're desperate—and so am I. Sarah, I don't know what to do. He's her guardian. We can't prove a thing, and Ronald Eversley doesn't land till Friday at earliest. I'd like to take you both away to-night, but if Geoffrey called in the police, I'd be done. I can't prove I'm her father till Ronald comes. And I'd give a good deal not to drag Lucilla and the family name into court. Geoffrey knows that. What am I to do?"

Sarah said, "I don't know."

He smiled suddenly.

"I did a stupid theatrical thing just now—I registered as John Hildred of Holme Fallow, right under Geoffrey's nose. I wish you'd seen his face. I'm afraid I'd do it again—just for that. By the way, did you know he wasn't staying here?"

She had known, but it came freshly and brought an overwhelming sense of relief. She said rather breathlessly.

"No—of course—he's got his flat—he wouldn't. He and Ricky will be at the flat. He said so. Oh, but then we'll be all right here—won't we?"

"It's the most respectable place on earth," said John Hildred. His voice lagged a little on the words. "I'm along at the end of the passage— No. 45. It ought to be all right. Now look here—I'm coming to the theatre with you to-night. I've told Geoffrey so, and he's offered me Ricky's ticket. Ricky is said to be at the flat, very seedy with a bad head. Bad conscience and funk, I should say. But anyhow he's off the map, and I'm going instead. Geoffrey was very polite, after looking as if his eyes were going to pop out of his head when I signed the register in my own name. He was very polite, and very upset about Lucilla. He rather gave the show away by saying he'd been anxious about her nerves for some time, and didn't I think she ought to see a specialist? He's a good actor, and I let him think it was going down all right, because I don't want to push him into a corner at this juncture. I've got to play for time. Now these are the plans for this evening, and you must back them up. We dine here, and we all go in a taxi together to the theatre. If Geoffrey's arranging a smash, he'll have to be in it himself—and I think he's a great deal too fond of his own skin, so that will be all right. Coming back, same thing. And if I have to go for a taxi, you and Lucilla don't leave the foyer till I come for you. Then we all come here, and Geoffrey can take the taxi on to his flat, which is only just round the corner. I think that's a pretty watertight arrangement. You both bolt your doors, and if you could bear it for once in a way, I think I'd like you to fasten the windows too. There's a sort of built-out place on the next floor below, and—I think I'd feel happier if your windows weren't open. Any active person could climb up by way of that bit of roof."

Sarah said, "All right." And then, "John, it's a bad dream. I'd like to wake up."

The dream-like feeling persisted through the evening. They dined together at seven, the four of them—Geoffrey, Lucilla, John, and Sarah. John Hildred had wondered whether Geoffrey would show up, but there he was, the agreeable host to the life, with no more than a shade of concern in his manner. He held Lucilla's hand for a moment and patted it. Sarah asked after Ricky, and they heard that he had gone to bed—a chill, Geoffrey opined, but considered that he would be all right in the morning. He continued to talk easily and fluently.

Lucilla wore her black georgette frock, but she wore it with a difference. She would not have come down to dinner at the Red House with her fair eyebrows darkened and shaped into a slender arch or her mouth painted in a scarlet cupid's bow. She had darkened her lashes too and faintly stained the smooth pallor of her cheeks with rose. The whole effect was very decorative, but Miss Marina would certainly not have approved of it. Sarah discerned the courage which flies all its flags in the presence of danger.

Dinner over, John's plan was carried out without a hitch. They had seats in the third row of the stalls, and sat in the following order—Geoffrey, Sarah, John, and Lucilla. Again, John's arrangement. It might, indeed, have been his party rather than Geoffrey's, and to Sarah's surprise Geoffrey took it all mildly enough, only smiling pleasantly when his offer of chocolates was very peremptorily refused.

"You think them unwholesome?" he said. "Now I wonder why—I really do wonder why."

Sarah thought the innocence a little overdone, and for the last time the question came beating at her heart, "Is it real? Is it possible that it's real?" Well, it was all part of the dream, and at some time and in some way the evening would be over.

The curtain went up and the play began. As it proceeded, Sarah found amazement struggling with indignation. What a piece to have chosen for a girl of Lucilla's age who was ostensibly to be cheered up and taken out of herself! It seemed as if Geoffrey must have guessed her thoughts, for when the curtain fell on the first act, he turned to her with an appearance of distress.

"I had no idea it was this sort of piece. Some friend of Ricky's recommended it. And of course it is very well acted—but I wanted to take Lucilla to something amusing—I had really no idea at all." He continued in this strain, and presently leaned across to ask Lucilla whether she would like to come away without waiting for the other acts.

The slender darkened eyebrows arched themselves in dismay.

"Come out? But why?"

His tone was solicitous.

"Well, it's rather a gloomy piece for you, my dear."

"Gloom doesn't matter when you're feeling cheerful. I'm feeling *very* cheerful, and wild horses won't get me away before the end. You and Sarah can go home if you like. The Preserver and I are staying." She hooked her hand inside John's arm and squeezed it.

Geoffrey Hildred sat down with a sigh and told Sarah all over again that he had had no idea what the piece was about.

It was certainly a very gloomy piece. There was a young man who was going mad, and a girl who tried to drown herself, and three very depressing middle-aged women who poured out the stories of their thwarted lives whenever any of the other characters could be got to listen, but as everyone in the play was entirely and exclusively preoccupied with his or her own feelings, this fortunately did not happen as often as it otherwise might have done. There was an elderly man who drank, and a girl of sixteen who doped. The piece was called *A Slice of Life*, and Geoffrey Hildred kept on explaining that he had expected it to be a farce.

It came to an end at last, and they drove back to the hotel according to plan. It seemed as if Geoffrey Hildred's flow of words had failed at last, for he sat silent in the taxi whilst Lucilla chattered about the play.

"They were all such idiots," she declared. "Why didn't they go and do something instead of just mooning around and talking about themselves? I do hate people who can't get a move on."

Geoffrey did speak then. He said in a curious flat, gentle voice,

"I hope it won't spoil your night's rest. You mustn't miss your sleep, my dear." And with that the taxi stopped before the hotel.

John sprang out with some relief. He said,

"You'll take the taxi on?" And then in a minute the three of them were there on the pavement and Geoffrey was being driven away.

Sarah felt a most blessed sense of relief. What had she been afraid of? He was gone, and the three of them were here together, she, and John, and Lucilla. They were a family. It was going to be like this always—she, and John, and Lucilla. It felt very good indeed.

They went up the steps and into the hotel.

Chapter Thirty-One

THE TAXI DROVE ON with Geoffrey Hildred round the top of the Square and out of the narrow street which runs in between Nos. 40 and 41. Another turn, and the taxi drew up before a block of flats. Geoffrey got out, separated the legal fare from the loose silver in his pocket, added a generous tip, and went in.

He rang for the lift, conversed affably with the porter who took him up, and, getting out at the third floor, let himself into his flat with a latch-key. He stood in the hall with his hand on the door-knob. It was as if for a moment he relaxed. The day had been a hard one. To be constantly on your guard; to contrive, fitting one bit of your puzzle so deftly to the next that there shall be no sign of a join; to hold pleasant converse through the strain of an awkward and dangerous situation; to dare in the teeth of risk; to be within an ace of succeeding and to fail, and, failing, to keep an unwavering purpose and show no sign—these things put a pretty heavy strain upon a man. Geoffrey Hildred leaned against the inner side of the door and eased himself from the strain.

The geniality of his expression was gone, leaving the features heavy with fatigue. The florid colour looked patchy and hard. The shoulders sagged into a forward stoop.

It was for no more than a minute. Then he straightened up, took his hand from the door, and walked into the first room on the right. It was a very comfortable sitting room—a man's room, with big leather chairs, a table strewn with papers and magazines, and a deep couch. There were Persian rugs on the floor, and a few really beautiful pieces of Chinese porcelain on the mantelpiece and in a cabinet which stood between the windows. The crimson curtains were drawn. A shaded reading-lamp glowed on a low table by the couch and showed Ricky lying there at full length. He had a magazine in his hand, but it was impossible to say whether he had been reading it. He started as his father came in.

Geoffrey Hildred had resumed his customary expression. He shut the door behind him, switched on the overhead light, and settled himself in one of the large arm-chairs.

"Well, my boy," he said, "we had quite a successful evening."

Ricky's face twitched. He flung up an arm to shield it and said in an uneven voice.

"What do you mean? What's happened?"

Geoffrey Hildred frowned. You had to use the material to your hand, but really Ricky's nerves—He shook his head a little as he said reprovingly,

"Nothing has happened. Nothing was due to happen."

Ricky sat up with astonishing vigour.

"I wish you wouldn't say things like that!"

Geoffrey's eyebrows rose.

"Why, I suppose the servants have gone, haven't they? But you're quite right—we mustn't be careless. Just make quite sure they're all off the premises, and then put the chain on the door."

Whilst he waited for Ricky to come back, his fingers beat a tattoo on the arm of the chair. He was going to have trouble with Ricky; he could see that. And he was tired—tired. He clenched his hand with a jerk. He wasn't too tired to finish the game.

Ricky came back.

"They've gone—and I'm going to bed."

"It's scarcely worth while, is it?" said Geoffrey Hildred.

Ricky came a step nearer.

"I'm going to bed. I'm not going on any farther. I don't care what you say—I'm not going on. I don't care if we're ruined. It's better to be ruined than dead. You're just trying to get me to put my head in a noose, and I won't do it. I tell you I'm through!"

"Well, well," said Geoffrey Hildred—" so you say. But have you the slightest idea what being ruined is going to be like? I'm afraid you haven't. I've tried to spare you, you know, and I'm afraid it's been a mistake. I ought to have taken you more fully into my confidence. Just shut that door and come and sit down. I don't think you'll really be quite so indifferent to being ruined when I've told you a little more about it."

Ricky plunged sulkily down on the sofa and stared at his father with shifty, nervous eyes.

"I know Jack can put you into court if he chooses. But he won't choose. After all he's a relation."

Geoffrey Hildred lifted his hand and let it fall again.

"My dear Ricky, that's puerile. He won't be able to help it. There is a settlement on Lucilla under his grandfather's will, and the fact that a good deal of it has gone will be beyond his power to hush up if he ever comes to go into the accounts. He would expose himself to the charge of being an accessory after the fact. So you see you are talking nonsense. There was a time about three years ago when I could have handed everything over and cleared enough to make us very comfortable for life. If Jack had come back then—well, I shouldn't have risked any further transactions. But with Henry at the other side of the world and no chance of his return—I used to get most deplorable accounts of his health—I was, most unfortunately, tempted to continue. And then, as you know, the roof fell in." He paused for a moment, waited to see if Ricky would speak, and then went on. "When you say you know that Jack can put me into court, you are a good deal under-stating what is likely to happen—what is bound to happen—unless we take steps to prevent it. I don't know if the idea of penal servitude attracts you. You would of course get a lighter sentence than I should. And you are young. You would probably be a free man again before your thirtieth birthday. That is still young, and I dare say you would be able to make a new start, though it's never easy for a penniless, discredited man to get on his feet again."

Ricky sprang up, quivering from head to foot.

"What do you mean? What are you talking about? *Prison?*" he said.

Geoffrey looked a mild reproof.

"My dear Ricky, don't you realise the position? Misappropriation of trust funds is, I fear, the name that will be given to my well-intentioned financial operations, and you will find that there is ample documentary evidence of your, shall we say, collusion? You may get off with a light sentence, but you will have no chance at all of convincing a jury of your innocence."

Ricky collapsed again upon the sofa and buried his head in his hands with a groan.

"What can we do?"

Geoffrey Hildred regarded him complacently.

"Why, what we planned to do. I think you must see that it is necessary and—" He made a slight gesture with his hand. "Forgive me, my dear boy, but I really cannot see what you are boggling at. It isn't as if it would be your first attempt, though I'm sure we both hope it will be your last."

Ricky looked up sulkily.

"What do you mean?"

"Well, I don't want to allude to past failures, but you did push her off the bank and under Miss Trent's car—didn't you? And without any prompting from me either. It was a bold stroke that might easily have succeeded, but after that you can't expect me to take your scruples very seriously."

Ricky stared at him gloomily.

"She'd made me mad. I didn't care what I did to her. I asked her to marry me, and she laughed at me and said—" His voice choked with rage.

Geoffrey Hildred nodded.

"Yes, she called you a white rabbit. Very silly of her, but she's still a schoolgirl."

Ricky sprang to his feet and began to walk about the room. "She made me mad, and I didn't care what I did. I pushed her, and I'd have been glad if she'd been killed. But I can't do it in cold blood, I tell you. Why don't you do it yourself if you're so keen on it?"

"I do wish you'd sit down," said Geoffrey Hildred, and as Ricky threw himself on the sofa again, he continued in a calm judicial voice. "I should just like to point out that up to the present most of the risks have been mine. I'm not complaining that it is so."

"You made me go down to that beastly school of hers and set light to her curtains."

"Well, there wasn't much risk in that, either to her or to you. There's one point about a school—you can always count on everyone being just where they're expected to be at any given moment."

"You made me put the screws in her pocket too."

Geoffrey Hildred laughed pleasantly.

"A most dangerous job, Ricky! Come, come, you must admit that so far the risks have been mine. That was a narrow shave at Holme Fallow, and a piece of real bad luck that Jack should have been so near. When Miss Trent turned her torch on and I saw him, I thought the game was up. Well now, my boy, about to-night—I would certainly undertake the job myself if it didn't involve climbing in at that bathroom window. I'm afraid that's a little beyond me. But really the whole thing is simplicity itself. You go round to the back, do the bit of climbing, which is easy enough for you, push back the catch of the bathroom window, and get in. You'll find this palette knife will do the trick. It's an old-fashioned catch and moves very easily. I have put the cylinder of gas all ready in your old rucksack. I don't think you'll find it at all in your way for the climb."

Ricky had his chin in his hands. He stared at his father and said nothing. Geoffrey Hildred continued in his equable voice.

"Leave the window unlatched and slip the bolt of the door. Then put on your gas mask—it is in the rucksack. If anyone does catch sight of you after that, you will be very well disguised. By the way, I should wear your Burberry. Everyone looks alike in a Burberry. Now listen carefully. You must deal with Jack first. He's in 45 at the end of the passage. Unless he's changed a lot, he's a sound sleeper—all the Hildreds are. There isn't any bolt on the door. If he's locked in, this little contrivance will turn the key from the outside. You'll be able to tell from his breathing whether he's deeply asleep. Bring the nozzle well down over his face and turn on the gas. When he's off, shut and latch the window, turn the gas fire on full, and leave him, taking care to shut the door. Then get back to the bathroom and lock yourself in again. This key opens the communicating door to Lucilla's room. I got the impression of the lock last time Marina stayed there. It's the room on the right as you come in. Repeat the process with the gas, shut and latch the window, make sure that the door is bolted on the inside, then turn on the gas fire and come away, locking the communicating door behind you and taking care to bring away the key. You then have only to unlock the bathroom door and climb out of the window, shutting it behind you. The fact of its being unlatched will occasion no remark. At least half a dozen people will have had baths, and any one of them might have left it like that. At the inquest it will be perfectly evident that Lucilla, in a fit of derangement, went along the passage and turned on the gas in her father's room, afterwards returning to her own room, where she locked herself in and once more turned on the gas. She will be found in a room with two locked doors and a latched window, and I think it is quite impossible that the least suspicion should be aroused. You will wear rubber gloves throughout, so there will be no finger-marks. Move the gas taps with the little instrument I gave you for turning the key. You don't want to disturb the prints which will naturally be there. I don't suppose anyone will think of looking for them, but it is just as well to be on the safe side."

Ricky stared at his father. He had a fixed, sulky look. He said,

"It won't go right. If you'd been going to bring it off, you'd have brought it off already. Look at this afternoon."

Geoffrey nodded.

"I know—very disappointing. But I wasn't counting on it. It was a good chance, so I took it, and if it hadn't been for Sarah Trent, it would have come off. There was just room for me to get my stick level with Lucilla's waist, and I got in a good hard push. They'd both have been under the train if Miss Trent had not interfered."

Ricky laughed unpleasantly.

"Your Miss Trent hasn't been a shining success—has she? If she hadn't brought that fellow Darnac down, we'd probably have got it fixed for up Cilla to marry me. I can't think what you wanted to drag them in for."

Geoffrey Hildred made a rather weary gesture.

"Oh, my dear Ricky—need we go over all that again? If you can't see how important it was to be able to show that we surrounded Lucilla with young companionship, that we did everything that was possible to counteract her morbid tendencies—" He shrugged his shoulders and sat up. "That's enough. If we bring off this job, we're safe. If we don't, we're done. Which is it to be? If Marina comes in for the property, we shall have the management of everything. She'll sign anything I put in front of her, and when she dies everything is ours. Come—you can't hesitate."

Ricky looked at him, a long angry look. Then he looked away.

"I suppose I'll have to do it," he said.

Chapter Thirty-Two

JOHN HILDRED WENT UP the hotel stairs with the two girls. At Lucilla's door he said, "I'd like just to make sure that your lock is in order." And with that he went in.

The door had an ordinary iron lock, and a small brass bolt—not the sort which can be slipped back from outside by a chambermaid with a pass-key, but the old-fashioned kind which can only be opened and shut from within. John looked relieved at the sight of it.

"Now, my dear," he said, "I want you to latch your window and lock and bolt this door. What about the one into the bathroom?"

"It's locked," said Sarah. "The chambermaid says there isn't any key."

He went over and tried the handle, and came back again.

"You'll do that, Lucilla?"

She nodded. Her eyes were fixed on him with a bright inquiring look.

"Good night, Uncle Henry," she said, and put up her face to be kissed.

Sarah leaned against the closed door and watched them. Her heart was beating rather hard. John Hildred put his arm round Lucilla and said gently,

"I'm not Henry, my dear."

She drew a little quick breath.

"Who are you?"

"Can't you guess?"

She gazed at him with a look which he found hard to bear. It held a piteous hope. He said,

"Don't, darling—it's all right. I'm your father." And all at once her weight came so heavily on his arm that he was afraid she was going to faint. Instead she winced sharply, cried out, and flung her arms about his neck.

"Oh, not really—not *really*! Oh, Preserver darling—are you *sure*?"

John said he was quite sure. He was so much moved that he took refuge in his quietest drawl. As for Lucilla, she hugged him, half laughing, half crying, kissed him again, and ran off to fling her arms round Sarah and kiss her too.

"Angel darling, did you know he was my father? You'll be a Step! That's worse than being a govvy, a million times! Oh, let us be joyful—joyful, joyful, *joyful*!" She turned back and caught John's hand. "It isn't really happening, is it? It's just a lovely sort of dream! But please, please, *please* don't let's wake up!"

John put his arm round her again, and again he felt her wince. He said, pressing his hand against her side,

"That hurts? Where his stick got you, isn't it?"

Lucilla pulled away, her breath coming fast.

"Oh!" she cried, and her colour flamed.

"Come and sit down," said John. "Let's all sit down. Now, my child—here's Sarah on one side of you and me on the other. There's nothing to be afraid of any more. We've got you safe, and we're going to keep you safe. He can't touch you. Don't you think you'd better tell us all about it?"

They were sitting on the bed, Lucilla white as a sheet after her sudden flush, Sarah and John each with an arm about her. She looked from one to the other of them, and was silent. A tremor shook her from head to foot. Then all of a sudden she said,

"You won't believe me. He said nobody would believe me."

"Lucilla, look at me," said John. "Now, my dear—Sarah and I will believe you. Have you got that? We shall believe you."

"He said anyone would think I was mad. He said I should be shut up—and I'd *rather* be dead."

"And that is why you were afraid to speak? We guessed that. Will you tell us now, Lucilla?"

She was looking at him with a steady, wide gaze that seemed to search, to weigh. Then, quite unexpectedly, she said,

"Why didn't you come home before?"

John Hildred met her look with one as steady.

"Yes, you've the right to ask me that," he said. "It's too long a story to tell you now, but I lost my memory, and when I got it back, it seemed too late to come home. Your mother had married again—and I thought I had better stay dead."

Lucilla went on looking at him. She said without any expression in her voice,

"You didn't think about me."

If he was startled, he did not show it. He answered her quietly and with honesty.

"No, I didn't. I'll try and make it up to you, my dear."

"They weren't—fond of me." Her voice was hard and bitter. She looked at him all the time.

"You can't always tell," said John Hildred.

"Can't you?" said Lucilla. "I can. They only wanted each other. He didn't like me—because of you. I *wish* you had come back."

"I've come back now."

"Are you going to be fond of me?"

"Very fond of you. We're going to be friends. We're going to be a very happy family."

She looked away at last and said in an odd wavering voice, "It's the nicest dream I've ever had—you and Sarah and me, and everything safe."

Sarah gave her a hug, and John said,

"Now will you tell us the whole thing from the beginning? I can take care of you better if I know just where we are."

Lucilla pulled away from them and got up.

"Can't do it all three sitting in a row like sparrows on a perch. You and Sarah can stay there, and I'll have the chair which was stuffed with potatoes when Queen Victoria was a child. It ought to be in a museum really." She pulled it forward as she spoke, an odd dumpy piece of furniture with a spreading seat and a narrow back. Then she sat down, her elbows on her knees, and laughed a little shakily. "You look awfully funny sitting there waiting for me to tell you the story of my life. Where do you want me to begin?"

"Well, I suppose nothing much happened before Henry died. Geoffrey would hardly get going before that."

A bleak look passed over her face. She said,

"No—that's where it begins. I was at school, you know. They wouldn't let me go back. They said I had tried to set fire to my room." She looked hard at Sarah. "Did he tell you that?"

Sarah nodded.

"What happened?"

"I don't know. I didn't do it. But they didn't believe me. It happened twice, and the second time they asked for me to be taken away. I really didn't do it."

John said, "I know you didn't. Would it have been easy for anyone to get into your room?"

"Oh, *frightfully* easy, but nobody seemed to think about that. It was just after the accident, and they said it was the shock. And Uncle Geoffrey came and fetched me away and told me not to talk about it, because people would think I was mad. But *he* told people—he told Dr. Drayton, and Mercer, and the Vicar, and Sarah. And then I was nearly killed out riding."

She looked at Sarah again.

"You asked me why I didn't ride. Well. that was why. The horse bolted. I don't know why I wasn't killed. Afterwards the groom told Annie—they were walking out together—he told her there was a thorn under the saddle. I told Uncle Geoffrey. He put on his shocked, grieved face and said he would never have believed that I would do such a thing, and how wicked it was, and that people who did that sort of thing were shut up. It was one of Mr. Raimond's horses, and they were all sold just after that. It frightened me. He didn't let me forget about it—he used to say things when we were alone, and—and hint. Then Ricky came down on a visit and began to make love to me. I just laughed, but Uncle Geoffrey rather slacked off and things were easier. I didn't *mind* Ricky, you know. He was a bit of an ass, but I thought he liked me, and he was someone to go about with."

She paused, frowned, dropped her chin in her hands, and went on again.

"The day Sarah came down to be vetted I went to the gate to meet Ricky. Uncle Geoffrey dropped him there and went on to the house. We were larking about, and all of a sudden he began to make the most awful ass of himself. He talked the most frightful mush, and he tried to kiss me. When I wouldn't, he said he'd make me. And I said if I wanted to kiss white rabbits, I'd keep some up in the stable." Lucilla giggled reminiscently. "And he simply foamed with rage and went stamping off. And then I heard Sarah starting her car, so I climbed up on to the bank to have a look. It was quite dark, but I thought I'd see her go by, and just before she came I heard someone behind me, and I called out, 'That you, Ricky?' And the next thing I knew someone hit me in the back and I went down blip in front of The Bomb."

"Ricky pushed you?" Sarah's voice was sharp with horror.

"I don't know," said Lucilla. She frowned. "*Someone* pushed me. Ricky had gone away. Perhaps he came back—I don't know."

"Well?" said John. "Go on."

She gave a little half laugh.

"The Thing that flapped against my window began that night. I was so frightened that I very nearly did what I suppose they wanted me to do, rush out of my room and scream the house down. It was rather beastly—wasn't it, Sarah?"

"I hated it like poison," said Sarah frankly.

"So did I. It didn't come every night, but when it did I just went under the bed-clothes and dithered till it went away." She looked at John intently. "You see, the worst part was not being sure whether there really was anything. It sounds awfully stupid, but I got to think— supposing I was just *hearing* things—I mean, supposing there wasn't anything that anyone else would hear. So when Sarah heard it too, it was like having mountains lifted off me, because then I was sure it was a trick, and I knew it would stop, because they wouldn't want to play tricks on Sarah and have *her* shrieking the house down. It would have rather spoilt the effect." She laughed again. "Well, that's all, isn't it? You know about the other things."

"Who put the screws in your pocket?" said Sarah.

Lucilla lifted her head with an impatient jerk.

"I don't know. Perhaps Ricky did. I think he'd have funked taking them off the bicycle. I think Uncle Geoffrey did that at home before we started, and Ricky just put them in my pocket to make it look as if I'd done it myself."

"And what happened on the stairs at Holme Fallow?" said John Hildred. "I thought there was someone there below you when you fell."

Lucilla shivered. She said,

"Yes." And then, "I couldn't help screaming. I was coming across the step to the balustrade, and I didn't know there was anyone there. And then somebody's hands came out of the dark—and caught my ankles—and tipped me off my feet—and I thought I was going to crash—" She jumped up, ran to John, and flung her arms round his neck. "I should have crashed if you hadn't caught me. You *are* my NOBLE PRESERVER! Do you mind if I go on calling you that? I like it a lot better than Father. You must be awfully strong, or you wouldn't have been able to catch me and lift me back. I say—*he* must have got away like lightning, mustn't he? And he's strong too—his hands were like iron. I couldn't help screaming."

"Why didn't you tell us the truth—*then*?" said John with his arm round her.

"Preserver *darling*! And have him fetch Dr. Drayton to say I'd got hallucinations, and how sad it was, but he was afraid I'd have to be put under restraint? That's what he'd have *done*. And we couldn't have proved he'd ever been near Holme Fallow. He's so frightfully clever. Look at this afternoon. How could you get anyone to believe that he tried to push us both under the train, when he was three rows away in a crowd? But he did. And he nearly brought it off."

"What did happen?" said Sarah.

Lucilla shrugged her shoulders.

"Dunno. I think there was a hole in the crowd. He got his stick through. I just felt the most awful jab in the ribs and I was over the edge. I expect I've got a bruise like a bullseye." She shivered again, held John tightly, and said in a sort of whisper, *"What do you think he'll do next?"*

A feeling of cold horror came over Sarah. John's quick "It's all finished" failed to reassure her. She wondered if it reassured Lucilla. She became conscious that she was very tired, and that Lucilla looked like a ghost in her black frock. When John kissed them both good-night, she said,

"I wish it was to-morrow."

Chapter Thirty-Three

BERTRAND DARNAC had dined merrily, and supped more merrily still. He had been the life and soul of a gay party. His manner advertised to all and sundry that he had not a care in the world. He paid extravagant attentions to a highly coloured brunette who was as unlike Lucilla as any girl could be. Yet, when the party broke up at about three in the morning, he was conscious of considerable relief. Laughter, music, dancing, pretty girls, and an evening that had gone with a swing, had not only failed to disperse the angry, miserable thoughts which held obstinate place below the surface of his mind, but appeared to have rendered them more aggressive. When he thought of Lucilla, he burned with anger, and with something which hurt more than anger does. When he determined not to think about Lucilla, a condition of so much inward gloom set in that it was only by talking, laughing and joking to an extravagant extent that he could maintain any headway against it. It was a relief not to have to make this sort of effort any more.

He started to walk to his lodging, and as he walked he allowed himself to think angrily about Lucilla, jealously about Lucilla, ferociously and miserably about Lucilla. Sometimes his anger burned so furiously that he found himself running to work it off; sometimes he found himself talking rapidly under his breath, his remarks being alternately addressed to Lucilla and to his own folly.

By the time the night air had had a somewhat cooling effect, he discovered himself to be very far out of his road. His preoccupation with Lucilla had had the effect of deflecting him in the direction of Millington's Hotel. When he pulled himself up at a street corner, hit himself on the chest, and informed an unheeding world that he was a species of imbecile, he was in fact no more than a quarter of a mile away from it.

Anyone not completely immersed in imbecility would have turned about and proceeded in the right direction, but Mr. Darnac, after calling heaven and earth to witness that he was a fool, continued along Randall Street and into Casson's Row.

Casson's Row leads into the top end of Portingale Square, and Millington's Hotel is about six houses down on the left-hand side. He was just about to turn into the square—and if anyone wishes to know why, I would refer them to the uncounted number of young men who in similar circumstances have gazed passionately, gloomily, or ecstatically at a parcel of bricks, mortar and window-glass behind which some lady is believed to be sleeping—he was just about to enter the square, when someone passed him, walking in the same direction, but on the other side of the street. A lover may be crazy enough to walk half across London in the middle of the night in order to stare at the unresponsive wall of an hotel, but he may retain enough sanity to desire a decent privacy for his madness. This was Bertrand's case. He therefore hung back a little and hoped that the other gentleman, whoever he might be, would get on with it and get away.

There is a lamp-post at that corner of the square where Casson's Row runs in between Nos. 40 and 41. The lamp-post stands outside No. 40. The other gentleman crossed over before he came to it. He wore a Burberry and a soft hat. He carried something which oddly resembled a rucksack, and he looked like Ricky Hildred.

Bertrand stood still where he was on the dark side of the Row and watched the hat, the Burberry, and the rucksack. He had no doubt that they adorned Ricky Hildred, and that Ricky was also making for Millington's Hotel. A perfect fury of jealous rage rendered him incapable of reasoned thought. He pursued the half seen figure swiftly, but with caution. He wanted to find out what Ricky was up to, and when he had found out he wanted to take him by the scruff of the neck and bang his head against a brick wall. He felt as if this would be an extremely soothing exercise, and he hoped very much that there would be no policeman at hand to interfere.

There is another lamp-post in front of the hotel. Ricky passed between this and the house—Bertrand was now quite sure that it was Ricky Hildred. He couldn't have said why he was sure, but he hadn't a doubt of it.

Just beyond the lamp-post a very narrow alley cuts in between the hotel and No. 29. Ricky disappeared into the alley and Bertrand followed him. The hotel has a tradesmen's entrance upon the alley. It has also the sort of old-fashioned double-leaved wooden gate which commonly leads to a stable yard. Coming on this, Bertrand discovered it to be open. His jealousy and his anger incontinently received a cold douche of suspicion and curiosity.

"What the devil is this Ricky up to?" was the question he was asking himself as he slipped through the half open gate into the back yard which lay beyond it.

He stood there, still angry, but more puzzled. The rucksack came back into his mind. Why the rucksack? Why Ricky at all? Ricky wasn't in love with Lucilla—well, not enough to notice anyway. But granted Ricky, why the rucksack?

His restless inquisitive brain took charge at this point, and it was a keenly wide-awake young man who now picked his way amongst the booby traps with which almost any back yard is encumbered. There are dustbins. There are tin cans and buckets. There are empty petrol-tins. There are rakes, forks, and brooms. There is washing on a line. But to these general obstacles Millington's added a small hand-cart placed diagonally across his path, a stable lantern, a very large coil of wire, some lengths of hose-pipe, and a compact little pile of bricks.

The advantage of following someone else is self-evident. It was Ricky who smothered a groan when the shaft of the hand-cart caught him in the diaphragm. It was Ricky who, treading on the bristle end of a broom, had his lip cut when the handle flew up and smacked his face. It was Ricky who stumbled over the stable-lantern and barked his shin on the bricks. The way of transgressors is proverbially hard. The virtuous Mr. Darnac, following in the transgressor's wake, and warned by his muffled groans, successfully avoided the worst of the obstacles.

His curiosity grew with every moment. Was it possible that he had been mistaken, and that this was not Ricky at all, but a cat-burglar? In which case, what an immense, what a superlative lark! Bertrand began to feel happier than he had done for some days. He stood in deep shadow and listened with all his ears. Ricky—or the burglar—was in process of climbing the wall against which he stood. As far as he could make out, it was the side wall of some room which had been built out into the yard, for it was only one storey high. The burglar—or Ricky—

was going up in the angle between this wall and the wall of the house. There was probably a convenient water-pipe—the burglar's friend.

Bertrand stood waiting. It was when the unseen climber had, by the very faint sounds that he was making, just reached the roof of the one-storey building, that not so much a new thought, but a new arrangement of his previous thoughts took place. It was Ricky—yes, assuredly it was Ricky. But at the same time it was also someone who broke in, and for a purpose which was assuredly criminal. He remembered Lucilla's headlong ride down Burdon Hill. He remembered her only just averted fall at Holme Fallow. And he began to edge along the wall, and having reached the corner, to shin up the water-pipe. There *was* a water-pipe.

Chapter Thirty-Four

LUCILLA WAS ASLEEP. She lay on her left side with one hand under her cheek. She was breathing softly and deeply, and she was dreaming a light, nonsensical, pleasant dream.

In this dream she was walking knee-deep in a field of buttercups. There was a faint but pleasant whirring sound in the air, and this was because hundreds of dragon-flies were circling, swooping, and hovering over the buttercups. The sun shone on the gold of the flowers and on the brilliant sapphire, emerald, turquoise, and chrysoprase of the dragon-flies' bodies. It was very hot and very pleasant. Lucilla herself was very comfortably dressed in a pair of shorts and a vest. Her feet were bare upon the grass, and her head was bare to the sky.

Ricky slipped the palette knife between the upper and the lower sash of the bathroom window and pushed back the catch. He began very cautiously to raise the lower half of the window.

In Lucilla's dream the sound became a loud whirring of wings, and one of the dragon-flies, grown to the size of an aeroplane and shining like all the jewels in the world, came down with a rush and caught her up in a swift breath-catching spiral of flight.

Sarah was not asleep. If you desire to-morrow too intensely, it is apt to recede down a vista of wakeful hours. She put out her light at half-past twelve and found her pillow too low. When she had reinforced it with a cushion, it was too high. At one o'clock she began to count sheep, but by half past one all the thoughts which she had been trying to keep out of her mind had come trooping in and were clamouring to be heard. She switched on the light and read persistently until three, when she really thought she had tired them out. She lay down in the dark again, and felt herself beginning to slip down into the shallows of sleep.

When Ricky moved the catch of the bathroom window, the sound he made was so very slight that even if she had been awake and listening, Sarah would scarcely have heard it. As it was, she stopped slipping down that dim incline and stayed without knowing why on the blurred edge between conscious and unconscious thought.

And then all at once she was awake. The window had made very little noise, but she was awake and up on her elbow, listening. And when she listened, she could hear that someone was moving in the next room. If she had been more fully awake, or more deeply asleep, this would not have troubled her. In the one case the sound would not have been enough to wake her up, and in the other she would have reasoned that sounds from a next-door room are to be expected in an hotel, and more especially when the room happens to be a bathroom. But in the misty half-and-half confusion of her mind the sound became linked with her fear of the night and her longing for the day. As she emerged from the confusion, the fear emerged too. She could hear a continuance of faint sounds from the other side of the party wall. The fear fastened upon these sounds.

Someone was moving, she thought furtively. There were none of the sounds which are natural to a bathroom. The noise of running water, the metallic click of the wire basket contrived to hold the vast out-moded sponges of an earlier day, the soft slapping sound of the rubber bath-mat being laid down, would have been music in Sarah's ears. Instead there came only the sounds which she thought of as furtive. She drew a long breath, slipped out of bed, and groped in the dark for her dressing-gown.

Bertrand Darnac reached the roof of the one-storey building, which was in fact an extension of the hotel dining-room. He lifted his head cautiously and stared about him. Several windows looked out this way. They were no more than four or five feet above the roof of the extension. The middle window was open and there was a light behind its down-pulled blind. The blind did not quite fit the frame. A line of light showed like a bright wire on either side of it, and the bottom edge cleared the sill by two or three inches. It was the bottom half of the window that was open, and the blind moved a little in the cool night air. Bertrand felt that he could bear to know what was going on behind that moving blind. He was angry, he was determined, he was apprehensive on Lucilla's account, and he was full of a most raging curiosity. He made his way across the roof and peered through the three-inch gap between the blind and the sill.

He saw the broad mahogany edge of an old-fashioned built-in bath. He saw the bath-taps, polished as very little brass is now polished. He saw about half of Ricky Hildred. He could not have sworn that what he saw was in fact Ricky, or any part of him. He saw about half of a Burberry, and suspected that Ricky was inside it. Then he saw a hand in a rubber glove, and immediately he was so very angry that it was only by the most heroic effort of self-control that he restrained himself from leaping into the bathroom and laying out the Burberry with a well-planted kick. He went on looking, and saw the hand which had gone down out of his sight come up again. It held an extraordinary but quite unmistakable object. Bertrand's anger went cold and savage as he recognized this object. It was a gas-mask. Inside that bathroom Ricky Hildred was putting on a gas-mask. "Very well then, my dear Ricky, we will give you time to put it on, and we will give you time to give yourself away. And we will give you rope—oh yes, we will give you rope to hang yourself."

Afterwards Mr. Darnac was pleased to remember that in such a crisis he had been able to recall so apposite an English idiom. It proved to him that his command of English was really unassailable. At the moment, he applied his eyes to the three-inch gap, and his mind to considering Ricky Hildred.

The hand came down again and up again. It still wore the rubber glove. When it came up again, the other hand had joined it. The two hands supported a metal cylinder with a short length of tubing leading from it. Next moment the hands and the cylinder were out of sight behind the Burberry, and the Burberry began to move away from Bertrand in the direction of the door.

Bertrand restrained himself. He gave himself orders not to move until this devil of a Ricky had gone out of the door. It was not enough to catch him with his gas-mask and his cylinder. He must let him go farther than that. He must let him go to the very edge of his crime and catch him there.

He saw the Burberry approach the door. He heard the faint sound of the rubber glove upon the handle. And then he heard another sound. There was a little click, and the bathroom light went out.

Lucilla was soaring higher and higher into the blue of a sky surcharged with light. The sound of the dragonfly's wings had dropped to a low soothing hum. She could see the wings from where she sat on the great emerald ring which joined thorax and head. They were just the colour of the bronze pollen on one special kind of grass. Nothing else had the brownness or the dancing iridescent light. She sang "Oh let us be joyful" in her heart. She did not hear the bathroom door open.

Ricky came out into the passage. It was very dimly lighted by a small heavily shaded electric bulb which marked the head of the stairs. It is perhaps a mistake to say that the passage was lighted. It was rather filled with a sort of orange-coloured gloom strongly reminiscent of a fog. Ricky hated coming out into it like poison. It was all very well for Geoffrey to tell him what he must do, but suppose someone came out of his room—or her room—while he was doing it. All very well to say they wouldn't, but suppose they did. With the utmost reluctance he took his hand off the knob of the bathroom door and began to make his way down the passage. He passed the head of the stairs and Lucilla's door. He passed two more doors, one on either side. The carpet under his feet was most reassuringly thick and soft. He began to feel a little better. After all, why should anyone come out of any room at half-past three in the morning?

Sarah put out her hand in the dark and felt for the knob of the door. Her fingers touched the cold metal of the small old-fashioned bolt, and she remembered with a sort of startled shock that she had bolted herself in—and why. She slid back the little brass tongue. It ran smoothly in its groove and made no noise at all. The handle was lower down. She found it, turned it slowly, and pulled the door towards her until she could look out into the passage. The first thing she saw was the orange light at the head of the stairs. The stairs came up very nearly opposite her room, and a little to the left the shaded light shone high up on the wall. She saw that first. Then she looked sideways and saw that the bathroom door was open, and that a man was coming out of it.

Her first natural impulse was to draw back. She had begun to do so, when she saw that the man was Bertrand Darnac. He was bare-headed and in evening dress. What light there was fell full upon his face and on his white shirt-front. His name sprang to her lips, but did not pass them, because even as they moved to let the sound of that whispered "Ran!" escape, she saw something else. Someone at the far end of the passage straightened up from a stooping position, turned the handle of the door immediately in front of him, pushed it open, and disappeared into the darkness beyond. The door was John Hildred's door, and the darkness was the darkness of the room in which he lay asleep. The door closed upon the darkness.

Sarah ran out of her room and caught Bertrand Darnac by the arm. She was quite past wondering how he came there. She held his arm hard, and said very quick and low,

"Did you see that?"

He nodded, and began to walk along the passage with a stride that was almost a run. Sarah had to run to keep pace with him. Her bare feet made no sound. Her voice just reached him and no more.

"Who is it?"

He said, "Ricky," and turning his head for an instant, he asked her urgently, "Whose room?"

She said, "John's."

When Ricky had closed the door between him and the passage, he experienced an illusory sense of safety. The most terrifying moments of his life lay behind him. The door had been locked. He had had to turn the key from the outside with the gadget which Geoffrey had given him for the purpose. The sweat had run down under his gas-mask—horrible cold sweat. His shirt was sticking to him now. His feet were cold, and his hands were cold and clammy.

He leaned against the inner side of the door, and the illusory sense of safety left him. The worst part of the job was still to come. Suppose Jack waked. Suppose he struggled. Suppose he called out. Geoffrey was safe at home. He took a faltering forward step and found himself suddenly and bewilderingly in a full glare of light. The light showed an empty bed, and John Hildred no more than a yard away with his hand just dropping from the switch.

Ricky made a sound. A sort of choking cry. He turned. He snatched at the handle of the door. He dragged it open. And bumped into Bertrand on the threshold.

Mr. Darnac was in a hurry. His impetus bore Ricky back into the room he was trying to leave and, having got him there, sent the two of them sprawling.

Sarah takes the greatest credit to herself because she did not scream. She began to scream, but she stopped it by pressing the back of her hand against her lips. When she was sure that she had stopped the scream, she came into the room. And shut the door. And leaned against it.

She really did need something to lean against. Bertrand and Ricky—if it was Ricky—were rolling over and over on the floor, and sometimes a masked head like something out of a bad dream was uppermost, and sometimes Ran's face, all furious, with the teeth showing like a fighting dog. It was only for a moment really, because John intervened, and then—it *was* Ricky, because the mask was off. He was half kneeling, half sitting, and they were holding him. He looked more like a rabbit than ever, but a rabbit that had been caught in a trap. And suddenly he crumpled, bowing himself forward and weeping aloud, sobbing for mercy, tumbling over himself to give Geoffrey away.

"I didn't want to—I didn't want to—he made me—it wasn't me!" And then more tears, more sobs, more hysterical writhings.

Lucilla stirred. Outside her dream Bertrand and Sarah were running down the passage. In her dream a black cloud—very black, heavy with blackness—had covered the face of the sky. A tremor went over her and over the dragonfly which was whirring her upwards. The light that had glanced in lovely iridescence on the bronze wings went out. The light on the emerald and sapphire and turquoise and chrysoprase of the body went out. All the light went out. She woke up in the dark, and felt the fear that was in the house.

It was horrible to wake like that.

No one need think that she was going to take it lying down.

She was out of bed without any plan in her mind. And then a plan came to her. She would go to Sarah.

She pulled back the bolt, opened the door, and saw that Sarah's door was open too.

And the bathroom door.

Three doors open in a row, and no one in any of the rooms.

She stood in the passage bare-footed in her thin pink nightdress which was just ankle length, and looked this way and that. Then she too ran down the passage towards John Hildred's room. And before she reached it she could hear Ricky's sobbing voice. Other people would have heard it too if the hotel had been less solidly built and if this end room had had other bedrooms to right and left of it. It had instead on one side a second bathroom, and on the other, first a housemaid's cupboard and then the entrance to the back stairs. She turned the handle of the door, and could not open it because someone was leaning against the other side. The someone moved, and then the door moved too.

Lucilla came into the lighted room and saw that it was Sarah who had moved away from the door. Then she saw her father, and Bertrand Darnac. Then she saw Ricky. The others were all standing, but Ricky was sitting on the ground. Sarah was in her dressing-gown. It was made of yellow crepe embroidered with bright little woolly flowers. Eleanor Manifold had embroidered it. She was very clever with her fingers. The Preserver had his arm round Sarah. He was in pyjamas. They had a blue and white stripe, rather wide. Bertrand, most surprisingly, was in evening dress. There were green stains on the knees of his trousers and a smear of blood on his chin. His tie was sticking up under his left ear. Ricky was sitting on the floor and weeping, in his very old Burberry. It had some new wet stains on it. His collar had come undone and was poking out at a raffish angle. It was all very surprising, like the most mixed sort of dream.

She shut the door because there was no sense in letting Ricky wake anyone else up, and said in her clear, light voice,

"What's the matter?"

Chapter Thirty-Five

JOHN HILDRED CAME OUT of his room and went along the passage as far as the head of the stairs. Ricky had made a clean breast of everything, and the question was, what next?

The police?

Nausea rose in him at the thought of Ricky in the witness-box—exposing himself—hurrying to swear away his father's life. No, not quite that, since, no thanks to Geoffrey, actual murder had not been done. Yet such a term of imprisonment as he would get would be the equivalent of a death sentence. And the name on every poster, in every flaring headline:

> THE HILDRED CASE. GEOFFREY HILDRED
> IN THE DOCK. RICHARD HILDRED
> IN THE WITNESS BOX.

What a mess!

Something might perhaps be done with Ricky. How far would he really have gone? He had probably had enough of meddling with crime.

O'Hara—suppose he could get O'Hara to try Ricky out. Suppose ... There wasn't any suppose about it. O'Hara would do it if he asked him. An open-air life, plenty of good hard work, and a tight hand over him might make something of Ricky yet.

But Geoffrey was another guess matter.

Geoffrey—

Just past the head of the stairs there was a telephone-box. John Hildred entered it, shut the door, and dialled a number. He had put on a dressing-gown over his pyjamas. He had sent Sarah and Lucilla back to bed. He had left Bertrand Darnac on guard over Ricky. He was now telephoning to Geoffrey.

Geoffrey Hildred roused at the sound of the bell. It was not sleep from which it roused him, but a heavy trance of fatigue and suspense. He was not at first sure what the ringing bell might be. It might have been the door-bell—but Ricky wouldn't ring. Who else would ring at four in the morning? He had an instant's shocking vision of dark blue cloth and a tall man helmeted, pressing with a gloved hand upon the bell.

The bell rang again—here in the room, from his desk where the table instrument stood. The shocking vision darkened and was gone.

He got up with a noticeable effort, went over to the table, and took the receiver off the telephone, but before he put it to his ear he fumbled for the chair and sat down. There were heavy pulses in his head. They made a noise. Through them a far-away voice said,

"Hullo!"

Geoffrey Hildred said, "Hullo!"

The far-away voice said, "Is that you, Geoffrey?"

At the sound of his name he knew who was calling him—Jack— Jack Hildred—dead years ago—come back to life—dead again to-night if Ricky hadn't bungled—

The line cleared suddenly—or was it his head?—and he knew that Ricky had bungled.

John Hildred was speaking—a living man and a stern one.

"That you, Geoffrey?"

He heard himself say, "Yes."

John Hildred said, "I'm letting you know that Ricky has failed you. He is here. And he's made a clean breast of everything. That's all." The click of the receiver followed.

Geoffrey Hildred heard it. It sounded as loud in his ears as the clap of a slammed door. There were thoughts in his mind—prison— misappropriation—trust—the dock—the Hildred case—a judge in a black cap. And then, "The Lord have mercy on your soul." ... But no one was dead. Lucilla wasn't dead. Ricky had failed. No one—was—*dead*....

He did not know that the receiver had fallen from his hand. He did not know that his forehead had struck the edge of the desk. They would find him like that in the morning, slumped forward in his chair.

John Hildred came out of the telephone-box and knocked on Sarah's door. She opened it at once. They stood there looking at each other. Then he said,

"Lucilla in bed?"

Sarah said, "Yes—she's here. We thought we'd stay together."

"Yes. But it's all over now. There won't be anything more."

She put a hand on his shoulder and leaned towards him.

"John, what are you going to do?"

"I don't know, darling—go back to my room."

"And then?"

He said again, "I don't know."

There was silence between them. He broke it when Sarah took her hand away.

"Sarah—"

"John—"

"Will you marry me very soon?"

"How soon?"

He said, "I think it takes three days to get a licence. Will you marry me in three days?"

Sarah said, "Yes, John."

She put up her lips and they kissed.

THE END

Made in the USA
Coppell, TX
25 January 2024

28160445R00125